VENDETTA

LEGEND OF THE IR'INDICTI SERIES, BOOK FOUR

CONNIE SUTTLE

To Walter, Joe, Larry, Lee, Dianne, Sarah and Mark.
Thank you.

ACKNOWLEDGMENTS

As always, this book is the result of collaboration. If it weren't for the support of my editor, my cover artist and my beta readers, it would be less than it is. All mistakes, as usual, are mine and no other's.

About the Author:
Connie Suttle lives in Oklahoma with her husband and a conglomerate of cats. They have finally banded together to make their demands, which has proven disconcerting to all humans involved.

You may find Connie in the following ways:
Facebook: Connie Suttle Author
Twitter: @subtledemon
Website and Blog: subtledemon.com

Blood Destiny Series:

Blood Wager

Blood Passage

Blood Sense

Blood Domination

Blood Royal

Blood Queen

Blood Rebellion

Blood War

Blood Redemption

Blood Reunion

Blood Destiny Series Boxed Set (Books 1-10)

Blood Recall

Blood Alliance*

Legend of the Ir'Indicti Series:

Bumble

Shadowed

Target

Vendetta

Destroyer

High Demon Series:

Demon Lost

Demon Revealed

Demon's King

Demon's Quest

Demon's Revenge

Demon's Dream

God Wars Series:

Blood Double

Blood Trouble

Blood Revolution

Blood Love

Blood Finale

Saa Thalarr Series:

Hope and Vengeance

Wyvern and Company

Observe and Protect*

First Ordinance Series:

Finder

Keeper

BlackWing

SpellBreaker

WhiteWing

~

R-D Series:

Cloud Dust

Cloud Invasion

Cloud Rebel

~

Latter Day Demons Series:

Hot Demon in the City

A Demon's Work is Never Done

A Demon's Due

~

Seattle Elementals Series:

Your Money's Worth

Worth Your While*

~

BlackWing Pirates Series

MindSighted

MindMage

MindRogue

MindMaster*

~

Black Rose Sorceress Series

The Rose Mark

Rose and Thorn

Black Rose Queen

Queen of Thorns and Roses*

Other Titles from SubtleDemon Publishing:

Malefactor

Transgressor

by Joe Scholes

*Forthcoming

FOREWORD

A note about the locations in this series:

Cloud Chief, Oklahoma is a real ghost town, located near Cordell, Oklahoma. All of the land is now privately owned and the Cloud Chief community portrayed in this book is fictitious in nature.

CHAPTER 1

"$\mathcal{H}$is father and Mr. Winkler won't allow it, that's why," Denise DeLuca dumped blueberry muffins out of a muffin pan with practiced deliberation. She was taking food to Adele, no matter what. Sali had an untouched can of soda sitting in front of him as he watched his mother work.

"But we need to do something for Ashe. Maybe a private service?" Marco, sitting opposite Sali at the kitchen island, suggested, his dark eyes searching his mother's face for an acceptable answer.

"Mr. Winkler said no, and the Grand Master is backing him up," Denise muttered, arranging muffins in a basket for Adele. Her mouth tugged into a frown as she worked, turning away from her oldest son's gaze and focusing on the task she'd set for herself.

"At least I don't have to go to work," Sali buried his head in his arms. He wanted to talk to Ashe so badly, and reminded himself (again) that Ashe was dead.

Jackson Pruitt was dead. Several of Mr. Winkler's wolves had died, too, in Zeke Tanner's attempt at kidnapping many of Star Cove's teens. If Ashe hadn't done as he did, half the community might have died as well.

Shirley Walker had suspended work for the Star Cove teens in the groves—the peach harvest was nearly over, anyway. She'd hired adults from Corpus Christi to finish it.

Jackson Pruitt's funeral had been held in the groves three days earlier. Marcie was heartbroken over her son's death and Jack's older brother Dustin blamed himself—he'd stayed in Dallas, working there with Winkler's Pack instead of staying in Star Cove.

Sali and Marco were asking about a funeral for Ashe, who'd burned himself and the enemy to save the Star Cove community. There wasn't even a thread of clothing or piece of Ashe's leather wallet left behind as a remembrance.

Dori, Wynn and Sali moved about numbly after the incident. Finally, they'd been allowed to remember. Ashe hadn't been an insignificant shapeshifter, capable of only turning into a tiny, bumblebee bat. He'd held amazing abilities. With Ashe's death, all that was gone. Sali sighed and lifted his head to gaze at his brother.

"Salidar, tomorrow is your birthday," Denise DeLuca reminded him.

"Yeah. Happy birthday," Sali mumbled sarcastically.

"And Jonas, Nathan and your father are interviewing for the Principal's position next week. We have to hire quickly or we won't be ready for the school year to start."

"I don't want to go to school."

"It'll be hard, Sali, I know. Ashe was always there." Marco sighed and looked away, remembering a time when he'd felt lost after James' death. "We all leaned on Ashe. We didn't realize we were doing it, but we did."

Marco turned back to Sali and lifted a muffin from the basket his mother prepared. He was staying at home for the present; Winkler had given him time off.

"It's too bad Dawn and Randy couldn't stay; it was easier to talk to Adele when they were with us," Denise fitted another muffin into the empty space left after Marco's theft.

"Randy always knows the right things to say," Marco agreed. "He's a good writer."

Dawn and Randy had remained in Star Cove for Jackson's funeral, then both had gone home afterward. The ruins of Winkler's beach house had been cleared away, too, and plans were made to rebuild quickly. Winkler was currently staying in Dallas; he, Trajan, Trace and the others had flown back shortly after the incident.

That's what they all called it—*the incident*. A page in their history that would never be recorded anywhere. Marcie and Jason had decided to buy Cordell Feed and Seed, so they could leave the bad memories of Star Cove behind. They'd already gone back to Oklahoma, staying in Clinton and driving to Cordell to run the store until the sale was finalized.

Denise had spent as much time with Marcie as she could, helping to pack things away and giving Jackson's belongings to charity. What Marcie could bear to part with, anyway. So far, nobody had touched Ashe's things. Aedan Evans wouldn't allow it.

"School is gonna suck," Sali said, running a finger through the ring of moisture his soda can left on the island.

"Been there," Marco sighed.

Winkler placed the paper copy of the email message inside a plastic sleeve. The fragile sheet was burned around the edges and threatened to crumble if handled directly. He'd read the message several time. Considered handing a copy to Aedan Evans several times. Something always held him back.

Anthony Hancock had discovered Ashe's dictionary in the rubble left from the beach house fire. Thick books were difficult to burn completely. The cover and edges of the heavy dictionary were singed but the inner pages remained intact, protecting the paper Ashe had slipped into the center of the book.

Tony hadn't seen the message—he'd handed the dictionary to Winkler, suggesting that Ashe's parents might like to have it. Tony had then returned to England and was likely on another assignment already. Winkler snorted at the thought.

Winkler, handling Ashe's dictionary carefully sometime later, found the paper Ashe had slipped between its pages. He'd glimpsed the corner of it protruding from the blackened edges. *Greetings*, the email read. *I am your grandfather*.

Ashe had never mentioned the contact to anyone. Winkler attempted to trace the email, but the trail had gone cold long ago. Nothing came of it, though he'd asked Matt Michaels for help. Now, Winkler waited for another sign. Had two or three of his best watching for it, in fact.

"We found nothing." Gavin Montegue placed a folder of information on Wlodek's antique desk. Wlodek, Head of the Vampire Council, sat in his richly decorated study, surrounded by books any collector would pay a fortune to procure and original artwork that would fetch millions.

A large Monet hung on one wall, a David portrait of Napoleon on another, in addition to other items that would sell quickly should they ever be offered. Wlodek had no interest in letting any of his treasures go.

Wlodek was nearing three thousand years in age, but with jet-black hair and eyes to match, he still looked young. All vampires did. Anyone would have to come quite close to Wlodek in order to see the depth of knowledge and millennia of experience in his dark eyes. Wlodek never allowed anyone to get that close.

Gavin, one of three Council Assassins, had worked with two of Wlodek's twelve Enforcers, searching for Wildrif's trail. Without blinking, he presented the information he had to the Head of the Vampire Council.

Gavin's quarry had managed to escape a maximum-security prison in Colorado and then succeeded in eluding human authorities and vampire trackers. None knew exactly how that was accomplished. Wlodek still wanted Wildrif. Mostly he wanted Wildrif dead, but he had to find him first.

Wlodek's worries concerning the quarter-blood Dark Elemaiya

was shared by the Vampire Council. They'd dealt with this threat before. The Dark Elemaiya, many of whom had been made vampire in the past, had almost taken down the U.S. government and many other world powers.

Wlodek and a handful of talented and vigilant vampires, with help from Weldon Harper, the werewolf Grand Master and some of his best wolves, had managed to track and eliminate those Dark vampires who sought to rule the planet.

A slight rift had occurred afterward—Weldon and Wlodek differed on how the Dark vampires had been destroyed. They'd called something of a truce, however, and agreed not to speak of it again.

"Unfortunately we do not have the resources to continue tracking him, but Matthew Michaels is also hunting this one since he escaped his government's imprisonment. Mr. Michaels has promised to keep me informed," Wlodek said.

Wlodek seldom revealed any sort of emotion. Vampires had a habit of never showing anyone what they were thinking or how they felt. Vampires were immortals after all, and it never paid to make an enemy of any of them.

"I shall take up the hunt again, should you wish it," Gavin nodded respectfully to Wlodek, keeping his dark eyes pinned to the older vampire. They gave nothing away. Gavin, as the Council's elite Assassin, also was adept at keeping his emotions hidden.

"I will consider it if we learn anything new," Wlodek replied. "Meanwhile, I hear we have a rogue in Budapest. Charles has information for you. See him on your way out." Wlodek terminated the meeting.

"Of course, Honored One." Gavin turned and walked out quickly. It never paid to try the old one's patience.

~

"Mr. Winkler, I heard a rumor." Jason held his cell to an ear as he walked down a sidewalk in Cordell. Summers could be quite hot in western Oklahoma and Jason Landers kept to the shade as much as possible, walking under awnings of small businesses that lined the street.

"You think it's a reliable rumor?"

"I'd check it out, I think," Jason said. "I left Marcie at the store—she doesn't know anything about it. She's still pretty torn up."

"I understand. I just hope your rumor bears some fruit."

"Me too. I hate to let both of 'em go like that."

"Yeah. I'll check it out, Jason. You stay with Marcie."

"Sure, boss." Jason sighed, tapped end on his cell and kept walking.

"I hold hope that my Jewels still live," Friesianna snapped at Parlethis. Parlethis did nothing to conceal his desire to work closely with the Queen as assassin and Sentinel. He'd worked his way up through the ranks of soldiers and guards surrounding the Queen. After the attempt to take the half-child, however, none of the Jewel brothers or the fifteen others had returned to the Queen's camp.

"Their talismans have not returned to me as they would have, had my Jewels perished," Friesianna informed Parlethis haughtily. "Surely you would not settle for the position without the power talisman. Those alone will guarantee an extra four relocations. They remain with my Jewels, I tell you. I have them not."

Rabis stood nearby, his head bowed as if in thought. The Queen had not ventured to ask his opinion on the matter. The talismans might not return for another reason, but the Queen had ignored the *Ekdi H'Morr* all along, calling it a book of myth and lies.

Rabis knew the Dark King's Destroyers hadn't returned, either, and their talismans had failed to come to Baltis. He held back a sigh of impatience. Friesianna might learn someday, when it was far too late, just what the terms *failure* and *comeuppance* actually meant.

"Should you not have a special guard at your side to do your bidding until the Jewels return, then? Someone to keep our beautiful Queen safe?" Parlethis was very persuasive when he wished to be.

"Perhaps," Friesianna pretended to think it over. "Yes. You may be correct. Perform well in your duties and when my Jewels return, we may consider a permanent promotion for you."

"That is all I ask, my lovely and talented Queen." Parlethis bowed low. Rabis wanted to gag. Steeling himself, he remained where he was.

~

Traci set the usual glass of ice water down in front of her customer, who seemed completely engrossed in the menu. "You don't have chicken and dumplings?" he asked, lowering the plastic-covered paper and lifting an eyebrow at the waitress.

"No, sir. Not today. I think we might have it tomorrow, though. The chicken-fried steak is good—it's the special for today."

"I'll have that, then." Weldon Harper handed the menu back to the waitress. Winkler said Betsy's was the best diner in Cordell. He was about to find out.

"What's the special?" Winkler slid into the booth on the opposite side.

"Chicken-fried steak," Traci said brightly. Two strangers, both handsome, had come in and sat at her table. She was hoping for a good tip and perhaps a little gossip—they didn't usually get two nice-looking strangers at once. The last time she'd gotten nonlocals, it had been a couple in their mid-fifties who were looking for the historical marker in Cloud Chief.

Traci and her fellow waitresses had snickered at the couple's questions—there wasn't anything left of Cloud Chief except the marker and a few crumbling buildings right off the road. The rest of the old ghost town was farmland.

Of course, the boy from Philadelphia had been killed not far from there, but everyone knew that was a rogue grizzly bear or something. Nobody had found the creature yet, although there were always rumors of sightings. A bounty had been placed on the creature but so far, nobody had claimed it.

"We're just passing through," Winkler waved away Traci's questions. She'd asked if he and Weldon were from the area. He and the Grand Master were on a mission, following up on Jason's theory. They would learn soon enough if their hunch bore fruit.

Weldon had flown commercial into Oklahoma City, while Winkler had driven up from Dallas. They'd agreed to meet at Betsy's Diner in Cordell for dinner before taking a short side trip.

"Ready?" Weldon asked after Winkler paid the check.

"Yeah. I'll drive." Winkler grabbed a toothpick on the way out of the small diner. Winkler had a more comfortable car than Weldon's rental—he'd driven his Mercedes.

Trace and Trajan had been left in Dallas, although they complained about letting him go without any guards. Neither knew he was meeting the Grand Master.

"I prefer North Dakota to this heat," Weldon felt like taking his shirt off.

"You're just not used to it," Winkler grinned, turning the air conditioner up a notch. Winkler backed out of the parking space and drove away.

"I left the power on, just in case," Winkler shut the car door quietly after they parked beside the Evans home in Cloud Chief. "Water was on a well and septic," he added, fishing for a note in his pocket.

There was no true front door to the house—the Evans family had always come and gone through the garage door. It was the vampire way of making sure a prospective break-in had as many solid walls placed between the outside and the residents inside as possible.

Winkler punched in the code written on the note and watched the garage door rise. Another code let him in through the back door and into the kitchen, with Weldon following close behind.

"Adele, I don't know what to do," Aedan sighed. "We could move if you want."

"I have no idea what I want at this point." Adele didn't feel like doing anything. Depression had come to call, she supposed. Laundry and housework were things she forced herself to do.

Had she considered taking college courses again? Ashe had urged her to do so. Now, information and enrollment forms were forgotten. Ashe's bedroom had been closed. Aedan refused to allow anyone inside.

"Winkler's insurance paid for Nathan's boat," Aedan said. "And the other boats, too. He must have some clout to get past the adjusters like that. I hear they'll start rebuilding the houses that burned down in a few days. Marcus says Winkler's contractor will be down soon. I hear he has several work crews hired already, to put things together in a hurry."

"We're supposed to meet Marcie and Jason at the mortgage company in four weeks," Adele said. "To complete the sale of the store in Cordell."

"It's hard to let all of it go, isn't it?" Aedan put an arm around Adele.

"It's like letting go of Ashe, all over again," Adele wept.

The sign might not have been evident to anyone else, but Winkler saw it. Two summer tomatoes were sitting in the kitchen window behind the curtain. He tapped Weldon lightly on the shoulder and pointed. Weldon nodded slightly.

Winkler turned to open the door that led downstairs and into the main portion of the house when the voice came, and then the body that went with the voice became solid. "I wondered if somebody would come," Ashe sighed.

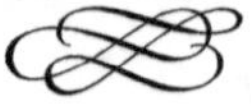

CHAPTER 2

"Ashe, your parents are devastated. They think you're dead," Winkler pointed out carefully. After all, Ashe could get away from all of them and there was nothing they could do about it.

Weldon sat quietly in the booth at Betsy's while Ashe ate stew and cornbread. He was quite hungry, as it turned out. He'd been afraid to use the debit card he had in his pocket and his cash had run out after the third day.

"I realize that," Ashe buttered half a piece of cornbread and bit into it, chewing thoughtfully. "Isn't that the best thing? Who else will come looking for me? Who else is going to die, Winkler? If they think I'm dead, then everybody should be safe."

"You have no proof of that," Weldon said quietly. "We all live our lives on an edge of some sort. None of us have guarantees. Think about who you're talking to, Ashe. Winkler and I have seen plenty during our lifetimes. Dead wolves, vampires, shapeshifters, humans. The world isn't an easy place, son. All we can do is make it better if we can. You have a gift that could help. If I understand correctly, there are a lot of people who work for the British Embassy who owe you their lives. Same with Winkler, Trajan, your parents, most of those kids you pulled off that island—they'd probably be dead now, if you hadn't been there. Dominic Pruitt was determined to get his son and the others with him, to help Ezekiel Tanner with his sick scheme to haul drugs across the border. You saved them from a terrible fate."

"I watched Jackson die," Ashe hung his head. "The first time he changed and he died because of it."

"But the rest of them are alive, Ashe. Think of that. And still with their parents instead of in a compound in Mexico, getting the sense beaten out of them if they didn't cooperate." Weldon sipped his coffee. Ashe went back to his food.

"I'm just asking you to come back with me; I'll take you to your mom and dad," Winkler pleaded softly. "Your mother sits around the house and cries all the time. At least that's what Marcus and Denise told me."

"You had to say that, didn't you?" Ashe's appetite had deserted him.

"Ashe, remember what I said—that you have to keep as much as possible as normal as possible? Let's take you back and do what we can on that front."

"Isn't the community moving again?" Ashe asked. "They know where we are."

"They don't want to. They like Star Cove," Weldon said. "In Marcus' words, we want to take a stand. They're not forcing us to move again."

"They think you're dead, too, I'm sure. So there's that," Winkler pointed out.

"Well, that's something at least," Ashe sighed.

"Come on, finish your dinner and we'll drive back. In fact, I'll let you drive the Mercedes to the Texas border."

"Really?" Winkler had said the magic words.

"Yeah. Here are the keys." Winkler passed them across the table to Ashe. "Eat. Then you drive."

"This is Weldon Harper, Mr. Evans," Weldon called the number Winkler had given him after watching Ashe drive Winkler's Mercedes away from Cordell. "We found your son in Cloud Chief. He was afraid he'd endanger the community again, so he ran away. They're on their way back now—he's driving Winkler's Mercedes to the Texas border."

"My baby's alive?" Weldon heard Adele Evans' voice clearly in the background. Aedan Evans was apparently too stunned to speak. "My baby's alive!" Adele was screaming, now.

"As you can see, this is good news," Aedan Evans finally said. "When can we expect him home?"

"I believe Winkler will have the jet warmed up and ready to go the minute they hit Dallas. And he'll call and give you an estimated arrival time," Weldon added. "It's good to speak with you again." Weldon terminated the call.

~

"We wanted to get you three together and tell you first," Adele was wiping her eyes with a tissue as Sali, Wynn and Dori sat on the sofa inside Marcus and Denise's media room.

Marco had gotten a text from Winkler, so he knew already. Wynn's hand was gripped tightly in Sali's as they waited for the news. "Ashe is alive," Adele wiped more tears away. Dori drew in a breath.

~

"Mr. Winkler, I can get myself home," Ashe pointed out as they stood outside his jet at the Dallas airport. "We don't have to waste the fuel."

"But we're coming back down," Winkler said, pointing to Ace, Trajan, Trace and two other werewolves Ashe hadn't met.

Winkler had driven straight to the airport after taking over driving duties at the Texas line. "Buck is sort of my Third, and he's my building contractor, too," he introduced a rather broad-shouldered werewolf with a good tan, light-brown hair and hazel eyes.

"We need Buck to rebuild my beach house and what we lost in Star Cove. And this is Andy, my personal assistant," Winkler nodded to the last werewolf. Andy was perhaps five-nine, with dark-brown hair and eyes. Ashe thought he looked efficient.

"We'll be setting things up to get the beach house rebuilt fast. Buck is a master at that. He'll make sure everything goes smoothly and gets done right. Andy will keep an eye on costs, so Buck doesn't go overboard." Winkler grinned.

"So there's a method to the apparent madness?" Ashe gave Winkler a curious glance.

"Yep. Buck will come back to Dallas for the next full moon and run the Pack for me if I don't come myself."

"The Pack knows Winkler will bust my butt if I don't do things right," Buck held out a large hand to Ashe, who took it. Ashe was surprised—few werewolves offered to shake with a young shapeshifter. Briefly, he wondered what happened to gruff Orville.

"Come on, kid, our bags are already on the jet," Trajan pulled Ashe into a headlock, hugging him quickly before letting him go. "We thought you were dead," he muttered close to Ashe's ear before stepping back.

"Yeah. I know," Ashe ducked his head. He was getting butterflies over seeing his parents. They'd be upset for sure and he hated to see his mother cry.

"Come on, they're ready," Winkler jerked his head toward the jet, which was revving its engines. Ashe climbed aboard, flanked by Winkler and Trajan.

"What can you tell me about Star Cove?" Winkler asked as Trace handed out bottles of water and soda before sitting next to Trajan. Winkler sat beside Ashe across the aisle. Buck and Andy took seats nearer the front.

"Which part?" Ashe asked.

"All of it, if you don't mind."

Ashe began to describe what he'd found the moment he brought the kidnapped teens back to Star Cove. He told Winkler about the four Bright Elemaiya who'd shielded themselves so they were invisible to everyone else.

"You could see through their shields?" Winkler lifted an eyebrow.

"He could on St. Joseph Island, too, boss," Trajan pointed out. "We couldn't see the camp from overhead. Ashe saw it and took us lower."

"You're right," Winkler nodded. "What then?" He turned back to Ashe. Ashe spoke about the four Dark Elemaiya and the vision he'd had when they threatened Randy Smith. Randy would have died if Ashe hadn't gotten him away.

Then he explained his next vision of Jackson, when he'd brushed against the four shielded Bright Elemaiya. The contact forced Jackson through the change for the first time. Jackson died from a hurled fireblast immediately afterward.

"I was out in the street as quick as I could get there, but Jack was already dead," Ashe sighed. "The four Dark Ones who threatened Randy followed me out of the house, and when they saw the Bright four, they started a firefight of some kind. There were other Elemaiya there, too, from both sides. Things weren't looking good, Mr. Winkler. They set a lot of houses on fire, I know that much."

"We're rebuilding those. Most of the important things were saved, kid," Winkler said gently. "We're even getting my insurance company to replace the boats. Doesn't hurt that I sit on the board of directors."

"I guess," Ashe shrugged. "In the middle of all the fireblasts," he continued, "Lavonna, Cori and Dori went after the Elemaiya, and Mom was diving down from overhead. I was afraid they'd be killed, just like Jackson was. I knew I was the target for both sides, so I started yelling. That got their attention right away. The Elemaiya came after me so I jumped to a boat in the canal. They came after me again, and that's when I set the water on fire."

"Uh, Ashe, did you just say you set the water on fire?" Trace stared at Ashe, disbelief plainly displayed in his eyes.

"Yeah. Those pages Tony Hancock gave me about the Elemaiya? The person who translated that stuff said something about manipulating the elements. He said somebody really talented in that area might be able to burn oxygen from the air. Well, water has oxygen in it, too. I just did a little extrapolation. I have no idea if there were any fish in the canal. If there were, they likely died of oxygen starvation." Ashe felt bad about that. He felt horrible about burning sixteen Elemaiya, too, but they were out to kill others and attempting to take him. Ashe couldn't let that happen.

"I didn't hear any reports of dead fish," Winkler said dryly.

"Mr. Winkler, I think I killed all those people," Ashe whispered. "All those Elemaiya."

"Ashe, you can't worry about that," Winkler's dark eyes raked Ashe's face. "They'd already killed some of ours and would have killed others, and then they'd have killed or kidnapped you. You did what had to be done; don't ever think otherwise." Winkler breathed a fatigued sigh.

"Kid, I've gotten research from Matt Michaels; he tallied up the number of deaths related to that fertility clinic. We estimate at least six hundred eighty-five deaths of children, ranging from preteen to early twenties, and those are the ones we can confirm. Those are murders, plain and simple. That doesn't include all the reported kidnappings, or the human boy who died outside Cloud Chief's boundary. Who knows how many other humans have died just by being in their way? This is a war between them, and they don't care who falls."

Ashe couldn't speak around the lump in his throat. He settled for nodding instead. "Here," Winkler tapped the water bottle on Ashe's table tray. Ashe removed the cap and drank.

He didn't say what he'd been thinking the past few days—that Earth looked to be the battleground the Elemaiya had chosen to pursue their wars. People like the Tanners fell right in with them, working together to take whatever they wanted in order to further their cause. He thought about Sali and Dori in the clutches of drug runners and shivered.

"Kid, it'll be all right," Winkler patted Ashe's shoulder lightly.

"Mr. Winkler, there's something else you need to know," Ashe heaved a shaky sigh.

"What's that?"

Ashe peeled back the left sleeve of his knit polo, revealing the biceps and triceps that Trajan had been working on in the weight room. Surrounding his upper arm, much like a tattoo might, were eight square gold medallions with unusual markings. They shone with the brightness of newly minted gold coins.

Winkler swore when he saw them. "What the hell is that, Ashe? Did you get a tattoo?"

"No, sir. These were on my arm the morning after the whole Star Cove thing. I went to sleep in my old bedroom in Cloud Chief and woke up with these. They're not tattoos. As far as I know, there's no ink that will come out gold like that." Ashe lowered his sleeve over the flat, gold images.

"They look like some of those transfers—you know—like the ones they wear at football games and stuff?" Trajan was up and lifting Ashe's sleeve again.

"But these don't scrub off—I've already tried," Ashe muttered. "They're not going anywhere. And if I pick at 'em, I start heaving."

"You're kidding?" Winkler stared at the eight medallions, moving Ashe's arm this way and that to see them more clearly.

"Not kidding. I don't know what they are, but they're here to stay." Ashe pulled his arm away. The medallions were beginning to itch and burn with all the handling. He felt immediate relief when people stopped touching them. Now more than ever, he wished that the Vampire Council had given him more information on the Elemaiya. The three pages they'd offered weren't nearly enough.

"I have to make a phone call," Winkler unbuckled his seat belt and walked to the front of the jet where Buck and Andy were seated. Ashe watched as the Dallas Packmaster pulled out a cell phone and made a call. With the noise of the jet and Trajan suddenly asking more questions about what happened in Star Cove, Ashe couldn't make out Winkler's words.

"He has eight square medallions circling his upper arm, like a tattoo," Winkler said. "He doesn't know where they came from and it upsets him if anybody touches them. He said he tried to pick at them and it made him nauseous. Is there anything in the information you have that explains this?" Winkler had dialed the Head of the Vampire Council immediately.

Night still lay over England—perhaps one or two hours remained before dawn arrived. Winkler wanted to insist that all information be given to Ashe, but knew better than to demand anything from the vampires. It was tricky dealing with them. At the moment, Winkler was playing his hand carefully with Wlodek. At least Wlodek was answering his calls. For now.

"Give us time to do research," Wlodek replied smoothly, making Winkler want to curse. Wlodek, like most vampires, had a very good memory and likely knew much already. For whatever reason, he wasn't willing to give information to Winkler.

"Thank you for your assistance, Honored One," Winkler said respectfully. Wlodek ended the call.

"Charles," Wlodek leveled a glance at his assistant, "Go through the records and learn what the precedents and adverse effects are regarding underage turning." Charles stood in shock for seconds before going to do as the Honored One requested.

"Mr. Winkler will bring him here; he has transportation waiting at the airport," Marcus reminded a restless Sali. The young werewolf stalked a path through the kitchen, media room and then through the patio doors to the deck. Marco shook his head at Sali's impatience.

Sali wanted to drive to the airport and meet Ashe there, but Marcus held him back. Nathan and Lavonna were doing the same— keeping Dori and Cori inside the house. Dori was also upset, for many reasons. Marco's cell buzzed.

"It's Winkler," Marco whispered and answered the call.

"We're on the ground. Probably be there in forty-five." Winkler hung up. Marcus heard Winkler's voice clearly on the other end.

"Come on, they'll go to Adele and Aedan's," Marcus jerked his head toward the door. Denise, Marco and Sali followed him as he left the house.

~

"Aedan, please stay calm. He thought to protect us," Adele's hands shook as she attempted to calm her husband. Aedan was pacing, much as Sali had been. When the doorbell rang, Adele went to answer it, ushering the DeLucas and the Andersons inside.

Marco had called Cori quickly as he followed his father out the door, and she'd shared the information with Dori and her parents. Now they were all gathering inside the Evans home to wait. Adele offered drinks, but there were no takers. All of them were waiting for Ashe to arrive.

~

"Winkler, I think the boy's about to be sick," Trajan warned. Sam Sheridan, Winkler's brother-in-law, had come to pick them up at the airport. He jerked the van over and Winkler shoved the door open just in time for Ashe to lean out and heave.

Winkler accepted a bottle of water from Trace and handed it to Ashe when the bout of nausea looked to be over. Ashe rinsed out his mouth, embarrassed that this had happened in front of a van loaded with werewolves, including Winkler, Trajan and Trace.

"It's understandable," Winkler offered a wad of tissues so Ashe could clean himself up. Feeling shaky, Ashe climbed back in the van and the journey continued. Twenty minutes later and feeling sick again, Ashe arrived at his home in Star Cove.

"Here he is, a little shaky and nauseous," Winkler said quietly as he and Trajan brought Ashe inside the Evans home. Ashe was grateful for Trajan's arm around his shoulders. He wasn't sure he could walk into the house on his own without it.

Adele ran straight to Ashe and hugged him while Winkler and

Trajan stepped out of the way. She was weeping, just as Ashe feared she would. His father stood nearby, a stricken look on his face.

Nathan, Marcus and both families were in the background. Sali was growling; Ashe heard it over his mother's crying. Adele finally stepped away. Ashe was about to apologize for worrying everyone when Dori rushed forward, slapped him as hard as she could and ran out the door.

~

"Son, we're all upset. We thought the worst," Aedan handed an ice pack to Ashe, who held it to his throbbing jaw. Who knew Dori could hit that hard? It stood to reason, though—she was an ocelot shapeshifter with a lioness mother and a vampire father.

Ashe figured there was more of Nathan in Dori than anyone knew. Adele hovered nearby—Nathan and Lavonna had hurried out the door after Dori. Cori, Marco, Sali, Marcus and Denise were still there, and Wynn had come in with her parents.

Sali was holding onto Wynn while they watched Ashe curiously. Winkler and his small group of werewolves were doing their best to stay out of the way.

"Dad, I didn't mean to hurt anybody. You have to believe that." Ashe's queasiness hadn't gone away—in fact, it was worse. He worried that he might have to mist to the bathroom.

"Honey, I know you were trying to protect all of us. But we're stronger than you think," Adele soothed. "We lost a few, but they lost a lot. Ask Mr. Winkler. That Tanner jerk brought at least fifty wolves with him, and he had Elemaiya there, too. Only three werewolves got away, and they were swimming. There's a good chance they didn't make it. Mr. Michaels had his agents send out boats, but we haven't heard anything."

"He found Congressman Jack Howard floating unconscious in a raft, but that's it so far," Winkler said. "The esteemed Congressman is now in an Austin jail, waiting to be sent to D.C."

He didn't add that the Grand Master had passed information to

Matt Michaels on Tanner's compound outside Juarez—only time would tell if that information paid off. He also didn't add that Jack Howard admitted to Matt's agents that Ezekiel Tanner was still alive. That fact was one of several reasons Winkler was back in Corpus Christi—Weldon Harper asked him to stay in the area in case help was needed to track Tanner.

"They need to lock that creep up forever," Ashe muttered, meaning Jack Howard.

"Honey, you shouldn't worry about that right now," his mother said. "Are you hungry? Thirsty? You look tired."

"He was sick on the way here," Trajan said. "Probably from not eating properly." Ashe silently thanked Winkler's Second for not saying it was nerves.

"Not hungry, Mom," Ashe mumbled. The ice pack was numbing his jaw nicely.

"He's been sleeping on the floor," Winkler pointed out. "Might be nice to lie on a bed for a change."

"Certainly. We can sort this out later," Aedan said. Everyone scurried from the Evans home shortly after, while Aedan pulled the ice pack away to examine Ashe's jaw. "Might be bruised a little," he assessed, allowing Ashe to replace the pack. "Take a shower and get in bed, son. We'll talk tomorrow."

"All right." Ashe slid off the barstool at the kitchen island and walked toward the stairs.

~

Ashe glanced briefly at his computer after stepping out of the shower and toweling off—it felt good to be clean. Sighing, Ashe ignored the computer, pulled the covers back on his bed and climbed in. He fell asleep immediately.

~

"Mr. Winkler is staying in the house Marcie and Jason had," Adele said at breakfast the following morning. Trace had arrived moments earlier and was now sitting at the breakfast bar, having a plate of food with Adele and Ashe. Trajan winked at Ashe as he settled on a barstool to eat breakfast.

"Trajan, Ace and I are staying in the house with Winkler; the others are moving into the empty house next door. We lost Gene on St. Joseph Island," Trace mumbled around a mouthful of food. "Gabe, too," Trace added before sipping coffee.

Ashe nodded. He'd liked Gene, Gabe and Spencer. They'd always treated him well, unlike other werewolves under Winkler's command. But Jimmy, Winkler's werewolf cook—Ashe would miss him most of all. "Mom, did they have a service for them? For Jimmy, too?"

"There was a nice service held in Shirley's groves, for all the fallen. Only the werewolves know where they're buried. To keep their secrets, you know, since some died as wolves." Adele settled at the island with a cup of coffee.

"Yeah. I understand that. What about Dominic Pruitt—Jackson's dad?"

"Dead, too. They buried the rogues at sea. Marcie identified him, since he died as wolf."

"He got his own son killed." Ashe had trouble accepting that. "Just signed right up with Tanner and his rogues. He was going to force Jackson to work as a drug runner."

"People do terrible things every day, Ashe. We can only do as much as we can do to stop all of it." Winkler walked in with Ace and Trajan. "We've got the weight and exercise room set up at the school. And, I haven't let you go, yet. You still work for me," Winkler ruffled Ashe's hair. "Andy could use your help, most likely."

"How did you get in here?" Adele gave Winkler a speculative glare.

"Master key." Winkler held up the key in question. "Sorry. Won't happen again. We just heard you talking and came on in so you wouldn't have to walk to the front door."

"Once is okay. Twice and I'll bomb you from overhead," Adele shook a finger at Winkler.

"Fair enough," he laughed.

"Feeling better today?" Trajan asked Ashe.

"A little. Want breakfast? We have enough eggs to serve everybody, I think."

"Yeah." Winkler and the others settled in at the island. Ashe helped his mother make bacon, eggs and toast for all of them. Adele poured coffee while they waited for food to cook.

"If you'll do breakfast most mornings, Adele, I'll pay," Winkler munched on crispy bacon.

"That's fine, what time?"

"Seven okay?"

"It's when we usually get up and around," she said. "That shouldn't be a problem. What do you like, so I can shop?"

"I'll make a list," Winkler replied. Adele handed over a pad of paper and Winkler pulled a pen from his pocket. "There'll be two more coming, too."

"I'll pull in an extra couple of chairs."

The doorbell rang, so Ashe got up to answer it. "Check who it is, first," Adele called after him. It was Sali. Ashe opened the door.

"Dude," Sali stood with hands in the pockets of his frayed shorts.

"Dude," Ashe said and stood back so Sali could come in. "Happy Birthday. Want breakfast?"

"Sure." Sali walked in, nodded to Winkler and his crew and accepted a plate of food from Adele.

"Nathan's thinking about opening a fishing business. He may hire Jonas and a few others to work with him. He'll still guard the community at night, but others can handle the business for him," Adele said.

"Really?" Ashe was surprised. The Star Cove community really was digging in its heels.

"Then I may have a proposition," Winkler grinned. "How about we take one of those lots where a house burned down and build a restaurant there? You could run it, Adele, with no trouble."

"Well, there's an idea." Adele poured more coffee for Winkler.

"And if you hired the people who cook for the school, you could provide lunches for the kids," Winkler added. "That will free up space at the school for a gym. It wouldn't be a hardship for the kids to walk to a restaurant nearby, now would it?"

"No. Not at all," Adele agreed. One of the burned houses was next door to the community center-turned-schoolhouse. "And it might be nice for them to get away from school for an hour."

"And their parents could have lunch with them, if they wanted," Trace teased. Sali blinked, a horrified expression crossing his features.

"Kidding," Trace held up a hand.

"We'll have a werewolf work crew in here, clearing the debris from the burned buildings and working to rebuild," Winkler went on, pointedly ignoring Trace. "That will mean more business for the restaurant. I'll put up the money, Adele, and you can run the place. If you want."

"I'll do it. But I may make time to take a night class or two in marine biology," Adele smiled at Ashe. Ashe shrugged at his mother, giving her a smile in return.

"You can take the early shift and knock off around three or four, as soon as lunch is over. Let somebody else handle dinner. The place can shut down around nine. That gets everybody home at a decent hour."

"Sounds good. I'll work it out with the others," Adele agreed. "It'll be good to have a business so close to home."

"I can get you hooked up with my sister's husband and father-in-law for fresh vegetables. They grow tomatoes, avocados, potatoes and other things to sell locally. The citrus they ship out."

"That will be perfect," Adele said. "Can I get a number?"

"Sure." Winkler wrote it down and handed it to her. "Just tell them who you are and that you talked to me about it."

"Are we going to meet your sister?" Ashe asked, curious. He'd seen Sam Sheridan twice but hadn't seen Winkler's sister.

"Whitney is pregnant, so Sam is overly protective," Winkler grinned. "I'm gonna be an uncle."

"A new Winkler?" Sali asked.

"Well, Sheridan, but it's almost the same thing. If we hurry on the restaurant, I'll bring her here for dinner."

"That will be so nice," Adele said. "We haven't seen a new one on the way for a while."

"Ashe, do you need to help clean the kitchen before we haul you to the dojo?" Trajan asked.

"He can go today, I'll clean up," Adele said.

"Good. Are you coming willingly, or do we have to put you in a headlock?" Trajan grinned. Ashe was glad that nothing seemed to have changed with Winkler's Second. Sali had barely said anything to him since walking inside the house.

"I'll come," Ashe said.

"Sali, you and Marco should come tomorrow—I'll start working with both of you," Trajan said. "We need all the muscle we can get."

"Really? I can?" Sali sounded excited.

"It's hard work," Trajan said. "But you'll be better off. You don't get out of running, either. We'll work on getting a track sorted out."

"I'll be there," Sali promised.

"Good. See you tomorrow, kid. Come on, indentured servant," Trajan pulled Ashe off his seat.

"You actually know what indentured servant means?" Ashe lifted an eyebrow.

"Ashe says stuff like that all the time," Sali grinned. "He even counts the syllables in my words."

"Then I'll employ the vast vocabulary," Trajan said. "Come on." He herded Ashe toward the front door.

"Vocabulary—five syllables," Sali laughed.

~

"Sit down, Ashe," Winkler had an office set up already in the house Marcie and Jason had lived in for such a short while. Ashe marveled at how quickly Winkler was able to get things done. Ashe slid onto one of Winkler's guest chairs.

"Now, you probably know as well as I do that it wasn't any accident this community was located so quickly," Winkler began. "There's a leak somewhere, and it's possible that even with all the killing, we still didn't eliminate it. I want you to put your mind to that, whenever you're not doing anything else. Find the traitor for me. It's possible he's still here inside the community. If that's the case, he could sell us out again." Winkler's hands tightened into fists. Ashe knew what that meant, all right. Winkler wanted the spy.

And he wanted him dead.

CHAPTER 3

"Have you shown those things to your parents?" Trajan nodded to the gold medallions wrapping Ashe's left upper arm.

"Not yet," Ashe grunted, lifting two hundred ten pounds. He'd taken his shirt off and now lifted weights dressed only in shorts and athletic shoes. "I don't know what Dad will say. Especially since I have no idea what they are or how they got there."

"Damnedest thing," Trajan muttered. "At least they're not ugly. And they might attract women."

"Doubt it," Ashe huffed, pushing the weights up. "You see how Dori slapped me and all. I guess it was doomed from the start. She wants Sali."

"For real?" Trajan settled in to talk.

"Yeah. I thought she was gonna have a fit when Sali started dating Wynn."

"Don't sell yourself short, Ashe."

"Why not? There's not much here," he said. "And since I'm back from the dead, well, they won't remember anything except the bat pretty soon. Sali's a wolf. That's more attractive than a measly bat."

"You think they'll modify memories again?"

"Story of my life. Nobody needs to know. So they don't."

"Kid, I don't know how you deal with it," Trajan said softly. Ashe's acute hearing caught the words anyway.

"Not everybody has a vampire for a father," Ashe observed. He didn't add his current fear—that the Council might be dictating his father's compulsion on the community. Surely, they could just order his closest friends not to tell anyone what they knew—that would make things so much easier. Instead, their memories were muted altogether.

Ashe was glad his father couldn't place compulsion on him. At least nobody was attempting to suppress his memories. He worried, though, that the Council might learn of his resistance to compulsion. He also wondered what they might do if they did know.

So much mystery surrounded the Vampire Council. His father, too, if he were honest. Would he ever know how old his father was? That was likely a no. His mother didn't know. Why should he?

"Ashe, buddy, you're done. Go do leg presses," Trajan brought him back to the present.

~

"Trace, I have to get something for Sali's birthday," Ashe breathed as they ran along the narrow beach near Star Cove.

"Ah, sixteen today," Trace grinned. "I hear Marco took him to Corpus to take the driving test."

"Then I know what I have to buy for him," Ashe said. "I have to find a Cadillac key ring. He's always admired vintage Cadillac convertibles. He used to say that someday I'd have one of those cars and he'd sit in the passenger seat as wolf and ogle people on the highway while I drove." Trace laughed at the image. "Sali likes to hang his head out the window," Ashe said, making Trace laugh louder.

~

"Yeah—that one looks good." Ashe accepted the key ring from the salesclerk. Trace had allowed Ashe to hop him to a nearby auto dealership, where a key ring could be purchased.

The fob was polished chrome with a gold inset and the Cadillac emblem on it. Handing the cashier his debit card, Ashe watched while the item was placed in a bag.

"If he doesn't pass the test, you'll be in trouble," Trace grinned as they walked out of the dealership.

"He'll just take the test again," Ashe said. They had to find a secluded spot where nobody might see so Ashe could hop them back to Star Cove.

Everybody stayed out of Zeke Tanner's way. He'd growl (or worse) at the slightest provocation. Two of his wolves sported healing knife wounds after failing to move fast enough.

The entire compound was in the process of packing; Zeke had reports from a trusted source regarding the visitors who'd come to call in his absence. Two of those visitors were vampires and he didn't want them invading his territory again. He'd have to move farther south—another compound waited for him there.

"Damage any of those heads or the taxidermic animals and you'll join them," he snarled at the hired movers clearing out his trophy room.

Of everything he owned, Zeke was particularly proud of the things he'd killed and stuffed. If he had his way, William Winkler's head, wolf or human, was going to join his collection.

He suspected that Winkler was personally responsible for Dom Pruitt's death, and was sure Winkler had called in vampires to help. Tanner had the greater number of wolves and they would have won the battle if Winkler hadn't had several of the vampire filth there to fend off the attack.

"Are you sure it was a good idea, setting Jack Howard adrift in that raft?" Hutch, Zeke's new Second, asked. "He could tell everything he knows about the werewolf race."

"You think I give a damn about that?" Zeke hissed. "Let the Grand Master explain to the whole world that werewolves exist. They're not gonna come down here and ask us about it." Zeke pulled a semiautomatic rifle from a gun cabinet and slung it over a shoulder. "Come on, we're driving to the new location. Now."

~

"What can possibly cause rat's hearts to explode?" Randy Smith looked over the reports from the veterinarian. She'd done autopsies on dozens of dead rats from Chicago's old underground narrow gauge rail tunnels. The rat's bodies seemed in good health—except for their exploded hearts.

"No idea. No traces of chemicals or anything else, and those wouldn't cause this kind of damage."

Sara Dillon worked for the city animal shelter. She'd been drafted into doing the autopsies after so many piles of dead rats were found in parts of the tunnels. "Honestly, rats are vermin. We should count it as a blessing, unless other animals start dying for the same reason."

"Haven't heard of any," Randy shrugged. Sara was close to thirty, but was very pretty and looked younger. Randy thought about asking her out. Her red hair was cut collar-length and curled riotously about her head. Green eyes and a pretty mouth smiled often. At Randy.

"Well, uh, let me know if you hear anything," Randy stammered uncomfortably. "About other animals dying the same way, that is."

"I will," Sara said brightly. Randy, shy suddenly, let the opportunity go. He waved and walked out of Sara's office, the folder of autopsy reports in his hand.

~

"Mom, how can I write an article about this?" Randy sighed. Dawn, his werewolf mother, had come to Chicago to spend a few days before going back to New Mexico. She worked for the Post Office there and had more than enough vacation time saved.

"About what?" Dawn pulled a pan of lasagna from the oven. Homemade lasagna was Randy's favorite meal.

"These autopsies show that the rat's hearts exploded. The vet says she has no idea how that happened."

"Really?" Dawn went to the fridge, pulling out mozzarella cheese to make garlic cheese bread.

Dawn's hair and eyes were a dark brown, while Randy favored his father, Terry Smith, who'd had lighter brown hair and green eyes. His Uncle Ted looked very much like Randy's father, too, and still talked of Terry's murder as if it were three weeks ago instead of three years.

Ted had never known of Dawn's heritage—Terry had kept that secret. Protecting the werewolf race was of paramount importance and every human who married a werewolf swore an oath never to reveal the werewolves to other humans.

Randy, too, had never mentioned it to his uncle, although he'd lived with Uncle Ted and Aunt Mary while attending the University of Illinois, finishing in three years instead of four.

"I could write a few words about dead rats and the mystery of exploding hearts and put up a few pictures, but what good will that do? We don't have a reason and that might cause people to panic. I can go back to the city and see if they're willing to send more of their work crews down there."

"Sounds good," Dawn replied absently, buttering French bread and spreading cheese over it. She then sprinkled garlic powder and a bit of basil on the top. That went into the oven for a few minutes. "Would you get the plates, Randy?"

Randy sighed and pulled two plates from the cabinet inside his small apartment kitchen, then scrounged for forks. Paper napkins came next. Aunt Mary had cleaned out her cabinets to give him enough dishes to get by until he could afford his own. A junior reporter's pay wasn't that great, after all.

"Too bad somebody can't do anything about the bugs; I saw a huge cockroach in the hallway this morning," Dawn muttered.

"I'll call maintenance. They spray once a month," Randy said. "It's not easy getting an apartment in this part of town. I don't have a car and this place is close to the train."

"You could come back to New Mexico with me. Newspapers are published there, too."

Randy didn't answer for a few seconds. They'd had the same conversation several times. In fact, he was sure it was why his mother had come to Chicago in the first place—to talk him into going home with her.

New Mexico didn't have anything for him. A position at a Chicago newspaper might get him something better later on. He'd been fortunate to get the job he had.

Besides, if he wanted to move anywhere, he'd go straight back to Texas. He loved spending time with the paranormal community. His mother probably wouldn't stay there, though; New Mexico was home for her. "Mom, let me do this for myself, all right?" Randy pleaded. "Let me make my own way. Besides, Uncle Ted is close if I need anything."

"But your Uncle Ted isn't your father. And Aunt Mary isn't your mother." Dawn sounded hurt.

"Don't you think I know that? I miss Dad every day. And there isn't a day that goes by that I don't curse Paul Harris for killing him."

"Randy, you know not to mention that name to me."

"Yeah. Sorry, Mom. I think the bread is ready." Randy nodded toward the oven. Dawn rushed to get the toasted bread out before it burned.

"Ashe, I'm sorry Dori hit you. She was upset that you didn't tell her." Cori stood beside Ashe's makeshift desk—he'd fit the tiny thing in a corner of Andy's office.

Ashe had spent the day going over accounts for Andy, checking figures for him. The task had turned out to be extremely dull work. It was nearly time to go home, too, when Cori arrived.

"I know," Ashe acknowledged Cori's sympathy as he checked

another line of figures against what was written on a page beneath his hand. Ashe knew it was payroll for one of Winkler's businesses.

Andy hadn't said anything about it, but Ashe figured he suspected something. Ashe was kept busy looking for the sewing implement in the traditional pile of hay. "I'd be mad, too, if somebody did that to me. I know she doesn't want to be together anymore but the truth is, Dori always wanted Sali. I can't do anything about that."

"Ashe," Cori walked away from his desk to stare out Ashe's window. It overlooked the small deck and backyard. "Things are never fair. But you know more about that than I do."

"Yeah. Is she gonna hate me when school starts? Like she used to hate Sali?"

"I don't know. But you could try an apology or something."

"I can send more flowers."

"No, do something else this time." Cori turned around, her arms hugging her waist. "Marco says there'll be burgers, cake and ice cream for Sali around six tonight."

"I'll come if it won't make Dori uncomfortable."

"What difference will it make? Sali is your best friend. You can't go around worrying what other people will think."

"Dori's your sister, Cori."

"And if Dori would use her sense, she'd know she's alive because of you. I know that," Cori tapped her chest. "Dori's letting her emotions get in the way."

"It wasn't meant to last. I have to deal with that." Ashe put his finger on another set of figures and it tingled. "Wait." Ashe went back to double check the numbers. "Cori, will you go find Andy?"

"Sure." Cori went off to find Andy, who'd taken a coffee break.

"What did you find, kid?" Andy was back and looking over Ashe's shoulder.

"These figures don't match." Ashe pointed out the numbers. "I mean the totals here do," he tapped the bottom line on the computer, "but these numbers in the middle don't."

"I see that. Looks like somebody got overpaid. A lot," Andy scooted

Ashe away from the chair and sat down. "I'll take care of this. Go ahead and go. We'll see you tomorrow morning. At breakfast."

"Okay. Come on, Cori." Ashe draped an arm over Cori's shoulder and they walked out together.

~

"Caught it right off the bat," Andy handed the paperwork to Winkler. "The accountant is overpaying one of the secretaries in Little Rock."

"I'll get somebody on it," Winkler took the folder. "I told you he'd find it right away."

"Yeah, but I thought you were exaggerating."

"Not about this one, Andy. Want a homemade burger with cake and ice cream?"

"Yeah."

~

"Look, dude," Sali waved his new license.

"Yep," Ashe took the license away and examined the photograph. "Too bad, man. It looks just like you." Sali elbowed Ashe in the ribs for the jab.

"Come on, let's eat," Sali walked toward the patio doors. Marcus was grilling burgers on the deck outside. Sali and Ashe grabbed plates, put burgers together and loaded any space left with potato salad, baked beans and chips.

"This is good, Mr. DeLuca. Mrs. DeLuca," Ashe said. He loved potato salad.

"There's plenty here, Ashe."

"Am I late?" Adele walked onto the deck carrying a bowl of fresh fruit.

"You're right on time," Denise found a place for the fruit. Ashe and Sali were dipping out strawberries and grapes immediately.

Wynn, Dori and Cori showed up at the same time, escorted by Marco. Wynn held a nicely wrapped gift in her hands. Ashe's small box had already gone into the pile at one end of the folding table. Wynn set hers down next to Cori and Dori's gift—they'd brought one together.

Throughout the evening, Dori stayed as far from Ashe as she could. Sali opened his gifts, admired the key ring from Ashe and then followed his parents outside. A nearly new import sat in the driveway. Marcus handed Sali the keys to the small, red car. Ashe sighed.

"Look at it this way," Marco dropped a hand on Ashe's shoulder. "Sali won't ever be able to travel the way you do."

"But wheels impress women," Ashe muttered.

"There's that," Marco agreed.

"It was really cool driving Winkler's Mercedes." It was—Winkler had a new Mercedes SLR McLaren in black. Ashe thought it drove like a dream.

"I've never gotten to drive it," Marco muttered.

"I think Winkler was hanging onto the handle the whole time," Ashe joked.

"We'll drive to Oklahoma in a few weeks to finish the sale of the store—Marcie and Jason are buying it," Adele hugged Ashe. "I'll let you drive if you want."

"So that's where they went," Ashe said. "That's too bad. I like Jason."

"We all do. But Marcie doesn't want to stay after Jackson died."

"Yeah." Ashe watched as Sali, Wynn and Dori loaded into the car and Sali backed out of the drive. They hadn't even asked him to come along. The sun was going down and Aedan and Nathan joined the crowd shortly afterward. Ashe started walking toward his home.

"Son?" Aedan was beside him in a moment.

"Sali didn't even ask me to go." Ashe told himself that he shouldn't be upset over such a trivial thing.

"Ashe, you can't take this personally. You've been separated from them for weeks now, working for Mr. Winkler, and then we thought you were dead. Things will smooth out."

"Sure, Dad."

"Mr. Winkler told me last night that you have something on your arm. I'd like to take a look at it."

"All right, but it gets itchy and burns if people handle it very much," Ashe said. "And when I tried to scrape it off, I got really sick. So don't try, Dad."

"I won't. I just want to see it for myself."

Ashe sat on a kitchen barstool later, having a glass of water while his father looked at the medallions circling his arm. "That's extraordinary, son," Aedan sighed. "And they just appeared?"

"I woke up and there they were," Ashe said. "I don't have any idea how, why or when."

"Perhaps all the Elemaiya get them—I don't recall ever seeing their bare upper arms."

"I wish they'd given me more information than those three pages," Ashe grumbled, lowering his sleeve. "Maybe that would explain how this got here."

"How are you feeling? Still queasy?"

"No, stomach's fine."

"Just the heart, then," Aedan allowed the accent to slip into his voice.

"Yeah. I hope it goes away soon."

"Ashe," Nathan walked into the kitchen with Lavonna and Adele. "I'd like to see the arm, too, if you don't mind."

Ashe peeled back his sleeve for the second time while Nathan, Lavonna and his mother all looked. Aedan warned them not to touch, so they didn't. Ashe was glad when he could pull the sleeve down again. Another discussion took place, much like the one he'd already had with his father.

"I'm sorry Dori hit you last night," Lavonna sighed.

"It's okay. I had it coming." Ashe slipped off the stool. "Dad, I think I'll go to my room. I have an early morning tomorrow." Ashe walked toward the stairs.

❧

"I don't have any idea and Winkler already called Wlodek, hoping to

35

get information," Aedan said. "I could have told him not to waste his time."

"He has information we may need and he's holding it back," Adele muttered angrily. The gold medallions were beautiful, but Adele didn't know what to think of them on her son's skin.

"We'll find out or we won't, it's as simple as that," Aedan soothed. "And I won't be angering the Head of the Council by asking a second time."

Baltis stared at the one before him. He remembered this one, with one blue eye, the other brown. A quarter child, he'd been forced away from the Dark camp years ago at age sixteen. Now he was back, although Baltis' new guards had been rough with him.

"What do you want?" Baltis demanded. "We have little patience with those who seek us out a second time."

"I have information, Dark King," Wildrif bowed low, his hands shaking. He was filthy and his clothing smelled—he'd traveled through sewers and then the old rail tunnels beneath Chicago's streets to locate Baltis and his temporary camp.

Most of Baltis' people were with his brother, Prince Beldris, in a remote area of Canada. Baltis wanted to be nearer to his spies. Chicago was a compromise.

"Tell me and be gone," Baltis commanded.

"Your Destroyers? They are dead," Wildrif informed the Dark King.

"You have no proof of that," Baltis snapped. "The talismans have not returned to me."

"They will not return. To you or to the Bright Queen, who has also lost her Jewel Sentinels. The talismans have found a new home. With the *Ir'Indicti*."

CHAPTER 4

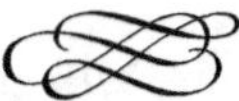

"There is no Ir'Indicti," Baltis was enraged at Wildrif's wild claim.

"No? Have you spoken to your sources? What have they said?"

"I have not spoken with them since the attempt we made met with failure. My Destroyers may be injured and making their way back slowly as a result."

"No. They will not return. Contact your sources. Find the truth."

"And if what you say is true?"

"Then you need a foreseer. You do not have one; I know this. You depend upon other means to gather information, now. Your former foreseer was also a Destroyer and could not see the Ir'Indicti. None can. To predict the movements of one we cannot detect, we must predict the movements of those closest to him. That I can do."

"Should you prove correct, I will consider this request. Do not count on it, or my patience." Baltis called a guard forward. "Contact my sources. Learn what you can." Baltis sent the guard away.

"May I have food and drink while we wait?" Wildrif asked timidly.

"See to his needs," Baltis commanded.

"Thank you, my King." Wildrif bowed.

~

Marco grinned as Sali's arms shook while lifting one hundred seventy-five pounds. "Come on, Ashe can do forty more," Marco said.

Don't make it a contest, Ashe sent mindspeech to Marco. Ashe was doing squats with Trace. Trajan watched Sali with a critical eye while Marco worked out with dumbbells. They went to run on the beach afterward.

"Come on," Trajan ran beside Sali, who lagged behind the others. "You run as a wolf. Now you run as a human, too. Don't expect to be perfect right away."

"Marcus, Nathan and Jonas are going to interview three candidates for the Principal's job next Monday, right after sunset," Trace informed Ashe as they jogged along.

"Do you know who's applied?" Ashe asked, his feet hitting the ground in a regular rhythm, accompanied by the swish of shoes meeting packed, wet sand.

"Somebody is coming from California, I heard. Another one from Colorado and the third from Kentucky. They made the short list."

"Do we know anything else about them?"

"Two are werewolf, one's a shapeshifter."

"Wow. They found a shapeshifter?" Ashe turned curious blue eyes to Trace's brown.

"Yeah. Don't know what he is when he turns, but he's a shapeshifter. The one from Kentucky is a female werewolf. If she gets the job, her husband will come with her."

"You're not giving the shifter a chance?" Ashe frowned at Trace.

"Ashe, it would take a really tough shifter to deal with werewolves, don't you think?" Trace turned his face forward again.

"So, a bumblebee bat just wouldn't be tough enough? Is that what you're saying?"

"Ashe, you know how they treat you. The other kids, that is. Even the shifter kids think it's a joke. I'm telling you that as a friend, not as a werewolf or a bigger shifter. Kids get bullied all the time because they don't fit into some cookie cutter ideal the others hold. Believe me; I know what I'm talking about. The Principal of any paranormal school has to demand respect. And get it. That way, when he challenges somebody for making fun of another kid, they'll back off and listen."

"And there I thought academic credentials and personal integrity were the guidelines," Ashe muttered sarcastically.

"It helps if they can read," Trajan ran up beside Trace. "Stop scaring the help," he jerked his head at his younger brother before dropping back to run beside Sali and Marco.

After his run on the beach, Ashe trotted homeward to shower before getting with Andy to see what the job was for the day. Coming out the front door later, he watched Sali climb into his car and drive away.

Breathing a frustrated sigh, Ashe loped down the street—Winkler's house and the community center were on the other side of the canal. He suspected that memories had been altered again. Shaking himself, he rang the doorbell at Andy and Buck's house.

"These are past year accounts," Andy handed a pile of file folders to Ashe when Ashe walked inside their makeshift office. "See if you can find anything wrong with any of them. We'll see about getting you a bigger desk—you're just too damn tall," Andy said with a grin. "On the bright side, though, Winkler says we can get a new computer for you. We'll take a trip to Corpus this afternoon and pick it up."

"Really?" Ashe felt a bit of excitement over buying a new computer.

"Yep. Get to work and we'll drive down after lunch."

Ashe took the pile of folders to his tiny desk and began to sort through them.

"These are the plans," Buck unrolled the large sheet of architectural drawings so Adele could see them. "We'll put the freezers here," he tapped the sheet where the kitchen lay. The building would take up the entire lot, including the back yard. "And Winkler asked me to tell you that he's buying a restaurant on the water in Port Aransas. He wants to hire you to run both."

"I think I'd like that—Ashe and I ate at Victoria's not long ago. We loved it."

"Funny you should mention that—Victoria's is the one he's buying. The owner wants to retire and just put it up for sale. Winkler got wind of it and was interested. He's got a lot of property in the area already."

"I'd like to keep the same menu," Adele said, offering Buck a smile. "We loved the shrimp and fish we got."

"There's a local shrimping business that's werewolf owned. They'll supply fresh shrimp and seafood, I'm sure. The Sheridans grow enough produce to keep two restaurants in business, plus some. And we have a line on any other fresh fruit and vegetables you want."

"This is exciting to me, Mr. Wilson," Adele said. "Please tell Mr. Winkler that I appreciate this opportunity."

"It's nothing. And call me Buck," he said, the corner of his mouth lifting slightly. "We're starting on this one tomorrow," he tapped the sheet again. "If the weather cooperates, we'll have it built just before school starts."

"That's wonderful. Thanks, Buck."

"No problem, Adele."

"Money's no object," Andy said as they looked through computers at the electronics store. A solicitous employee stood nearby, hoping for a very good sale. Ashe was busy reading the specs for two that he'd narrowed down.

"I want a better printer," Ashe said, pointing out the desktop he'd selected.

"Not a problem," the employee agreed.

After Ashe and Andy packed the new computer and accessories into a Winkler Security van, Andy drove to an office-supply store.

"Pick out a desk. You'll get the office we're in right now. I'm moving my office to the media room. Buck is putting a TV in his bedroom so you won't have to share your office."

"Really? I feel special," Ashe grinned.

"Yeah. Come on; let's find something that will accommodate those long legs of yours."

"This is as good as Christmas," Ashe said later, rolling an ergonomic chair across the tile floor. "I like this one."

"We'll take it. And the desk and credenza," Andy told the salesclerk. Another load went into the back of the van. "I think Winkler wants to talk to you again when we get back," Andy said quietly as they climbed inside the vehicle.

"What about?" Ashe couldn't imagine what the Dallas Packmaster might want this time.

"Not sure," Andy lied. Ashe knew that Andy knew but wasn't going to point it out. He was used to it.

"All right." Ashe buckled up, settled into his seat and watched the van drive past gulf waters.

～

"Ashe, I know we've asked an awful lot of you, and I realize your age, but I have a proposition for you," Winkler said.

"What's that?" Ashe was certainly curious.

"You took the SAT already, didn't you?" Winkler asked.

"Yeah—took it at the end of the school year, as practice. Did pretty good on it, too."

"Good. That's what I was hoping for," Winkler nodded. "Now, what I really want to propose is this; take and pass the GED, start taking online college courses and work for me part-time, permanently."

"What?" Ashe stared at Winkler. "I thought you had to be eighteen or older to get your GED."

"There are conditions for a sixteen or seventeen-year-old to get one, but I can pull a couple of strings. We can get a waiver, but you have to pass the test on your own. Besides, young prodigies and geniuses get into college all the time. Take the GED, Ashe. Pass it."

"I can pass," Ashe muttered, staring at his hands.

"Yeah. I know that too," Winkler said. "But the college courses are a must. I want you to enroll in at least nine hours and pass with a B average or better. I'm paying."

"You're serious about this?" Ashe lifted his eyes. Winkler's dark-brown eyes were quite serious. "What about Mom and Dad?"

"I talked to your mother this morning while you were out running. And with the way things are going with your classmates," Winkler shrugged.

"Yeah." It still stung that Ashe had been ignored by Sali, both the night before and earlier in the day. "Mom was okay with this?"

"She didn't object. She said Aedan would have to agree, but there's really not much of a downside, in my opinion. I don't doubt for a second that you can do this, Ashe. It's like testing out of your junior and senior year. They give the GED test at a community college in Beeville—it's the closest place," Winkler said. "Think it over. Talk to your parents if you want, but I think this is a very good solution. You can travel with me, too. Between here, Dallas and a few other places. I have meetings coming up in D.C. with Matt Michaels. I want to be in on the questioning of Jack Howard, as Weldon's representative."

"I see," Ashe said softly. Ashe's talents might get Winkler more information than normal questioning might ever get.

"I see the wheels turning, Ashe," Winkler said. "Go home for the day. You can let me know tomorrow."

"Thanks, Mr. Winkler." Ashe stood and turned to go.

"Tell your mother that we'll be settling on Victoria's restaurant earlier than we thought. She'll have it next week."

"Wow—you're buying a restaurant?"

"It came up for sale. It's a good investment," Winkler laughed. "Your mother will be managing two for me, when all's said and done. She's proven that she can manage a business and turn a good profit. It'll be fun and I don't have to pay for my meals if I show up in either place," he added.

"But there's COG to think about," Ashe waggled a finger at his employer.

"Ashe, I'm not surprised you know what Cost of Goods is," Winkler grinned. "Go home. We'll talk tomorrow."

~

"Sali, I didn't think you remembered who I was," Ashe grumped when he let Sali in the door fifteen minutes later. He'd just settled down to watch his mother prepare spaghetti sauce for dinner.

"I remember," Sali said.

"But *what* do you remember?" Ashe muttered despondently.

"Ashe," Adele gave the warning without turning away from stirring the sauce. Ashe figured she was cooking for Mr. Winkler and the others—the pot was huge.

"Who do you think we'll get as Principal this time?" Sali accepted the soft drink Ashe offered and took a seat at the island.

"You heard what Trace said this morning. The shapeshifter probably doesn't have a chance," Ashe said. "That's too bad. I think I'd like to see a shifter in charge of the school."

"What do you mean; the shifter probably doesn't have a chance?" Adele placed a lid on the pot and turned the heat down.

"Trace said a shifter would have to be capable of staring down the werewolves," Sali answered. "Can't see a bat doing that," he snickered. Ashe sighed helplessly at Sali's statement. He now had solid evidence that Sali remembered the bat—and nothing else.

"It may interest you to know that the Grand Master recommended this particular shifter," Adele informed Sali, who straightened up right away. "The letter was with his application."

"The Grand Master recommended him?" Ashe stared at Sali. Sali shrugged. "Mom, what is his animal?"

"We don't know, hon. How about setting the table for Mr. Winkler and the others?"

~

"Sali, things may be different this school year," Ashe said. He and Sali sat on the deck behind the house, eating plates of spaghetti and garlic bread. The others were eating and talking in the dining room inside.

"How?" Sali swiped the last of his sauce with a piece of bread and stuffed it in his mouth.

"Mr. Winkler wants to keep me on part-time and asked me to take online college courses. That means taking the GED and skipping the rest of high school."

"What?" Sali swallowed his food and stared at Ashe.

"What I said," Ashe blew out a breath. "He likes my work, I guess. Enough to keep me on."

"Dude, that's just, that's just—wow. No more high school homework? That's outstanding."

"But there's no graduation, either. Not from high school. College maybe, somewhere down the road."

"I'd be happy to give that up," Sali insisted.

"You can do me a favor, though," Ashe said.

"What's that?"

"Drive me to the bookstore in Corpus, so I can buy a GED study guide."

"I'll go with them," Trace volunteered when Ashe walked inside to get permission from his mother.

Marco went as well, and since Sali's car wasn't large enough, Adele allowed Ashe to drive Aedan's SUV. Ashe weighed different versions of the study guides later in Corpus Christi's largest bookstore.

"Here," Marco handed a frozen coffee drink to Ashe. "It's decaf."

"This is good—now I know why everybody gets addicted to these things," Ashe slurped at the caramel mocha concoction.

"Dude, aren't you done yet?" Sali walked up with an identical drink in his hand.

"I can't decide which one to get," Ashe said, tapping the books under consideration.

"Get both, Winkler's buying," Trace said, holding up a company credit card.

"Good. I can get the new book in my favorite series, too," Ashe laughed. "Winkler can get these," he handed both guides to Trace, "and I'll buy what I want."

"You read entirely too much," Sali grumped.

"Wait till you get in college," Marco teased.

"Dad won't let me out of it?" Sali begged.

"Don't give me pitiful puppy eyes. You're going," Marco said.

"Winkler won't hire you without college credit," Trace whispered beside Sali's ear.

"Really?" Sali sucked on his frozen drink.

"Yep. So get to work, slacker." Marco slapped Sali's back.

"Sal, your grades are decent so far," Ashe pointed out. "And if you worked at it, they'd be even better. That could get you into any school you want. Think of the girls."

"Yeah," Sali sounded bitter.

"Ixnay on the irls-gay," Marco made a cutting off motion with his hand.

"Huh?" Ashe stared at Marco.

"Let's go find that book you wanted," Marco hauled Ashe away from the reference section.

"Sali and Wynn broke up this afternoon," Marco hissed when they arrived in the sci-fi section. Ashe pulled the new hardcover he wanted off the shelf as he listened to Marco. "You saw the bracelet Wynn bought Sali for his birthday? He didn't want to wear it all the time. She got upset and now they're history."

"Well, Dori might get what she wants after all," Ashe muttered bitterly.

"Ashe, you can't let this bother you. I had at least eight girlfriends before graduating from high school. And in a small paranormal school, that's a lot."

"But you were cool. Sali's cool. Ashe Evans?" Ashe pointed to his chest. "Definitely not cool. And I don't have wheels, so I'm doubly not cool."

"I wish you'd stop looking at yourself in that light. Coolness isn't measured by what you have or drive. Anybody who looks at someone else that way is too shallow to waste time on."

"I know. But you see where we are and all? I can't go anywhere without a bodyguard. What if I want to go on a date, Marco? Is Trace coming along for that?"

"That does present a problem," Marco rubbed the back of his neck uncomfortably. "You could always flash that tattoo you have and your girl might not mind going on a double date."

"It's all moot at this point, I don't have a girl," Ashe pointed out the obvious. "And not likely to get one, either."

"Chad and Jeremy don't have any either. And not likely to get any," Marco chuckled.

"Where are they?" Ashe asked. "I haven't seen them around."

"On vacation. Jeremy's parents went to Florida and took Chad and Jeremy with them. Those two won't head back to school until the end of August."

"And Mr. and Mrs. Booth are such nice people," Ashe said.

"You think somebody dropped a cuckoo's egg in their nest?" Marco grinned widely.

"It can happen," Ashe agreed.

"Yeah, you'd know, all right. Let's go; Trace is probably seeing double, surrounded by so many books."

"Dude, you don't like to read?" Ashe asked Trace as they loaded into the SUV.

"I'm a little dyslexic," Trace admitted. "I had a tough time getting through school."

"But you're a smart person," Ashe said.

"Yeah, but the words on the page? They just scramble when I try to read them. I listen to audio books," he said. "I enjoy good mysteries when I have free time."

"I didn't realize wolves could be dyslexic," Ashe said. "Sorry, man."

"Not a problem. I like what I do. It suits me."

"Someday, maybe you'll teach me that Kung Fu stuff," Ashe said.

"We're working on that," Trace nodded.

"Are you sure this is what you want, Ashe?" Aedan leaned back on the glider with Adele.

"I think it is, Dad," Ashe said. "I mean, nobody really knows me anymore." He couldn't keep the bitterness from his voice. "What difference does it make how I finish high school?"

"Son, I don't know what to say," Aedan sighed. "It's almost too much. We've destroyed your friendships, I know. That's the only reason I'm allowing this now—perhaps you'll have new friends with Mr. Winkler's group. A few of them know what you are and what you can do."

"I like Trace, Trajan and Marco."

"I know. Don't give up on Sali just yet. He's been a good friend all along. Perhaps things will work out eventually. In the meantime, I expect you to study and pass that test. We'll look into online courses over the weekend. You'll work four hours a day, Monday through Friday, for Mr. Winkler. The rest of the time you can devote to your studies. You won't have a teacher reminding you to turn in homework, son—you're on your own. Fail any class and this all goes away."

"Got it, Dad."

"I'm off to do patrol," Aedan rose and walked through the patio doors.

Ashe waited until he heard his father leave the house. "Mom, why is it always doom and gloom whenever I do something different? Does he expect me to fail now? I never have before."

"Honey, he's vampire," Adele said and left it at that.

"I think I'll go work out for a while and then study a little." Ashe stood and walked into the house.

"My Queen, your Jewels will not return." Friesianna had finally consulted Rabis. Even with injuries, her Sentinels should have returned or sent mindspeech. Her efforts to contact them had met with silence. If any had been conscious, they would have replied.

"That cannot be," Friesianna turned away from Rabis, but he'd confirmed what she'd begun to suspect. "The talismans," she whispered.

"I cannot see them," Rabis replied.

"What does that mean?" She whirled angrily, prepared to blow Rabis away from her.

"That can only mean one thing," Rabis bowed low. "I know of your opinion concerning the Ekdi H'Morr. But it speaks of this."

"Go," Friesianna said coldly. "Get that cursed book and read it to me. Now!"

"Yes, my Queen," Rabis bowed and hurried away.

"Honored One, I know your mind is made up, but I disagree," Charles ventured.

"I gave him fifty years. That ended yesterday. Can I help it that he wasted so much time?"

"But the boy is only sixteen, Honored One. Surely he needs his father close."

"Aedan is a very good Enforcer. One of my best. Draft the message and bring it to me before you send it."

"I think he expected an extension, sir." Charles knew not to beg. "Like the others received. He believed, I think, that you would allow him to remain where he is until his wife's death. Another fifty years is nothing to a vampire."

"Except I need him here. He should be thankful I'm not recalling Nathan as well."

Charles wanted to moan in exasperation, but that was conduct unbecoming. Wlodek had his mind made up and nothing would sway him. The information Charles gathered on underage turning had not revealed anything positive on the subject. The youngest turning on record was age twelve, and that had ended in disaster—the child became insatiable and was hunted and killed.

Older children tended to be morose and depressed following their turning, choosing to walk into the sun not long afterward. Besides, Charles had read the information on the Elemaiya. Ashe Evans was already immortal. The vampire race had nothing to offer him.

Wlodek hoped to keep the boy under his thumb by compulsion—vampire law prohibited the turning of any human less than eighteen for a reason. "I will do as you say, Honored One," Charles left Wlodek's study.

"But you don't like it," Wlodek muttered at Charles's retreating back.

"My King, I was able to speak with one of our sources, after much effort," the guard stood before Baltis, panting with the exertion required to return to the King's quarters. "He has already spoken with the other spy and reports strange happenings."

"What sort of happenings?" Baltis asked.

"Water turned to fire to kill your Destroyers, my King. The Queen's Jewels died as well."

"May the gates be kind," Baltis muttered.

CHAPTER 5

"I heard you bought a study guide," Winkler said at breakfast Friday morning.

"Two," Ashe held up two fingers. "Already started reading them. They have sample tests I can do online, too."

"You're scheduled to take it three days before school starts here," Winkler said. "I got it set up this morning. Flunk and it's Star Cove Combined for you."

"I won't flunk, Mr. Winkler."

"See that you don't. Let's go. I think you still have some files to go through."

"Yeah. I do." Ashe got up and followed Winkler and the others out of the house.

Ashe listened to the rumble of heavy construction equipment most of the day—a crew had come to pour the foundation after more electrical and water lines were laid. He watched for a few minutes after coming back from lunch. Buck was there, wearing a hard hat and supervising to make sure everything was done correctly.

Ashe handed the folders to Andy by the end of the day, pointing out two that had problems. Andy was quite happy with the results. "I think we'll have more for you on Monday," he said. "Winkler wants to take everybody to Victoria's tonight for dinner, including your mother. Be ready around seven; we'll pick you up."

"Will do." Ashe waved and walked out of the house. Buck waved, too, when Ashe walked past on his way home.

⁓

"The candidates for Principal will be here tomorrow afternoon," Winkler announced over a dinner of lobster, shrimp and pasta.

The restaurant employees had already heard rumors that Winkler had purchased Victoria's and there was no lack of service at the table. Adele watched how they served the tables around them, since she'd be supervising the employees soon.

"We'll put the applicants up with Marcus, Nathan and Jonas," Winkler added, accepting a drink from a solicitous waiter.

"That should make Sali happy," Ashe said. A guest meant Sali would be turned out of his bedroom, and Ashe wasn't sure he wanted to invite Sali for a visit while the candidate slept in Sali's room.

"We'll take the candidates out for a meal on Sunday," Trajan said. "Just to feel them out. It'll be a late dinner; we'll wait until Nathan is up for that one. Then the official interviews will take place on Monday night in Winkler's office."

"If we don't hire him, the shapeshifter has another interview in Missouri," Winkler said, dipping a chunk of lobster in warm butter before eating it. "Lissa used to tease me about eating two lobsters."

"So she really was rare," Ashe observed. He remembered Winkler telling him that female vampires were extremely rare.

"Only fifteen or sixteen like her," Winkler nodded. "And they married her off to Hancock's sire." Winkler didn't look happy about that. "He made her life miserable."

"An arranged marriage?" Adele asked. "I'm not surprised."

"Sold to the oldest and highest bidder, that's what I understand," Trajan grumbled. "Lissa saved my neck, once. I wish you could have seen that." He smiled at the memory. "Winkler was challenged outside the full moon, and the challenger wanted the Seconds to fight. Old

Karl brought in a werewolf blademaster as his temporary Second, and I only fight with my hands." Trajan held up the hands in question—they were large and capable, but they'd never held a sword. "Lissa stepped in for me that night, and it was something to see," Trajan shook his head in amazement. "I wonder what happened to that video Hancock had? Thomas Williams was there as a witness, wearing a lapel camera Hancock provided."

"You know, I think you may have to tell me the whole story, sometime," Adele said. "You're making me curious."

"Any time," Trajan said.

"Lissa was the only vampire to be Pack," Trace explained when Ashe climbed out of Winkler's van later. "She saved the Grand Master's life, too."

"But if they married her off to an assassin, was she an assassin, too?"

"Ashe, walk with me a little way," Trace herded Ashe down the street while Adele stayed behind to talk with Winkler and Buck about the restaurant they were building.

"Lissa wasn't sanctioned by the Vampire Council when she was turned. Her sire didn't report it. That made her rogue. The Council sent Gavin Montegue after her. He hauled her in after watching her for a long time. She was working for Winkler, back then. The vamps almost killed her outright. Ashe, she had Elemaiyan blood. A quarter, if I understand right. She could mist and mindspeak. Gavin kept her on a short, tight leash, and they sent her out after the worst of the worst. That terrorist, Rahim Alif? She took him down. Several others, too, that Hancock or his successor, Bill Jennings, took credit for. And she took down the ringleader of all the Dark Elemaiyan vampires. I don't know that entire story. Winkler knows more, but he doesn't talk about it much. Somebody convinced her to go after another batch of bad ones after that. She died, killing them. Winkler wouldn't talk to anyone for a month after she was killed. Her grave is in Oklahoma, but there's nobody in it."

"Because vampires turn to ash when they die."

"Yeah. Let's go back. It's dark and I figure your dad will be out and about soon."

"He already is; I hear him talking to Nathan," Ashe said.

~

"I got a good feel for the restaurant tonight," Adele told Ashe's father when they met him outside the house; they'd walked around to get home. "The lobster was really good, too."

"I'm glad you enjoyed it," Aedan slipped an arm around Adele's shoulders. "Walk with me for a little tonight, my love."

Ashe walked into the house, watching as his parents strolled down the street, their arms around one another.

~

"We got a hit on the kid's email," Matt Michaels was on the phone the moment Winkler walked inside his temporary home.

"Did you get anything?"

"Oh, we got something, all right. I forwarded it to you. I'll wait while you get into it and we'll talk."

"Trajan, Trace, take a walk," Winkler jerked his head at his Second and chief of bodyguards. Both of them hurried from the house. Winkler settled in with his laptop and pulled up a private email account. He opened the message Matt forwarded immediately.

Hello, I am Ashe's grandfather, the message began. *This message is for you and not my grandson. Never fear, you will not trace this sending. The boy must be protected. The Bright Queen and Dark King are only now learning what he is, and his life may be forfeit if they can devise a way to take it. Guard him closely if you value your lives and your planet—R.*

Winkler cursed, then slammed his fist on the desk in anger and frustration before cursing again.

"I feel the same way," Matt Michaels offered dryly. "And that Wildrif nut? He's probably with those homicidal idiots now, telling them anything they want to know."

"We need to find them. I don't look forward to doing it a second time, but it probably needs to be done. In secret, if at all possible."

"I know. I want to get Ezekiel Tanner out of the way, too. He's still out there, according to Jack Howard."

"I'll be in D.C. next week, Matt. I'll bring the boy with me. We'll do some questioning, too. I want to find out as much as I can about Wildrif and the Elemaiya Tanner dealt with."

"Sounds good. I look forward to your visit."

Winkler ended the call with a heavy sigh. "Can things get any worse?" he mumbled to himself before going to find Trajan and Trace.

"The source says his father guards the community and his son is never far away," Baltis said. "Therefore, we will gather a few of our own and go after his father very soon. Wildrif will tell us where the father is and we will go after him. I suspect that they may move the child to keep him away from the others. They surely know he has been our target all along."

"That sounds logical, my King," the guard bowed low before Baltis. "Let me know when you wish to strike and we will go at a moment's notice."

"I depend upon you to do so." Baltis waved the guard away. "I must think for a while. Bring Wildrif to me tomorrow. The later, the better."

"Of course, my King."

Adele was frightened when the courier knocked on the door early Saturday morning. Signing for the letter with shaking hands, she closed the door quickly and leaned against it.

Thankful that she didn't have to make breakfast for Winkler's crew, she reread the return address before making her way into the kitchen. A postal box in London was listed as the sender. Adele knew what that meant. The Council had sent something for Aedan. Shoving it inside a drawer when she heard Ashe walking downstairs, Adele put on a brave face and began preparing breakfast.

"What do you have planned today, honey?" Adele asked as she put a plate of eggs and toast in front of Ashe.

"I was going to take one of those practice exams online and see how I did on it," Ashe said. "And then do some studying."

"That sounds good. Are you sure Sali doesn't have something going?"

"He probably does," Ashe replied glumly. "But I don't know about it. Sali and Wynn broke up," he added.

"I heard from Sharon," Adele said. "But they fought each other through so much of their lives, I'm not really surprised."

"Yeah. But I think Dori may take Wynn's place soon. She likes Sali."

"Hon, I'm sorry."

"Don't be. I think we were doomed from the start. It was nice while it lasted, though."

"I can barely remember being that young," Adele sighed. "Ashe, I was already a hundred years old when I met your father. That was more than fifty years ago."

Ashe sat, stunned, his fork halfway to his mouth. "You're a hundred and fifty?" his voice squeaked in an embarrassing manner.

"Yes, hon. I'm that old. No matter what happens, I'll always love you and your father. Don't ever forget that."

"When did you go to college?" Ashe whispered.

"I graduated just before I met your father. Going to London was what I'd saved for, back then. We met and that was that."

"You've been married for fifty years?"

"We were married by the Head of the Council. For a fifty-year period, that could be renewed afterward. Unless something happened."

"What do you mean, unless something happened?"

"Your father was an Enforcer for the Council. Wlodek said that if there were an emergency, your father could be called back into service. I'm worried, now. I got this from them this morning. Special courier."

"So they won't renew?" Ashe stared at the letter in his mother's hands. She'd pulled it from a kitchen drawer.

"I didn't intend to show you this, but you're old enough to know," Adele said. "According to the Council, our marriage expired six days ago. If this isn't a renewal, then your father will have to go back to London."

"He won't be my dad anymore?" Ashe felt like crying. Was struggling not to.

"He'll always be your dad. I'll always be your mother. No matter what." Adele was weeping now.

"Mom, don't cry," Ashe was up and hugging his mother. He didn't know what to do or who to call for help with this. He sent mindspeech to the first person who came to mind—*Winkler*.

Winkler walked into the house moments later, Buck right behind him. "Come, sit down, Adele, we'll get this sorted out," Buck led Ashe's mother to a barstool and settled her on it. "Ashe, get a cool wet cloth for me, please?" Ashe went to do as asked, quickly handing a damp kitchen towel to Buck.

"Ashe, let's go out back," Winkler led Ashe toward the patio doors and the deck beyond. "Now, what happened?" he asked. Ashe explained about the fifty years and the unopened letter. Winkler swore.

~

"Wlodek's doing this to pull the boy to him," Weldon said when Winkler called later.

Buck, Trajan and Trace had taken Adele and Ashe to the beach for a walk after Adele calmed down. "He can't turn him until he's eighteen, but this could serve to force Adele and Ashe to go to London, just so they can see Aedan once in a while. Wlodek will have that boy placed under compulsion before you can blink, and ready to come when called if he needs him."

"Then we'll have to work faster here," Winkler said. "I don't want to force that boy into anything. Matt wants him too, as soon as he's of age. The boy should get to make up his own mind."

"I agree. I'm sure we could work something out among all of us. Offer to pay for special assignments and such. If he were older, I'd send him back to Mexico with Grady and Clayton. I think Ashe could get Zeke Tanner for us easily."

"Lissa could have. She was older and not susceptible to compulsion. Poor Ashe, he won't know what hit him if Wlodek gets his claws in that boy."

"You saw what he did to Lissa."

"Wlodek has a lot to answer for," Winkler agreed. "But he wasn't the one who got Lissa killed. Her father did that."

"I still don't understand that." Weldon had no idea how anyone could set their child against an enemy that they knew quite well would kill her.

"Neither do I. She's beyond anyone's reach, now. Ashe—we have to watch over him. He's so young, still."

"I agree, but this is a delicate situation. Wlodek and the Council may think they're entitled to Ashe. They're wrong, but we still have to tread carefully. We can't allow the truce between the races to fail because we disagree over this."

"I know. If we resume the war with the vampires, we'll all die. Grand Master, I have to go—the candidates for the Principal's position are waiting at the airport. I'll call back when a decision is made."

"Good enough. Let's put some thought into this. If Ashe goes to London, we'll likely never see him again except as vampire."

"Yeah." Winkler ended the call and walked out of the house, nodding to Ace and Andy, who waited outside. They climbed into the van with him, Ace driving. Trajan, Trace and Buck were still with Ashe and Adele.

～

"Mom, what are we going to do if they make Dad go to London?"

"Honey, that's complicated," Adele said. Trajan, Trace and Buck walked around them, giving them enough space to have a conversation while guarding them. Ashe and his mother had arms about one another as they strolled slowly down a deserted stretch of beach.

"Can't we go to London with him?"

"We could, but that's the complicated part, Ashe. Your father still has a home outside London—he's kept it all these years and has somebody taking care of it. Think of it this way—Enforcers are always busy. You'll likely get to see him just as much here as there. In an entire year, he might have two weeks when he's free to do as he likes. Even then, he'll be on call. Your father and I have talked about this in the past—when he was willing to answer questions. Radomir went straight from Cloud Chief to the Council to make his report and then went right out on another assignment. That's the way it works."

"I think I hate the Council."

"As do I. We just can't make this harder on your dad than it already is. If he has to go, then he has to go. I think our home is here, Ashe. Perhaps we might visit London sometime if we know Aedan is free, but we have no way to know if or when that might be."

"Mom, this is the worst. The Council knows that not everybody has time like they do. Are they that nasty and vindictive?"

"They're used to playing a very long game and it's usually to get what they want in order to protect the race. It's one of their fundamental laws—one of the things that drives them as a whole. The race war killed off more than half of the population on both sides, werewolf and vampire, so of course they'll be very interested in whatever will preserve and protect what is left."

"But can't they make more vampires?"

"That's a very difficult proposition. There are specific rules to follow before a vampire makes another vampire. They have laws governing how many others a single vampire might make. They're immortal unless someone manages to kill them or they walk into the sun, so that's another reason. They're very powerful, honey. They can't turn just anyone—imagine what would happen if a criminal was turned. He would continue with his crimes but as a vampire, he could cause all sorts of trouble. That's why there is such a need for Enforcers or Assassins—at times even the best of them succumb to the thrill of power."

"They don't turn women?" Ashe was very curious as to why there were so few female vampires.

"They try. Most of them don't live through the turn for some reason. Those who do usually don't live long—Aedan said once that a lot of them walk into the sun before they reach one hundred years of age." Adele looked troubled over that.

Ashe watched her face—his mother looked very tired. Suddenly he knew that his parents had discussed this—the possible turning and how that might come out. Ashe knew without asking that his mother had already considered the idea and decided not to allow the attempt; it would likely fail anyway.

"So they're going to separate us. No matter what." Ashe stopped and kicked at a clump of dried seaweed. Piles of the stuff littered the beach on most days. Tractors came and raked up much of what washed up on the public portions of the beach early in the day, but more was deposited by unceasing waves afterward.

Ashe squinted across the gulf waters, which seemed to stretch endlessly toward the east. He felt no different from a pile of seaweed at the moment; it held no control over the sea which birthed it.

"Ashe, I don't think there's anything in that envelope other than a summons for your father," Adele sighed.

"Yeah. I get that idea, too. What about Nathan? Will they call him back?"

"I haven't heard anything, and Lavonna has never said if Nathan was an Enforcer like your father."

"I just assumed that they were the same, somehow. I don't know why I thought that," Ashe shrugged and started walking again.

"We'll just have to learn how to do without your father," Adele brushed a tear away. Ashe hugged her closer and they walked in silence for a while.

∼

"Do you want someone to be here?" Sharon O'Neill had come to check on Ashe and Adele. Jonas was at home, entertaining the shapeshifter candidate for the Principal's position. Marcus and Denise were hosting the female werewolf and her husband; Lavonna had her hands full with the single male werewolf—until Nathan rose for the evening, anyway.

"We have to deal with this, Sharon. But I appreciate the thought," Adele sat at the kitchen island with a box of tissues at her elbow.

"If we didn't have to entertain the candidates for Principal tonight," Sharon grumbled. "What will we do without Aedan? We've always leaned on him. We depend on him and Nathan to keep us safe while we sleep."

"I don't know," Adele sniffled. "Nathan can't do it by himself. He and Aedan were stretched to the limit as it is."

"I always thought they'd replace Old Harold. That never happened," Sharon agreed. "Surely there's someone somewhere who can come. The Council agreed to help support these communities. As I see it, they haven't done a lot lately. At least not for this one."

Ashe sat and listened while his mother talked to Sharon. He'd looked forward to Saturday—had planned to relax and study. Now it was turning into something he couldn't identify, forcing his world to twist itself into a shape he no longer recognized.

How could the Council take his father away? It made no sense at all. He sat gloomily at the kitchen island, sipping ice water and watching the clock. It was midafternoon and his father wouldn't rise for another six hours.

"Mom, I'm going out to the deck," he said and walked toward the back of the house.

∼

Ashe was preoccupied, dusting sand off his athletic shoes when a voice spoke right beside him, causing him to jump. He hadn't heard anyone approach and this man—tall, brown-haired and hazel-eyed, sat in a deck chair beside him. "They can't offer you immortality, you know," the man said while Ashe stared into his eyes.

"Who—who are you?" Ashe didn't know whether to be frightened and stay or be frightened and mist away.

"Who I am isn't important and generally I don't interfere with anything. Not long ago, however, I was informed that the giving of some information might not be interference. What you do with that information is up to you. The vampires can't offer something you have already. Remember that."

"Are you my grandfather?" Ashe worried that this was the person who'd sent the email message.

"No. I'm not your grandfather." The man smiled, making his eyes crinkle around the corners. It was a genuine smile, Ashe decided. "But I will say this—if William Winkler saw me, he would certainly recognize me. I must go." The man patted Ashe's shoulder and disappeared.

"What the—dang," Ashe breathed. Whipping out his cell, he hit Winkler's number.

"Ashe?" Winkler answered right away.

"Mr. Winkler, there was a man here just now. Just appeared from nowhere. He was tall and had brown hair. Sort of greenish-gold eyes. Said you'd recognize him if you saw him, but he wouldn't tell me his name."

Winkler cursed. "Ashe, what did he say to you?" Winkler demanded.

"He said that the vampires couldn't offer what I already had," Ashe replied, beginning to feel shaky.

"Where are you?"

"On the deck behind the house."

"I'll be there in a minute." Winkler hung up. He was there in little past a minute. "He was just here?" Winkler asked. Buck, Ace and Trajan were with him.

"Yeah. I didn't hear him come up or anything. One minute I was alone, the next he was sitting beside me. Who was that?"

"What did he mean; the vampires couldn't offer what you already had?" Winkler answered Ashe's question with one of his own.

"He was talking about immortality. What's that supposed to mean?"

Winkler muttered under his breath for a moment. "Ashe, I have it on pretty good authority that the half-children of the Elemaiya are immortal, just as the full bloods are. The quarter children aren't and that causes problems at times. I don't know why he chose to appear and tell you that, but it's true. If the Vampire Council says they can give you immortality by making you vampire, that won't be the whole truth. You already have that." Winkler sat in the same chair the other man had occupied.

"But who was he?" Ashe persisted.

"Ashe, how old did he look to you?" Winkler said.

"Maybe thirty. Might be a little younger. Why?"

"He's more than a hundred thousand years old," Winkler said. "And he can cause more trouble than you can possibly imagine."

CHAPTER 6

Josiah Dunnigan watched his crew unload boxes of electronics. He had another truck waiting and it was nearing time to quit for the day. He didn't want to be kept late, just because his crew couldn't move a little faster.

He didn't need the overtime, after all. Obediah Tanner had paid him well over the years—for information in addition to the occasional capture of a hapless shapeshifter for one of Obediah's lucrative hunts. Josiah was a member in good standing of the Amarillo Pack and he wanted to keep it that way.

He'd gotten away from the game preserve long before Obediah's bunch had been attacked and taken down that fateful night. He was now passing information to Zeke Tanner, Obediah's older brother.

He didn't come by the information himself—he had several carefully placed informants, willing to help for a fee or the promise of revenge. They all fed him information and Zeke was perfectly happy to pay for what he received.

In fact, if Josiah could manage to do this latest thing Zeke asked, he'd never have to work again and he'd be away from Ezekiel's demands. A ranch in Wyoming sounded very good and he could afford that, along with spending the rest of his life in leisure if he pulled this off.

"Bring William Winkler's head to me and you'll have ten million, free and clear," Zeke had said over the phone. Josiah intended to do just that, only he was planning to have one of his sources do it. He could blackmail them, after all. Threaten to go straight to the Grand Master with what he knew. They'd cooperate, all right. *Piece of cake.*

"Hurry it up," Josiah shouted at his forklift driver. "We don't have all day, here."

~

"Keep it quiet—it's not something your father or Nathan can do anything about," Winkler advised Ashe regarding the unexpected visit.

"But what can you tell me about him?" Ashe asked.

"Kid, this is going to sound really strange, but knowledge of that race protects itself," Winkler sighed. "So I couldn't tell you much at all, other than what I've already told you."

"That's messed up," Ashe stared at Winkler. "Are you saying that even if I knew anything, I couldn't repeat it?"

"That's exactly what I'm saying," Winkler agreed. "They may tell you all sorts of things about themselves, but there's no way you can tell anyone else unless that person knows what you know already."

"Is there anything else you can say about them? Since there's not just the one? You said *them.*"

"I did, didn't I?" Winkler's mouth tugged into a half-frown. "I think I can tell you they don't lie. Ever. But they word things carefully at times, so you have to pick through whatever they say."

"Are they dangerous?" Ashe searched Winkler's face for clues.

"Yes and no," Winkler said and left it at that. "Come on; let's go meet the candidates for Principal. You can tell me what you think."

~

Ashe shook hands with Catherine Copeland and her husband, Barton, from the Louisville Pack, learning that Catherine had been Vice-Principal at one of the school districts there. "I've already examined the test scores," Catherine said to Winkler as they settled in the DeLuca's family room. "They're all right but I think they can be better." Ashe disliked her immediately.

"Which scores?" Ashe asked. "There aren't very many students. Which scores are you talking about?"

"That's *to which scores are you referring?*" Catherine corrected his English. Ashe mentally intensified his desire to pass the GED.

"My apologies, ma'am," Ashe nodded politely. "To which scores are you referring? And how will your feelings toward shapeshifters affect your ability to run a school such as Star Cove Combined?"

"I will only answer those questions for the interviewing panel," Catherine replied haughtily.

"What if I want to know?" Winkler lifted an eyebrow. Catherine Copeland's head swiveled toward the Dallas Packmaster. She'd been courting him the entire time, Ashe knew. It was Mr. Winkler this and Mr. Winkler that, but when a prospective student opened his mouth, she became cold and arrogant.

"Children will be treated the same in my school," Catherine insisted. Ashe wanted to point out the lie, but held his tongue. He imagined that Winkler could smell a lie just as easily as he could.

"Of the seventy-eight students here, how many are werewolf and how many are shapeshifters?" Winkler asked innocently.

"Fifty-six werewolves and twenty-two shapeshifters," Catherine replied promptly. Winkler had asked that question for a reason, Ashe knew. If the race truly didn't matter, then she would have pointed that out. It was obvious that she'd studied this—had looked through the records already and knew which students were werewolf and which were shapeshifter. Ashe didn't want another bigot in the Principal's office. He'd seen enough of that already.

"How do you feel about moving to Texas?" Winkler turned his attention to Barton, Catherine's husband.

"Not a problem. I've been promised a position by the Grand Master if Catherine gets the job."

"What position do you think that might be?" Winkler straightened the crease in his black jeans. Ashe wanted to smile. Winkler dressed casually unless he had a business meeting, but he always looked tailored and well-dressed anyway. Ashe figured the jeans alone had cost quite a bit. The snakeskin boots? Probably made to order for the werewolf Packmaster.

"Some sort of administrative position, I think," Barton replied coolly. "Perhaps assisting Catherine in her work. I ran an insurance office in Louisville."

"Did you like selling insurance?" Winkler asked.

"Of course. I still do that part-time. If you have any insurance needs, I can give you one of my cards."

"I'll consider it," Winkler inclined his head. Ashe knew what that meant—Winkler was dismissing Barton Copeland politely. He was seeing a bit of the Winkler who sat in boardrooms and important meetings. This was a colder, more calculating Winkler. The Dallas Packmaster had already assessed Catherine and Barton Copeland, finding them shallow and inadequate.

"Ashe, are you ready to go?" Winkler stood with an easy grace.

"Yeah." Ashe stood as well and followed Winkler out of the DeLuca's house. They walked past Ashe's home on their way to the Anderson's. Ashe hadn't seen Wynn anywhere and imagined she might be with Dori.

Dori's home was Winkler's next objective; he strode purposefully toward the Anderson home, leapt up the steps leading to the porch and rang the doorbell with a flourish, turning to wink at Ashe while they waited for someone to answer the door. Ashe's assumption proved correct—Dori and Wynn both answered the door.

"We're here to visit with Dexter Beesley," Winkler announced, smiling at both girls.

"He's in the kitchen, schmoozing Mom," Dori muttered, refusing to look at Ashe. He wasn't surprised, either, to find Sali, Marco and Cori sitting at the island with Lavonna Anderson.

Dexter Beesley slid off a barstool and introduced himself to Winkler first. He wasn't as tall as Winkler—his hair was a medium brown with eyes nearly the same color. Dexter was dressed in a suit, even in such hot weather.

"Dexter Beesley," he pumped Winkler's hand enthusiastically. "From the Boulder, Colorado Pack. I've always wanted to meet you, Mr. Winkler." Winkler managed to pull his hand away, resisting the urge, Ashe figured, to wipe it on his jeans afterward.

"And who is this?" Dexter Beesley turned his smile on Ashe, extending his hand again. Ashe took it and everything shifted.

"Just keep him guarded," Winkler ordered. Trajan, Ace and Marco watched Dexter Beesley struggle with the silver handcuffs and ropes that bound his hands. He sat in a chair beside Winkler's desk, growling and angry.

He'd shouted at first, but Winkler threatened to end him so he was quiet for the most part afterward. Winkler had already spoken with the Grand Master and now they all waited for Nathan to wake and place compulsion. Weldon Harper merely wanted verification of what Ashe had already seen. Winkler stalked out of his office and went to find Ashe.

"Ashe, they've been hunting this guy for two decades," Winkler settled on the sofa next to Ashe. "His victims—all those young girls— have disappeared throughout the past twenty years. I think that's how long he's lived in the Boulder area. If we figure out where he was before then, well, other things might come to light. Matt Michaels is working on this, too. His contacts at the FBI may be able to close the books on this tonight."

"Winkler, that was the most horrible," Ashe shuddered at what he'd seen, unable to complete the sentence. Dexter Beesley had already marked Wynn as his next victim when Ashe and Winkler met him at the Anderson's. Ashe's throat closed up every time he saw those images replayed in his mind—Beesley had mentally planned Wynn's murder.

"Kid, I'm just glad I decided to bring you along," Winkler admitted. "I didn't like him from the start but I wouldn't have known why."

"What will happen to him?" Ashe asked. He was almost afraid to know the answer, but after what he'd seen in the visions, he wanted an answer of some kind.

"If everything comes out under compulsion, he'll be executed. If Marcus doesn't want to do it, Trajan or I will take care of it. Weldon was clear—no vampires on this one. This is werewolf justice."

"This time, I don't disagree with that." Ashe felt nauseous. The day had gone from really bad to much worse.

"Ashe, this is the way we have to dispense justice. You and I know that werewolves and vampires are different. They're too powerful to be placed in a human jail. It doesn't work; we've tried it in the past. This is fast and everybody knows what will happen if they run afoul of the laws and get caught."

"Mr. Winkler, you don't have to convince me. I saw too much of what he did."

"I wasn't sure we were going to get you back for a while," Winkler grimly agreed. "I was calling your name for minutes afterward; you wouldn't let go of Dexter's hand. He was screaming there at the end."

Ashe didn't tell Winkler what he'd done—he'd tried to give as much pain back to Dexter Beesley as Dexter had given to his victims. Dexter begged to be taken away from Ashe after Winkler finally pulled him off. "Come on, there's still one more candidate to speak with," Winkler patted Ashe's knee. "Let's go see what he's about." Ashe followed Winkler out of the house.

"Alvin Wright," the shapeshifter extended his hand to Winkler. Ashe stared. The man was huge. Nearly as tall as Trajan, Alvin Wright was broad across the shoulders and looked like a powerful, shaggy wall. "But people call me Bear," Alvin Wright grinned. His smile was nearly as big as he was.

"Bear Wright?" Ashe gaped. "That's what the GPS says every time it wants us to go in that direction." Ashe wanted to clap a hand over his mouth after he'd said the words—Bear Wright might toss him into a wall with a careless swipe of a hand.

"Yeah. I laugh every time," Bear's grin grew wider. "But they called me that before those things were invented. Maybe I should sue for infringement."

Ashe couldn't help grinning back at the man. He was dressed casually and seemed muscular and fit while thick, light-brown hair stood out from his head, lending a more rugged cast to his bearing.

Ashe couldn't help but think Bear Wright might fit well in a photo ad for outdoor clothing or equipment. Bear's nose, too, was slightly crooked—as if it had been broken a time or two. Warm brown eyes were still laughing as he pumped Ashe's hand, his grip firm and confident.

"You know the Grand Master?" Ashe asked as they took seats in the O'Neill's living room.

"Yep. Weldon and I got into trouble a time or two when we were younger."

Sharon O'Neill served glasses of iced tea and soft drinks to her guests. Jonas, normally quiet, was content to listen as Winkler and Ashe talked with Mr. Wright. "Got into a big fight with some sailors at the docks in San Diego during dubya-dubya two," Bear said. "Weldon had eight or ten on him. I was a yeoman at the time. I waded into that crowd and dispensed a little justice."

"The Grand Master was in the Navy?" Sharon sounded surprised.

"Nah. He was a Marine. I was Navy. He could have taken them down on his own, but how could you explain that afterward? With my help, no explanation was necessary."

"Quick thinking," Winkler said.

"Had to do something. Couldn't allow a fellow shifter to get in trouble, could I?"

"Uh, could you tell me—do you mind telling me, that is," Ashe began.

"I'm a bear," Bear Wright grinned. "Hence the nickname."

"And what do you think of shapeshifters who turn into tiny bats?" Ashe had to know.

"Kid, every shifter can do amazing things. I don't care if they're a gerbil. Ever see the damage a gerbil can do to walls and carpet? They'll try to tunnel through anything."

Ashe tried to cover a snicker, and then just let the laugh go. "Heard you had a bad day already," Bear Wright observed when Ashe stopped chuckling. "Don't let things get you down, kid. We're in this together."

The hour or so that Ashe had spent with Bear Wright was the highlight of his day. Now the uncertainty was back as he waited in the kitchen with his mother. Nathan would be asked to deal with Dexter Beesley when he woke—Aedan usually handled those assignments but there was the letter to consider. Marcus had already told Adele that he'd have some of his werewolves patrol the community. Aedan had the night to spend with his family.

Aedan always knew when something was wrong. Adele sat at the kitchen island, staring at her hands. Ashe had never seen her so defeated. "What is it?" Aedan sighed as he took a seat beside Adele.

"This." Adele pulled the letter from the drawer and handed it to Aedan. Aedan hesitated, as if he could hold off the news and keep his life as it was for a few moments longer. Finally, his fingers grasped the envelope. Ashe watched as the weight of it settled onto his father's shoulders. Slitting the envelope open with a slightly extended claw, Aedan pulled the folded paper out and opened it.

"Take him to Shirley's groves," Weldon instructed on Winkler's speakerphone. Nathan had placed compulsion, Winkler asked questions while the Grand Master listened in and now Dexter Beesley was scheduled for termination. "I'll call the Boulder Packmaster and schedule a meeting. Winkler, how hard will it be to bring Ashe to Colorado in a day or two?"

"Let me get back with you on that—I don't know if the Council is recalling Aedan and how quickly he might have to leave if they do."

"Understood. Let me know."

"Will do," Winkler muttered. "Come on, filth," he hauled Dexter Beesley from the chair he'd sat in for questioning. Nathan watched the Dallas Packmaster, his Second and three other wolves carry Dexter Beesley out of the house. Sighing, he walked out behind them, hurrying to get to Aedan's home.

"I go tomorrow," Aedan said. Ashe watched his father pace on the deck behind their home. "The Council's jet will be here to take me to New York, and then from New York to London on Monday night."

"Aedan," Nathan had come to join them.

"Nathan, it's time they knew," Aedan raked fingers through his hair. Ashe and his mother stared at Aedan. "You have to watch over them, son."

"What?" Ashe started to say something else when Nathan agreed quietly.

"I'm Nathan's sire," Aedan admitted, sitting beside Adele on the glider. "I'm eight hundred sixty-seven years old, Ashe. You've always wanted to know—there it is. Nathan, I charge you with taking care of Ashe and his mother."

"I will, father."

"Aedan, don't put this on him. What if they want him back, too?" Adele stood and walked to the edge of the deck, arms folded tightly across her chest.

"Adele, they renewed Lavonna and me last year," Nathan sighed. "Wlodek may be an ass at times, but he seldom goes back on his word."

"So we're not married anymore?" Adele whirled on Aedan. "Go on, say it. Say we're not married anymore." Ashe felt like crying. His mother was in pain and there wasn't anything he could do about it.

"Only in the Council's eyes." Aedan was beside Adele in less than a blink.

"Ashe," Nathan had his hand on Ashe's shoulder, urging him up. Ashe rose from his seat and followed Nathan into the house. "We'll patrol the perimeter while your parents talk," Nathan said.

Ashe dutifully followed Nathan from the house and walked beside him as Nathan navigated the street through the Star Cove paranormal community. Worried over what his parents might be discussing, Ashe shadowed Nathan as Nathan sniffed his way through the addition, looking for anything unusual or out of place. Finally, Ashe spoke.

"Nathan?"

"Hmm?" Nathan's focus was elsewhere.

"Dori was able to send mindspeech to me," Ashe said. "I think that's something that ought to be kept away from the Council." Nathan stopped dead at Ashe's words.

"When?" Nathan's eyes shone silvery in the moonlight.

"When the others were kidnapped and held on St. Joseph Island. I was trying to send mindspeech to her and Sali. I didn't get anything from Sali, but I did from Dori. She probably doesn't remember that now, so forget I said anything."

"Ashe," Nathan sighed, "Send mindspeech to me. I'll try to send something back. That runs in families, you know."

Can you hear me? Ashe sent. Nathan tried to send something back, but was unsuccessful.

"No luck," Ashe sighed. "I couldn't hear a thing." Nathan pulled his cell phone from a pocket and dialed. Lavonna's voice came through clearly to Ashe's enhanced hearing. "Love, will you meet me in front of the Dodd home?" Nathan asked.

"I'll be there in a moment," Lavonna answered and hung up. Ashe, worried that he might have stirred something up unintentionally, waited while Lavonna made the trek to the other side of the neighborhood, finding Nathan easily in the dark.

"Love, Ashe will send you mindspeech. When you receive it, see if you might send something back. Concentrate hard, my darling."

"All right," Lavonna nodded. *Can you hear me?* Ashe sent.

I can hear you! Lavonna's mental voice indicated her astonishment. Ashe was no less surprised to get something back from her.

"It's from you," Ashe whispered, staring at Lavonna Anderson.

"We will not speak of this outside this circle," Nathan instructed softly. "No one else is to know."

"I understand," Ashe said. He did. Nathan didn't want his wife to be targeted by the Council, any more than he might. With the information he'd gotten from his mother on the attempts to turn women, Ashe worried that Lavonna's life might be in danger.

"This is important," Nathan said, gripping Lavonna's shoulders.

"Nathan, I know what they're doing to Adele and Aedan. There's no way I want that to happen to us. The secret stays here." She patted Nathan's cheek gently and walked away.

"It stays with us," Ashe agreed and began walking down the street.

"Ashe, they'll try to pull you to them," Nathan said. "I had a choice when Aedan made me. He asked me as I lay dying upon the road. I was attacked by thieves," he added. "Aedan appeared and asked me if I wanted to live, no matter what. I said yes. I woke four days later thirsty for blood. You, on the other hand, may not be given a choice."

"Yeah," Ashe nodded, staring at his shoes. "Nathan, I'm sorry if your life has been difficult." Ashe nudged a small rock with the toe of his athletic shoe. It skittered down the paved street a short way before rolling to a stop. Ashe sighed as he watched it.

"It has been bliss, the past fifty-one years," Nathan replied softly. "I hope for another fifty years or more with my Lavonna. And my daughters."

"I hope you have that and more," Ashe said.

"I won't ask that you forgive the Council or any vampire, Ashe," Nathan said. "They can be quite selfish at times in their desire to protect the race."

"I'm glad you won't ask," Ashe said. "Because I won't forgive them. When Dad leaves tomorrow, I don't think things will ever be the same again." Ashe walked away from Nathan.

"If it ever comes to it, try not to let them know you're not susceptible to compulsion. Unless you're ready to defend yourself against them," Nathan called out softly.

"Don't worry about that, all right?" Ashe walked faster.

~

"Who wants to take this?" Winkler eyed Dexter with distaste. Trajan, Trace, Marcus, Marco and Ace had all come to a vacant portion of Shirley Walker's groves. Plowed ground and piles of dead vegetation surrounded them as Dexter Beesley's fate was considered.

"I'll take it," Ace began to unbutton his shirt.

"No. Dad," Marco looked at his father. "It's time I bloodied my muzzle."

"Then do it, son. Don't stop until it's finished," Marcus commanded. Marco jerked his head in a brief nod.

"Come on, filth," Marco growled at Dexter. Winkler and Trajan began to remove the chains from Dexter Beesley's hands and feet. "Get out of your clothes and turn."

~

When Ashe arrived at his home late the evening before, his parents had taken the SUV and driven away. He didn't hear them come in until nearly daybreak. Ashe didn't know what that might mean.

His mother had gone to bed immediately after, his father had locked himself inside his underground shelter. Ashe, lying in bed awake, hadn't gotten to speak with either of them.

He tiptoed out of the house after putting breakfast together and walked past the DeLuca's house to get to the beach for a run. Bear Wright was just coming back from a walk, carrying a few shells in rather large hands.

"This is a lettered olive," Bear held up a brown-patterned shell. It was two inches long and appeared smooth and shiny. "Olives are like that, right after the animal dies. If they lie in the sun too long after washing up, the shell will be bleached white."

Ashe fingered the smooth shell in his hands. That's what he felt like that morning—an empty shell. He might appear smooth and normal on the outside, but his insides had been emptied out. He was hollow. His life would never be the same. He knew that, now.

"Looks like you had a successful hunt," Ashe handed the shell back.

"I heard that one of my fellow candidates was eliminated last night. I spoke with the Grand Master," Bear said, his eyes searching Ashe's face. "And I hear your father has been called back by the Council."

"I think I hate them," Ashe muttered, his eyes settling on the water between Star Cove and the barrier island that lay eastward.

"Hate is a strong word," Bear cautioned. "It's best to know what it is you hate, before you say that word and mean it."

"You're saying I should study the enemy before I slap a label on him?"

"Something like that. Try to keep an open mind. Your father is vampire, after all. Do you hate him?"

"No." Ashe turned his gaze to his feet. He'd need new athletic shoes soon. Running on the beach had nearly worn them out.

"I don't believe you hate Nathan Anderson, either."

"No."

"Study your enemies. Make sure that they're not your allies before you apply the H word," Bear advised. "The Council isn't just one vampire." Bear Wright, candidate for Principal of Star Cove Combined, walked toward the paranormal community, leaving Ashe behind to run and think.

"Dude," Sali was standing in Ashe's driveway when Ashe arrived at the house after his run.

"You should have gone out to run with me," Ashe said before he thought. He had to think of Sali in different terms, now. As an acquaintance and not a friend.

"You didn't ask," Sali pointed out.

"Would you have gone?"

"Don't know," Sali hunched his shoulders. "Marco. Marco—he uh," Sali stuck his hands in the pockets of his shorts, uncomfortable, suddenly.

"What is it?" Ashe was concerned, now. "Is Marco okay?"

"Marco's good—a few bites and bruises but that'll heal up while he sleeps," Sali muttered. "Marco bloodied his muzzle last night."

"What?" Ashe stared at Sali in incomprehension. He drew in a breath when the realization hit him. "Marco took the execution?" Somehow, Ashe hadn't thought of Marco in those terms. He did now.

"It's a mark of accomplishment," Sali said, scuffing his sneaker on the concrete of Ashe's driveway. "A sign that you're looking to move up in the Pack."

"Sali, come in the house but be quiet. I hope Mom's asleep," Ashe said. "I'll get you some juice and eggs."

Ashe dumped scrambled eggs onto a plate for Sali, handing that plus a plate of buttered toast to the sixteen-year-old werewolf. Sitting down with a glass of juice, Ashe watched Sali dig into the pile of cooked eggs before speaking again.

"I keep forgetting that everything is different from what we see on television," Ashe sighed. "That werewolves and vampires hand out their own justice. That shifters won't ever lead a completely human existence. Humans outnumber us, Sali, and it confuses things. They're considered the norm, so I expect things to fit into that norm. And that won't ever happen as long as we are what we are."

"We get lessons from Dad on how to be werewolf. About the laws and protocol governing the werewolf race. Every pup is expected to learn and recite those laws. You move up in the Pack if you seek Pack justice, under the Packmaster and the Grand Master, of course," Sali stuffed more eggs in his mouth.

"Dude, I've never heard you talk like that. Your intelligence is showing, Sali."

"Doesn't pay so much to be smart if you're an omega wolf," Sali muttered. "Marco might be a beta—a Second one day. Me? I'll be farther down the food chain. I'll just be muscle for Dad or some other Packmaster. That's it."

"That's a terrible attitude," Ashe said, pulling paper from a drawer and digging around for a pen. His mother always kept pens, paper, envelopes and stamps in a kitchen drawer so they'd be found easily. "Dude, you could be a werewolf physicist or something. Surely, the Grand Master would recognize that. That werewolf doctor who came from Chicago? Man, I'd like to have his money." Ashe pulled the cap off the pen and settled in to write.

"You think I could do that? Be a doctor?" Sali stopped eating for a moment.

"Yeah. Dude, I always said you were smart. You just have to believe that for yourself. Study hard in biology and science. Do a few extra assignments. Read up on those science fairs and stuff." Ashe worried his lower lip as he struggled to write something appropriate.

"So, Salidar DeLuca, M.D.?"

"Sounds good. It'll look great on a plaque outside your office." Ashe scribbled through what he'd just written.

"Somebody's at the front door," Sali interrupted Ashe's censorship.

"Dang," Ashe disappeared in front of Sali and appeared on the front steps. Dori had a hand poised to ring the doorbell. "Mom's asleep; we don't need to wake her." Ashe hauled Dori against him, turned her to mist and landed her in the kitchen a second later.

"Ashe, what did you just do?" Dori and Sali stared at Ashe.

"What I've been able to do all along. Except the vampires don't want you to remember. So you don't. Now, if you want to remember what you just saw from now on, you have to keep your mouths shut, all right?"

CHAPTER 7

*D*ori fumed quietly while Ashe begged her not to be angry with her father. "Dori, do you want to know this or not?" Ashe snapped without meaning to. "Your dad loves you and Cori. More than you can possibly imagine. He's just trying to keep you safe from the ones who hunt me and from the Council. There may be others, too. I'm trusting you with an awful lot, here."

"But how?" Sali was still trying to come to terms with what Ashe could do.

"Elemaiya. I'm half. That gives me a little extra." Ashe, Sali and Dori were all sitting on Ashe's bed while Ashe attempted to explain what he was.

"But I thought," Dori whispered.

"Mom and Dad had to arrange for a fertilized egg. That egg came from the Elemaiya."

"Holy, cow, dude." Sali flopped onto his back a hand over his eyes. "This is messed up. What *are* you?"

"Here." Ashe pulled three sheets of paper from his desk drawer and handed them to Sali. "This is what the Council sent me. I think there's a lot more they're holding back." Sali sat up and read the first page quickly before passing it to Dori, who also began to read. Dori was gasping in a breath and staring at Ashe shortly after. Sali handed the second page to Dori, who read that and then the third when Sali was finished. "How many of these things can you do?" Sali asked in a hushed voice.

"I've always had acute hearing," Ashe pointed out that talent on a page Dori held. She nodded in agreement. "I have mindspeech, I can mist, I can do this," Ashe tapped relocation on the second page. "And I can shapeshift. Shapeshifting is all they'd let you remember before."

Ashe didn't tell them about the talents of illusion or manipulating elements—one could get him in trouble and the other was just too scary. Images of water burning and Elemaiya dying were imprinted on his mind.

"Dude, that says you're royalty, if you can do four or more. You have five, man."

"Yeah. For all the good it does. Sali, you have to keep this secret or we'll all be in trouble. Dori, I'm sorry I hurt you. Can we still be friends?" Ashe begged.

"We can be friends," Dori sighed. "Ashe, we just thought," Dori didn't finish.

"I know. I wanted you to think that, too, because I didn't want you to be in danger because of me. Believe me, it was the worst few days of my life."

"We'll have to tell Wynn," Dori said.

"Why don't you and Sali tell her? If she has questions, tell her to come and ask me," Ashe added. "And she has to promise to keep this secret. You can't tell Hayes or Jeff or anybody else."

"We know that," Sali huffed.

"Ashe, I just remembered why I came to see you," Dori said, even as Sali pulled her against him, wrapping his arms around her waist. Ashe hid his surprise as well as he could.

"What's that?" Ashe asked, ignoring the budding relationship.

"Chad and Jeremy are transferring to Corpus Christi University," Dori said. "They won't be going back to school in Little Rock next month."

~

"So he's leaving without a backward glance," Denise stared at Marcus.

"Aedan has been summoned by the Council. You don't ignore a summons from that bunch of old vamps."

"I can't imagine what Adele is feeling over this."

"Ashe, too."

"Hasn't he been through enough? Marcus, how many of us might have died if he hadn't done what he did—I've never heard of anyone burning water. I've heard of oil burning on top of water, but burning oxygen *from* the water? That's incredible."

"I can't believe the Council is pulling Aedan away," Marcus said. "But that may make it easier for them to take Ashe whenever they please without fighting his father."

"I'm glad Anthony Hancock went home when they all thought Ashe was dead," Denise went to the coffeepot. "Want some, hon?"

"Sure." Marcus took a seat at the kitchen island and waited for the coffee to brew. He'd had a late night, after all. Marco was still sleeping after taking the execution.

Marcus had been surprised by his oldest son's offer. Denise had responded to the news with a tightening of her mouth. Marco wanted to move up in Winkler's Pack instead of coming home eventually and joining with Marcus. Marco was twenty-one, though, and old enough to decide for himself.

~

"Wynn, it's all just a big plot." Dori had taken Wynn to the new school and now they sat behind it on a small, covered porch. They'd been inside the building a time or two while a crew of werewolf construction workers put up walls, built classrooms and a library.

The new cafeteria was being built next door, which meant a gym was going in now. A weight room had already been installed—that's where Ashe and Sali were working out most mornings.

"But why did he keep it from us?" Wynn was upset that Ashe hadn't come forward before.

"I think they told him not to," Dori pulled at a blade of grass. A few stray clumps of the reedy stuff grew next to the concrete porch and Dori had yanked up a bit of it. "Are you sure you're not upset over Sali and me?"

"Huh," Wynn scoffed. "He was at the right place at the right time. You're welcome to him. Just watch out. And don't buy him any jewelry."

"Yeah. Sometimes he's a butt."

"Sometimes?"

"Well, we should probably agree not to talk about Sali."

"Yeah. So—Ashe can do some pretty serious stuff." Wynn lifted one of Dori's grass stems and chewed on it.

"Looks that way. We can't tell anyone, Wynn. It will get all of us in trouble."

"I know. At least we know again." Wynn wasn't happy that their memories had been altered.

"I feel bad for Ashe," Dori whispered. "And I hit him."

"You sure did. Sali said his jaw was sore afterward."

"I didn't mean to hit him that hard," Dori admitted. "But I was mad."

"Remind me not to make you mad like that," Wynn snickered. "And Ashe said I could go talk to him?"

"He said so."

"I think I will." Wynn stood and brushed dust from the back of her denim shorts. "Want to walk with me?" Dori rose without a word and followed Wynn.

"Let's go have lunch in Port A," Ashe suggested. He was doing all sorts of things that Sunday, most of which would get him in trouble. Sali had caught up with Wynn and Dori as they walked toward the Evans home, joining the girls as they'd made their trip to see Ashe. It was early afternoon and nobody had eaten lunch, so Ashe suggested they leave the house and go out to eat.

"Let me tell Mom," Sali pulled out his cell. Wynn and Dori did the same. Ashe, who still had paper and pen on the kitchen island, left a note for his mother. A few minutes later, they were inside Sali's import and on their way to the Aransas Pass ferry, which would take them to the barrier island.

Ashe hadn't been invited to ride in Sali's car until then. He climbed out of the car once they were on the ferry and pointed out the dolphins to Wynn. She stood next to him, pulling long, white hair from her face when the sea winds whipped it about.

"Look," Wynn was bouncing on her feet as she pointed out the gray backs of three dolphins as they came up for air. Dori, standing next to Wynn, had Sali's arm draped over her shoulder. Ashe watched her and knew she was happy. He wasn't about to begrudge that. Besides, he was happy enough just to stand next to Wynn as she watched the dolphins, an expression of wonder clearly on her face.

"This is amazing," Dori said as they walked into Victoria's Restaurant. The glass windows operated like garage doors and all of them were lifted to allow the breeze off the water to circulate.

"Winkler's buying it," Ashe whispered when they were seated at a table near the outside deck. A fishing boat and a sailboat went past, floating toward deeper gulf waters. "And Mom is going to manage this and the restaurant in Star Cove," he added.

"This is so cool," Wynn said, looking around at the décor. Everything had a beach or nautical theme, with shells, antique fishing equipment and boat oars hanging on the walls.

Ashe glanced toward a nearby table, filled with young men staring at Wynn and Dori. Dressed in shorts and T-shirts, they'd likely been on the beach already, leaving it long enough to eat before going back.

Dude, those guys are staring at Dori and Wynn, Ashe sent the mental message to Sali. Sali cut his eyes toward the table before reaching out to rub Dori's back. Wynn, reading over the menu before deciding, seemed oblivious of the stares and subsequent whispers.

"Still planning on taking the GED?" Sali asked, ignoring the nearby table. He and Ashe both heard the whispered conversation between the young men. "They're drunk," Sali said softly, knowing Ashe would hear.

"Yeah. I get that," Ashe agreed softly. He didn't want to hear anyone saying those sorts of things about anyone, especially Dori and Wynn. "I'm studying the manuals I bought," he said in a normal voice. "Winkler says the GED test is three days before school starts in Star Cove. I have to pass it before I can enroll in any online courses at the University of Texas."

"You're going to work for Winkler part-time and take online college courses?" Wynn lifted an eyebrow in surprise. She hadn't heard this before and was understandably curious. Sali had to explain after bringing it up.

"I think so," Ashe said. "And since Chad and Jeremy are staying in Star Cove now, well, I think I'd like to beat them at their own game."

"Those creeps," Wynn sniffed. "I heard Jeremy met a girl at the mall in Corpus."

"Is that why they're staying? True love?" Sali laughed.

"Jeremy wouldn't know love if it bit him on the ass," Dori muttered. Ashe had to stifle a snicker.

"Get what you want, I'll buy," Ashe said as Wynn and Dori continued to discuss menu items and what they might be able to afford.

"Ooh—shrimp cocktail," Wynn said. She and Dori shared the appetizer while Ashe and Sali split fried cheese sticks. Ashe had grilled shrimp for lunch, Dori and Wynn chose fried shrimp and Sali had the catch of the day—flounder.

"This is so much fun," Wynn sighed after they'd left mostly crumbs and a few bits of food on their plates. "Can we go to the beach now?"

"Maybe for a little while," Ashe agreed. Sali was already nodding. The table of young men had left earlier.

Ashe was happy to see them walk out the door—they'd been rude in their comments, wondering aloud if Dori and Wynn were available, in addition to other, less savory remarks. Sali had growled a time or two while they ate; fortunately, Wynn and Dori were chatting at the time so they hadn't paid attention.

Ashe paid the check, leaving a generous tip—the waiter had treated them very well, smiling and joking a little. Ashe noticed he didn't do the same with the other table. Those patrons had been loud and obnoxious, demanding more pitchers of beer and then arguing that they'd been charged incorrectly at the end. Ashe was glad they were gone.

"Ride up front with Sali," Ashe told Dori when they reached Sali's car in the parking lot.

Sali pulled his shirt off the moment they reached the public beach, tossing it into the front seat. Without thinking, Ashe did the same. Wynn stared at him after Ashe dropped his T-shirt in the open window.

"Did you get a tattoo?" Wynn stared at Ashe's left arm.

"Uh, I guess," Ashe said uncomfortably.

"Dude, what is that?" Ashe recalled that Sali hadn't seen it either. Sali, Dori and Wynn were scrutinizing the eight gold imprints on his skin. "That is so cool," Sali breathed. "Mom and Dad won't even consider letting me get one."

"This was an accident," Ashe muttered, feeling embarrassed.

"A good one. That's amazing. Come on, let's take our shoes off and walk in the water," Dori pulled Sali toward the surf. Sali only halfheartedly protested.

"Want to go?" Wynn stood before Ashe, shading her eyes and looking up at Ashe.

"Sure. Can't let Sali wander off too far—he'll get lost."

"Just what I was thinking," Wynn grabbed Ashe's hand and hauled him along.

"Mr. Wright found one of these this morning," Ashe handed the sun-bleached olive shell to Wynn. "Only his still had color. This one is bleached out."

"Still pretty," Wynn said, putting it in a pocket. She and Dori had worn shorts and flip-flops, but the flip-flops were left behind in the car. Sali and Dori, arms about one another, walked ahead of Ashe and Wynn.

"Look what showed up." Ashe jerked his head around—he'd been watching Wynn as she searched for shells on the sand. The pack of young men from the restaurant now stood in front of Sali and Dori. They were likely still drunk too, Ashe thought. "And it's the one with boobs," one of the young men taunted Dori.

"Look, it's the stupid jerks from the restaurant," Dori said before Sali could stop her. "Didn't your mother tell you it was rude to refer to women as body parts? Oh, wait—you don't have a mother. You have a zookeeper. Escape the leash today?" Sali was doing his best to keep Dori back—she was about to land on her tormenter.

"You let her do the talking for you?" Sali was being taunted, now. The young man looked to be around twenty-two or so, as did the others. All wore swimsuits, no shirts. Ashe imagined they thought highly of their abilities if it came to fighting. Sali growled.

Dude, settle down, Ashe hissed mentally. Sali could likely take on all four of them; as a werewolf, he was stronger than he looked. Dori, too, could hold her own against humans. Ashe didn't want to start a fight with four drunken frat boys on the public beach, though. He stepped forward.

"Man, what's wrong with his eyes," another of the would-be assailants asked when Ashe came to stand before them.

"You will leave," Ashe commanded. "And you will forget you ever saw us." All four turned obediently and walked away.

Ashe and the others watched as they climbed into a car parked a short distance away. Spinning tires sprayed sand in their haste to get away. Sali pulled Dori close and they resumed their walk on the beach, but the day had soured after the confrontation.

Ashe was silent, pondering a frightening new ability as he walked beside Wynn. He'd only meant to scare the young men away—he was taller than all of them and hoped his presence might seem intimidating. Instead, he'd commanded and they'd obeyed. As much as he hated compulsion, it had turned into a blessing in this case.

No mention of compulsion was made during the trip home. Sali draped his shirt over the back of the driver's seat and leaned against it, shirtless, to drive away from the beach. Ashe had slipped his on again, hiding the medallions on his arm.

"You okay, Wynn?" Ashe turned to her as Sali navigated his car onto the ferry.

"I'm fine, Ashe. I thought it would be enough to ignore those jerks at the restaurant." Wynn brushed platinum hair behind an ear and gazed out the window.

"They were drunk," Ashe said.

"Yeah. It wouldn't have been a fair fight. I wanted to punch that blond one so bad." She'd named their main adversary.

"Wynnie, maybe you and Dori should work out with Sali and me," Ashe said. "Trajan can teach you self-defense."

"Really? You think Trajan would do that?" Wynn turned and flashed a smile at Ashe as they opened the doors to get out of Sali's car. The ferry flew smoothly through the water as Ashe and Wynn searched for dolphins again.

"I think he would," Ashe smiled back.

"Dude, was that compulsion?" Sali asked after they'd dropped off Dori and Wynn at the Anderson home. Sali parked in his driveway but walked with Ashe toward the Evans' home.

"I guess," Ashe shrugged. "It could be the weakest thing in the world, though. Those guys were pretty drunk. Even I could smell them."

"Yeah. They were blitzed, all right."

"Dude, I know you would have beaten all four of them to a pulp," Ashe turned to Sali. "But we don't need the notoriety. And your dad doesn't need to come bail us out of jail."

"I know. But it might have been nice to punch 'em a time or two."

"Yeah. I feel the same way. There's no cure for rude or stupid, Sali. Come on, let's go to my house and get something to drink."

"What are you going to do when your dad leaves?" Sali turned his glass of iced tea around, watching the damp ring it left on the granite island.

"What can I do? He won't be here. I'll have to live without my dad." Ashe had been avoiding that subject throughout the day. Sali was now asking about it directly.

Sali's phone buzzed with a text. "Dude, I better go," Sali said. "Mom's texting."

"Yeah." Ashe agreed. He followed Sali to the door and waved as Sali trotted toward his home.

❀

"Ashe?" Adele walked into the kitchen looking a bit rumpled. She was dressed in an old T-shirt and jeans—something she used to wear when gardening.

"Mom, are you all right?" Ashe hurried to get a glass of tea for his mother.

"I'm fine. Is there anything to make a sandwich?" She sat at the kitchen island.

"Yeah. Ham okay?" Ashe pulled ham and mayo from the fridge.

"That's fine. Hand me the tomato and I'll slice it." Ashe slid a plate, knife and the requested tomato toward his mother while he spread mayonnaise on two slices of bread. Adele had a sandwich in no time.

"Mom, I have a proposition for you," Ashe breathed while his mother ate. He'd been thinking furiously ever since Sali left.

"What's that, hon?" Adele looked up from her meal.

"Pack a bag. Go with Dad for a couple of weeks. You can clean out his house or something. Mr. Winkler can find somebody to watch over Victoria's until you get back. Just give me a little time to work on this. Dad can't just leave. They have to reconsider."

"Your father says they won't," Adele dropped half her sandwich on the plate and dusted crumbs off her hands.

"Finish your sandwich, Mom. Give me two weeks. Give Dad two weeks. Then you can come home and we're no worse than we were. I think Mr. Winkler would have my head if I don't behave while you're gone."

"I don't know," Adele lifted her sandwich again.

"You could come home anytime, but two weeks is sort of standard for a vacation, don't you think? You can take pictures with your phone and send them to me. There's plenty of time to mess with the restaurant here and with Victoria's when you get back. Come on, I'm sure we can come up with something in two weeks. I think the Council just wanted to do this quick so they could catch us off balance. They're counting on our emotions getting in the way of reason. If they send Dad out right away, then you can do some sightseeing during the day and shoot anybody that walks through the door at night. Unless it's Dad."

"How much time do I have before sunset?" Adele glanced at the kitchen clock.

"You have nearly two hours," Ashe said. "Enough time if we hurry."

Adele was dressed nicely and had two bags packed and ready by the front door when Aedan hauled two bags of his own from the bunker beneath the garage. "What's this?" He frowned at Adele's bags.

"I'm coming with you. For two weeks. I haven't been to London since we met, Aedan. I'm taking a vacation now. If those vampires don't want me on their jet, I'll find a flight out tomorrow and follow anyway," Adele said. "Ashe said two weeks. I'm taking his advice."

"Ashe," Aedan was now frowning at his son.

"Dad, there's a way around this. There has to be. That old piece of shoe leather isn't breaking up my family."

"You're calling the Head of the Council an old piece of shoe leather?"

"Yeah. Mom should go with you. If nothing happens, she'll come home after two weeks. I already booked a flight from London; here's the ticket information." Ashe handed an envelope to Aedan. "I'll miss you Dad, but I'll miss you more and I'll kick myself if I don't at least try to get you back. Now, I have one question before I drive you to the airport."

"What's that, son?" Aedan stared at Ashe.

"Was I born with pointed ears?"

"The doctors said it was just a slight deformity. You had surgery when you were two," Adele said on the way to the airport. "I put away all those photographs so you wouldn't see them and think you were abnormal."

"But I am—abnormal, that is." Ashe sat in the back seat—his father elected to drive on the first leg. Ashe would drive back.

"Son, we don't know much about what is normal or abnormal for the Elemaiya. I hope to learn more while I'm in London."

"I hope you learn more, too. Some of this stuff is driving me crazy."

~

Radomir waited at the bottom step leading to the large jet sent by the Council. "Those vampires must have some money," Ashe breathed as he pulled one of his mother's bags behind him.

"Good to see you again, young one," Radomir smiled slightly at Ashe. Ashe handed the bag to his father.

"Mr. Radomir, I think about you sometimes," Ashe said. "And I hope you're doing all right when I do think about you."

"That is kind of you," Radomir inclined his head. Ashe wondered how old Radomir really was. His father was pushing nine hundred, after all. "Are you not coming with your parents?" Radomir asked politely.

"No. I have things to do. Mom's only coming for two weeks. She's taking over a restaurant and building another. And just so you know; taking my dad away like this is bullshit." Ashe turned and walked away.

Sorry, Dad, Ashe sent mentally. He could almost see his parents staring in shock at his retreating back as he strode toward Aedan's SUV.

"You're not half, you know," the brown-haired man was back—appearing in the passenger seat beside Ashe as he drove toward Star Cove. Ashe did his best not to jump and wreck his father's vehicle in the process.

"A quarter? I thought you said I was immortal. Halves are immortal." Ashe might have thought the man was lying, except Winkler said he couldn't lie.

"Quarters are most certainly not immortal. Think for a moment. What else might be immortal?"

"Only a half-blood or better," Ashe scoffed. "I'm half."

"No. You are not half."

"The only thing left is a pure-blood," Ashe pointed out.

"Now he gets it." The man smiled and disappeared.

"Where are those papers?" Ashe searched frantically through the records his father kept in a fireproof safe. It wasn't hard to mist inside, gather everything he needed and then mist right out again. He finally came to the folder he wanted—he'd scanned through it once before but he didn't have as much information then as he did now. "Ah, here it is—dang. Both donors listed as anonymous." Ashe flopped the paper onto his father's desk with a sigh.

Winkler expected Ashe to sleep at his temporary home—it was one of the conditions his father had set before he'd allow Ashe to stay behind in Star Cove. Ashe would have given anything to go to England with his parents. On vacation. Perhaps that might happen someday. Ashe strode from his father's study to pack a bag.

~

Ashe ate tacos at Winkler's kitchen island with Trace, Trajan and Winkler. "Trajan, Dori and Wynn want to come and work out with us," Ashe said as he dumped taco sauce on a third taco. "They want to learn self-defense."

"That's a good idea," Trajan agreed. "They're welcome anytime. As are any of the others."

"Mr. Winkler, I had another visit from that man. He showed up while I was driving home from the airport."

Winkler carefully set his taco down—he'd been about to take a bite of it. "What did he do this time?" Winkler's dark eyes were concerned.

"He says I'm not half."

"He said the last time that you were immortal. That spells half, Ashe." Winkler cursed softly to drive home his point. "You're not a quarter, I'd bet money on it."

"He said I wasn't a quarter, either."

"But what's left?" Trajan grabbed another packet of taco sauce.

"Full." Winkler had gotten there first.

"Yeah. I went through the folder of information my parents have locked up and both donors are listed as anonymous," Ashe muttered.

"So the egg was donated by a female and then fertilized by a male Elemaiya. That's the only way this might have happened," Winkler observed.

"Yeah. I was born with pointed ears and everything. Mom said they did reconstructive surgery when I was two. The surgeon said it was only a slight deformity."

"A slight deformity." Winkler rose and went to the fridge to pull out a beer. Trajan and Trace got one, too. Ashe asked for another soda.

"Will it bother you that I'm not a half?" Ashe asked.

"Kid, I don't care if you're a stink-eyed humpback," Winkler said, making Ashe laugh. He had no idea that Winkler had gone to see any of a popular movie series, which depicted many fictional characters.

"Read the books, too," Winkler said. "To my kids. They couldn't get enough of that stuff."

"I caught him reading ahead—several times," Trajan whispered theatrically.

"How's Marco doing?" Ashe asked.

"He's fine. Coming to terms with his place in the world," Trajan opened up the box containing their dessert—a pineapple upside-down cake from an Aransas Pass bake shop.

Ashe accepted his slice of cake with a glass of milk. He cleaned up the kitchen afterward, too.

"Have everything you need? Clothes? Toothbrush?" Winkler stuck his head inside Ashe's office, where a cot had been set up for him.

"Yeah. I got it," Ashe said.

"Don't stay up too late," Winkler warned. Ashe was flipping through one of his study guides.

"I'll be in bed by eleven," Ashe promised. Winkler closed the door.

"The father and mother are in transit," Wildrif bowed before Baltis. I will tell you when they settle for more than three days. Then you may send your guards, my King."

"Do so. Leave me now, I wish to think on this in peace."

"Of course, my King." Wildrif bowed a second time.

"Send word to my brother. Have Dauntless brought to me. I will send you, Dauntless and four others after the boy's parents as soon as they remain stationary." Baltis extended the royal seal to Fearless, his personal guard.

"Shall I carry any other message, my King?" Fearless asked.

"Yes. Tell my brother to remain hidden. We will take the boy for our own and Beldris will instruct him in our ways. He will either obey us or die."

"You do not believe the H'Morr?" Fearless asked.

"Faugh—that worthless bit of prophecy? You saw what happened to its author, did you not?"

"Saldis, my King? Of course I know what happened to him. He

died at the hands of Diamond, the Queen's Chief Sentinel, when he refused to serve her after the coup against her predecessor."

"Didn't see that coming," Baltis laughed at his own joke. "Go now and visit my brother."

"As you say, my King." Fearless bowed respectfully before relocating.

CHAPTER 8

"What happened?" Ezekiel Tanner asked Josiah. Zeke contacted Josiah after the relocation of Zeke's compound outside Juarez was complete.

"Dexter managed to get himself caught, that's what," Josiah grumbled. "But my source says that the vampire didn't question him about anything other than his little indiscretions. We're still in the clear on that quarter."

"But we were going to pair him with your other source," Zeke muttered angrily. "Who do you have to replace him?"

"Nobody available at the moment. I may go myself."

"Might be risky. Winkler may suspect the Amarillo Pack. The Grand Master didn't ask any of you to help take down my brother. Find someone else if you can. If not, then go to Corpus Christi but remain hidden as long as possible. I want Winkler's head hanging in my trophy room—wolf or man, doesn't matter."

"I'll arrange it, Mr. Tanner," Josiah promised.

Ashe was already on the weight bench the following morning when

Sali walked in with Wynn and Dori. Ashe was surprised that Wynn didn't bear animosity toward Dori or Sali, but she didn't.

Trajan put the new arrivals to work right away. Sali worked out with the butterfly machine while Wynn and Dori lifted dumbbells. Trajan wanted to build their arm strength before setting them harder tasks. Ashe thought Trajan might be underestimating Dori—she'd hit him with a good right hook.

Trajan pushed them hard that morning, with Trace working with Sali and Ashe while Trajan watched over the girls. Ashe thought Dori might balk when it came to running down the beach, but she gamely kept up with Wynn, who was used to running on the full moon. Dori, as the ocelot, went prowling with her mother's lioness and Cori's panther, when Cori was home.

"You're running better, bro," Marco ran up at the last, Cori trailing him gamely. Ashe spared a grin for Cori, who'd been noticeably absent for the past two days.

"Went to enroll for the fall semester at Corpus Christi University," Cori said. "Got everything transferred down, I just had to finalize my classes."

"Good for you," Ashe said. "I'm going to take online courses with the University of Texas. Winkler insisted, and since he's paying," Ashe shrugged.

"Have to pass the GED first," Sali poked Ashe in the ribs.

"Sali, wait up," Dori moaned behind him.

"Sorry, baby," Sali dropped back to run with Dori.

Baby? Ashe mentally poked at Sali.

"You had your chance, dude," Sali grinned.

"Don't forget to stretch again," Trajan called after Dori, Wynn and Sali as they walked toward their respective homes later. Sali, nearly out of breath, waved at Trajan and kept walking.

"So—a man now and all?" Ashe stretched beside Marco. Cori was nearby, listening.

"A calculated risk, Ashe," Marco huffed as he pulled a leg up from behind to stretch it. "He wasn't going to live, one way or another. I decided to take it."

"He was a terrible person," Ashe nodded. "I'm still glad I didn't see it."

"Pack law dictates that executions are all Pack, unless someone from another race is instrumental in the capture. You could have gone if you wanted, Ashe. We didn't figure you'd want to."

"Yeah. You were right." Ashe shivered in the early-morning light. He still had a few screams in his head he couldn't easily banish after seeing Dexter Beesley's memories. "Marco?"

"What?" Marco was pulling the other leg up this time.

"Who killed Paul Harris?"

"Ah. Well, Dad took that one himself."

Ashe nodded. "I'll get in the shower," he walked toward Winkler's house. "Oh," he turned back to Marco one last time. "I still don't understand how Billings thought he could take on your Dad. I don't know much about him, but if I were a werewolf, there's no way I'd make a challenge against Marcus. Unless I wanted to commit suicide."

"And you'd be right to think that," Marco agreed. "I'll see you for lunch, maybe."

"Yeah." Ashe walked through Winkler's front door.

"We'll take a trip to Boulder on Tuesday, and continue to D.C. on Wednesday," Winkler sat beside Ashe's desk. Andy had found a chair somewhere so Ashe could have an occasional visitor. "Someone will go with you to pack more clothes tonight after work. Pack some nice stuff, too. We can go out to eat afterward."

"What are we doing in Boulder and D.C.?" Ashe asked. While he waited for Winkler to answer, he handed two folders to Andy. No information was contained in either folder to tell him whether these were Winkler Security divisions or something else. Ashe decided he didn't want to know. "I circled the questionable entries," Ashe said. Andy flipped the top folder open, nodded and walked out.

"Weldon wants to meet us in Boulder and question the

Packmaster. We want to know if he had any inkling of what Dexter was doing and just failed to report it."

"How am I supposed to help with that?" Ashe asked. "I thought interrogation was your area."

"It is. But it seems that Sali told Marco about an incident on the beach yesterday. I'd like to see how that might help us out—in Boulder and D.C. After all, a vampire is only awake during the night. You're available twenty-four-seven."

"Does everybody tell on me now?" Ashe rose from his desk chair, angry immediately.

"I didn't say that to upset you," Winkler attempted to calm Ashe. "Marco has sworn oaths as a member of the Dallas Pack. He's loyal to me and tells me what I ask of him."

"Is that how it works?" Ashe snapped. "I haven't sworn any oaths, Mr. Winkler."

"You're too young and you're not Pack. Werewolves do the oaths the first time they run with the Pack. Human children or mates of werewolves do a different oath and they have to be at least eighteen to take it."

"But the people I think are my friends can betray me at every turn? Is that it?" Ashe was prepared to go to mist. He wanted to scream and cry. The bitterness almost overwhelmed him. Sali had promised. He'd *promised.*

"Ashe, no." Winkler had him gripped in an embrace quickly. "We're the people who care about you."

"Yeah?" Ashe hopped to the other side of the room, away from Winkler's hug. "All I see are people trying to use me." He wiped dampness from his cheeks. "The Council takes my dad, because that's a way to take me. The Elemaiya hunt me because they want to kill me or bend me to their will. I can't trust anybody, can I?" Ashe disappeared before Winkler could stop him.

"Teenage hormones," Trajan set a cup of coffee in front of Winkler.

Winkler muttered a rude oath and lifted the cup. "Now, we just have to figure out how to find him."

"If he's not back by ten tonight, call his cell," Trace suggested.

"I know now not to tell him that Marco is bringing me information," Winkler blew out a sigh.

"He thinks of Marco as a friend. You just ended that friendship," Trajan observed.

"You think I don't know that? Sometimes I should have a lock on my mouth."

"The relationship with Sali was tenuous, too," Trace said. "And that may be over as well. After all, Marcus would have been hauling Sali out of jail if he'd jumped those drunks. Ashe took care of the situation."

"And he'll figure out that we know he told Sali, Wynn and Dori what he can do. He needs peers who know what he can do and understand him better because of it. Not somebody who's gonna run to the older folks every time they see something out of the ordinary," Trajan added. "We betrayed a trust, boss. Big time."

"Yeah. I get that." Winkler rubbed the back of his neck uncomfortably. "I don't want to report to his parents that we managed to lose him in only a day."

"He doesn't have a soul to confide in, now," Trace said. "At least I had Trajan and Jason to talk to when I was in school. We ruined things for Ashe, boss."

"Randy, it's better if you don't know how I got here," Ashe sat at Randy's tiny kitchen table drinking a soda.

"It's good to see you. Mom went home three days ago. Tried to talk me into going back to New Mexico with her. I don't have any good memories of that place, Ashe." Randy shuddered.

"Yeah. I know that," Ashe nodded and sipped his drink.

"Tell me why you're here, man." Randy said.

"Can't. And I have to go back before they call out the dogs. You know what I mean."

"Yeah. Been there," Randy grumped. "Life's not great here, either. I'm still trying to figure out how rat hearts are exploding in the old train tunnels beneath Chicago. Nobody else is reporting rat deaths by the hundreds."

"Their hearts are exploding?" Ashe jerked his head up. He'd been staring at his soda can, tracing a finger through the condensation on the side.

"Yeah. Know anything about that?"

"Not for sure," Ashe hedged. "Randy, stay away from those tunnels. You can take that warning to the bank. I'll have to let Mr. Winkler know—if I can stomach talking to him. Gotta go." Ashe stood. "Thanks for the soda." Ashe walked toward the door of Randy's tiny, slightly untidy apartment. "Find another story, Randy. Leave the rats alone for now."

~

"Don't say another word to me and keep Marco and Sali away. They're not my friends. Never have been." Ashe threw clothing into a roller bag much harder than necessary. Trajan had been watching for lights to come on in the Evans home. He'd been rewarded around nine that evening. Now he watched Ashe pack for the trip, anger in every movement.

"Ashe, I could give you all kinds of reasons for what happened, but they won't mean a thing to you right now. I will say that Bear Wright was offered the Principal's job late this afternoon. He accepted. Catherine and Barton Copeland went home in a huff." Trajan lifted an eyebrow at Ashe's messy packing but didn't comment.

"Too bad. She was prejudiced. Like a lot of werewolves," Ashe snapped.

"Some of them are," Trajan agreed. "And some shifters are as well. We won't even start on the humans or other races. It's something we all have to learn to live with. We know it's wrong. They don't."

"You know what else is wrong? Having your best friend sell you out." Ashe flung T-shirts into the bag.

"Look, I know that hurts. And I know you'll be suspicious of all of us from now on. That's a terrible place to be. Next time, go directly to Winkler. He knows how to keep secrets."

"Fat chance," Ashe said, wrapping shampoo in a plastic bag and tossing it into the suitcase.

"Things keep changing for you. You hold some amazing talents. You have to tell somebody."

"Nope. Not falling for that again."

Trajan sighed. "You have no idea how much Winkler cares about you. How much Trace and I care about you. You're like the little brother Trace and I never had. And Winkler—he thinks of you as another child."

"I'm not werewolf, Trajan. Nor will I ever be."

"We know that. We don't care. Does it matter that much to you—that people who care about you—love you, even—are werewolf?"

"Keep Sali and Marco away from me," Ashe zipped up the bag and hefted it off the bed.

"We'll be in Boulder around ten tomorrow morning—jet is scheduled to leave around seven. We'll fly to D.C. first thing Wednesday. You won't see Sali or Marco the whole time we're gone."

"If you're counting on absence making the heart grow fonder," Ashe pounded down the steps to the lower level, "then you're wasting your breath."

"He's back, boss, and he's mad," Trajan announced as he and Ashe walked into Winkler's temporary home. Winkler didn't attempt to say anything as Ashe stalked past, heading toward the bedroom that Trace had cleared out for him, wearing an angry scowl.

"Has he had dinner?" Winkler asked as the door to Ashe's new quarters slammed shut.

"I don't think so. And he's very sure he never wants to see Marco or Sali again."

"Too bad you can't rewind this whole thing, boss," Trace drawled.

"Trace, go get a pizza. We'll slide it under the door if we have to." Winkler handed cash to Trace.

"What kind?" Trace took the money and pocketed it.

"Pepperoni, what else? Get a sausage and mushroom too, just in case."

"Will do. I'll grab Ace on the way out."

"You do that." Winkler shooed Trace out the door.

"Ashe is pissed." Marco sat beside Sali at the kitchen island. "Found out this morning before Winkler hauled him off to the airport."

"About what?" Sali dipped up scrambled eggs and stuffed them in his mouth.

"At whom," Marco sighed. "He's so mad at both of us he could spit. Winkler let the cat out of the bag. Ashe knows I've been informing Winkler."

Sali swallowed his mouthful of food with difficulty. "He didn't. I promised Ashe, Marco. I promised him I wouldn't tell. He knows. Ashe knows everything. He's not stupid, Marco."

"I know that," Marco muttered. "And when Cori finds out, well," Marco shrugged. Cori wouldn't be happy, he knew that much. Cori liked Ashe. A lot.

"She won't be that mad at you."

"Don't bet on it."

"Kid, things will go a lot better if you're not so mad at all of us you can't see straight," Trajan observed dryly as he settled his lean frame into the seat beside Ashe. "And we'd all feel better if you'd eat something."

Ashe stared out the window of Winkler's private jet, ignoring Trajan. He'd refused pizza the night before and snubbed the offer of breakfast at a restaurant in Corpus Christi. "Ashe, you don't have any weight to spare. At least eat. We all acknowledge that you have the right to be angry."

"And you'll do the same thing again, when the opportunity comes," Ashe muttered.

"What are you planning to do, Ashe? Marco will continue to work for Winkler."

"Are you forcing me to speak with him?"

"I won't. I don't know what Winkler wants to do." Trajan looked past Ashe at the mountains they were passing over. The jet would be landing in Denver soon.

"I promised Mom and Dad that I'd stay with Winkler while Mom is gone. When she gets back I may rethink my employment options." Ashe misted out of his seat and appeared in another at the back of the jet. Trajan breathed a frustrated sigh.

"Trace is riding herd on him," Winkler informed the Grand Master. Weldon had driven down with two bodyguards. They met Winkler at the airport with a rented van. Weldon could see Ashe and Trace at a tiny pizza restaurant inside the Denver airport. Ashe was buying a slice of pizza, refusing to allow Trace to pay.

"He threatened to quit?" Weldon turned to Trajan.

"He said he'd rethink his employment options," Trajan repeated. "Grand Master, we stripped every bit of privacy away from him and he thinks he has no friends. None that he can trust, anyway."

Weldon cursed softly. "What can we do?" he asked.

"No idea," Winkler said. "He's not one of my kids, though I'd adopt him in a second if he didn't have parents already. My gardener put him through hell; he blistered his hands laying new sprinklers and never complained once. He's not one of those kids who goes looking for trouble."

"And you say Griffin told him he's pure-blood Elemaiya? Winkler, this means that none of us can lay claim to him." Weldon wanted to curse again.

"Bear told us in his interview that he's looking to put a shifter council together. He has a lot of contacts, Weldon. If anybody can get that disorganized bunch together, it will be him." Winkler didn't sound happy.

"You're upset that they might finally organize and lay down some rules?" Trajan stared at Winkler.

"No, he's upset over the fact that they might have as much pull with Ashe as anyone else," Weldon pointed out judiciously. "A Shifter Council could be very influential with Ashe—his mother is a shifter and they haven't betrayed him in any way. If shifter Enforcers are created, he could go to them if we don't fix this. Face it; we all need him, Trajan. Desperately. I just don't want him turned to vampire without his knowledge or consent. He'll belong wholly to the Council after that and be forced to live under Wlodek's thumb. Like Lissa."

"And asleep every day, all day," Winkler agreed. "We don't need that. We need that talent available during day hours. If Wlodek had any sense, he'd see it, too."

"I think Wlodek worries that he might not be able to completely control Ashe. It's a valid concern," Wlodek said.

"They're coming," Trajan whispered. Ashe had devoured two large slices of pizza while Winkler and the Grand Master spoke.

"Ashe, you can't let a bunch of clueless wolves upset you," Weldon said when Ashe and Trace walked up. "We don't know everything and don't claim to. Winkler and I have made mistakes in the past and likely will make more in the future. Son, I think the wolves here would give their lives for you and I don't say that lightly."

"You trust them. I can't trust anyone," Ashe muttered, ducking his head.

"You can trust them not to let that information go any farther," Weldon said. "Trust us that much at least. In the meantime, let's go talk to the Packmaster in Boulder. If he or his Second knew or suspected what Beesley was doing, then I want to know. You can see the sense in that, can't you?"

"Don't need somebody who can ignore that kind of crime anywhere near a position of power," Ashe grumbled. He still had visions of deaths in his head and none had been merciful.

"Ashe, you're really smart. Sometimes we forget that," Winkler placed an arm around Ashe's shoulders. "Help us out, son."

"I'll go."

"Good. Great. Load up and let's get to Boulder," Weldon ordered. Halfway there they pulled over to get the Grand Master a cup of coffee. All of them slid into a booth at the truck stop restaurant and ordered drinks. Ashe, refusing to look at the others, idly played with his soft drink cup when their order came.

"Lissa told a funny story once," Winkler said, causing Ashe to lift his head. He'd been staring at his glass of juice, tuning out the conversation around him. "She said that she and her human husband went to a restaurant in San Francisco on vacation. The waiter brought a huge, live lobster out on a tray for everybody to stare at. Her husband felt sorry for the lobster and shouted 'Let my people go,' in front of a large crowd. They were asked to leave by the staff."

Ashe blinked at Winkler and then laughed. "Kid, I'm sorry," Winkler apologized. "Maybe we should talk more often. I'll tell you things, you can tell me things. We'll leave out the middleman. Don't be upset with Marco. He was following orders. I don't control Sali. You'll have to work that out yourself."

"I won't trust them again." Ashe had gone from smiling to sullen in the space of a blink. Winkler sighed.

"Come on, kid. Let's get some air," Trajan said, pulling Ashe from the booth at the coffee shop. Trace followed as they walked outside. The air was thinner where they were, Ashe realized. Cooler, too. Mountains surrounded them and Ashe saw bits of white on the tallest peaks.

"Trajan, Trace," Ashe looked from one werewolf brother to the other before grasping arms and hopping them to one of the peaks.

"Holy crap," Trajan turned in a circle, standing in knee-deep snow.

"Ashe, send mindspeech to Winkler and tell him we'll be back in a minute."

Winkler, we're on the side of a mountain, Ashe couldn't keep the amused exultation from his mental voice. *Trajan says we'll be back in a minute. Maybe I should let 'em walk back.*

"Ashe!" Trace shouted, just before Ashe was pelted with a huge snowball. Ashe scooped up snow and launched one back, causing Trace to duck and laugh. The second one came swiftly on the first's heels, smacking Trace in the ear. Trajan's cell rang.

"Boss?" Trajan answered the call. Ashe and Trace both listened to the conversation as Winkler growled at his Second for allowing himself to be hauled to the top of a mountain.

"Not his fault," Ashe called out.

"Not Marco's fault either," Winkler replied. "Let's declare a truce. I'll stop chewing on Trajan if you'll agree to stop blaming Marco."

"I'll put the blame on Sali and I still won't speak to Marco."

"Kid, we'll work this out. I promise. Finish your snowball fight and then join the rest of us mortals." Winkler ended the call. Trajan no sooner had his cell put away before Trace lobbed a snowball at him.

Clumps of snow were still dropping off clothing and melting from shoes when Ashe transported both werewolves back to the restaurant. Winkler was glad to see that Ashe landed them between vehicles so they wouldn't be seen.

"Done with the rebellious activities?" Trajan tousled Ashe's hair.

"Till the next time," Ashe grinned. Trajan pulled Ashe into a tight hug.

"Why am I not comforted?" Weldon sighed piously. Winkler laughed.

~

"I will not renew the marriage," Wlodek snapped at Aedan. The sun had set a bare hour earlier, he was plagued with rogues in Paris and Amsterdam and here was Aedan Evans asking for his marriage to be renewed, although he promised to take up his work for the Council again.

"May I have a reason, Honored One?" Aedan asked respectfully.

"Because I do not wish it," Wlodek replied coldly. "Charles has information on the nest in Amsterdam. Go now—the jet is waiting at Heathrow. Do not ask me again."

"Very well," Aedan dipped his head and left Wlodek's study quickly.

~

"Wlodek is sending me to Amsterdam," Aedan tossed clothing into a bag.

"Then I'm coming with you," Adele said, gripping Aedan's arm anxiously.

"Adele, these are vampires I'm chasing, and criminal vampires in addition to that."

"I can track anything from overhead," Adele pointed out. Aedan looked into his wife's eyes. She would always be his wife, he didn't care what Wlodek said or did. He just didn't want to upset her with Wlodek's statement. "You can come if you promise to only go out in daylight," Aedan offered his solution.

"I promise," Adele agreed. "I can order room service if I'm hungry after dark."

"We'll be staying at a safe house."

"Then I'll stock snacks or something."

"That's fine. It may have a small kitchen. Some of them do. It will certainly have a refrigerator, stocked with bagged blood."

~

The flight crew didn't want Adele on the jet, but Aedan growled at the younger vampires, who stood aside eventually and allowed it. "I'm surprised these things are as luxurious as this," Adele ran a hand over soft leather and settled into the comfortable seat.

"Wlodek travels with the fleet now and then," Aedan leaned back and stared ahead at the vampire attendant.

"I see," Adele replied. She knew not to add anything to that—her words would likely be reported to the Head of the Council as soon as they landed anyway. She didn't want to give the Council any fuel to harm Aedan.

"My love," Aedan turned before leaning in to kiss Adele.

CHAPTER 9

$\mathcal{A}$she was surprised to see that Matt Michaels and two agents had arrived already at a building located on the outskirts of Boulder. There wasn't anything to distinguish this particular brick and stone building from others nearby.

Two men waited in the lobby as they walked inside, reading magazines from a table located between seats. Ashe realized that both were quite nervous and jerked to attention as soon as Weldon and Winkler appeared.

"Grand Master," the brown-haired werewolf dipped his head respectfully to Weldon Harper. Ashe wondered what his scent told the Grand Master.

"Dan," Weldon didn't give anything away to the Boulder Packmaster. "This is William Winkler," Weldon nodded toward Winkler.

"I remember; Dan Garber," he introduced himself and held his hand out to Winkler, who shook it briefly. Dan Garber was more than six feet tall. Ashe was taller but the Boulder Packmaster had at least fifty pounds on Ashe, who was still on the thin side.

Garber was dressed in a suit somewhat out of date but it fit. His dark eyes watched the Grand Master and Winkler warily. "This is my

Second, Keith Simpson," the Boulder Packmaster made introductions. The Second had nearly black hair, hazel eyes and thinning lips. Ashe thought Garber's Second looked older than his Packmaster.

Trajan and Trace stood behind Winkler while introductions were made; Matt Michaels stood back while Weldon and Winkler spoke with the two who ran the Boulder Pack. "This way," Matt led everyone toward a room down a hall moments later.

"Who's the kid?" Ashe heard Dan Garber whisper to Weldon Harper. Ashe hadn't minded that he'd been left out of the introductions; this was Pack business. He wished he were a million miles away. He didn't want to know the truth of what he already suspected. Not after Dexter Beesley.

"Winkler's ward—a shapeshifter," Weldon replied. "I asked for him." Trajan's hand dropped on Ashe's shoulder and kept him moving down the hall tiled in marble.

The room Matt Michaels led them toward was located at the back of the two-story building. He flipped the light switch as he walked inside. A conference room was revealed when Ashe walked in, flanked by Trajan and Trace. A wide table was centered in the windowless room, with two chairs positioned on the far side of the lengthy table. Six chairs were on the opposite side, near the door.

Matt Michaels' guards walked in last and took positions on either side of the door. They didn't bother to hide the fact that they were armed, either. Weldon sat near the center of the six chairs while Dan and Keith took the two seats on the far side, facing the Grand Master.

Winkler and Matt Michaels took the seats beside Weldon while Trace and Trajan sat beside Winkler. Winkler's Second patted the empty chair next to him and nodded to Ashe. Ashe sat next to Trajan without a word.

"You know Dexter Beesley was executed three nights ago," Weldon began. "We discovered he was guilty of unspeakable crimes and responsible for the disappearances of at least fifteen young girls from this area over the past twenty years or so. Now, when he joined your Pack, did he petition the Pack here in Boulder? I don't have those records in my files."

"An oversight, Grand Master. He came highly recommended from the Casper Pack, and none of those girls disappeared from the school where he worked." The Boulder Packmaster's eyes didn't quite meet the Grand Master's.

"You told me that over the phone. It's too bad the Casper Packmaster has died since then and the Pack dissolved. I'm having trouble finding any of those former Packmembers. Do you have any idea why that is?" Weldon watched carefully as Dan Garber worked to meet his gaze. Ashe's skin itched.

"I know it was hard with Dexter Beesley," Weldon turned to Ashe. "But I want you to put your hands on our Packmaster here and tell me what you see."

~

"Adele, I want you to stay here. I have a lead to follow and it requires speed and stealth," Aedan said. "My cell will be turned off. Do not attempt to contact me—it can place both of us in danger."

"I understand," Adele nodded uncomfortably. Aedan had been trained to do this, but he hadn't done it officially for fifty years. Adele was frightened. Aedan kissed her absently and stalked out of the safe house, his mind already on the task ahead.

~

"Cori broke up with me." Marco sat heavily on the sofa inside the DeLuca's media room. Marcus sat in an old recliner nearby. Denise was visiting Lavonna Anderson while Sali was out with Dori. Marcus and his oldest son were alone in the house.

"What happened?" Marcus tapped the remote, muting the television program he was watching.

"She said I owed Ashe and hadn't paid him back very well. She poked me in the chest and told me Sali could be dead or running drugs across the border if it weren't for Ashe. She's right, but I swore an oath to Mr. Winkler."

"Marco, the oath you give your Packmaster supersedes anything else. That's the way things are for any werewolf," Marcus frowned as he studied Marco's face, his dark eyes betraying no emotion. "How many other friendships outside the Pack have been fractured because of Pack Law? You can't have everything the way you want it, son. Some things are going to conflict with the laws we follow. If you hadn't reported it to Winkler, that could have cost you down the road. You don't need that black mark against your name as you're starting to make a place for yourself. Membership in the Dallas Pack carries a lot of prestige, son. I had hopes that you'd come back to the Star Cove Pack, but I think you have a better future with Winkler, now."

"Yeah. I wish Sali hadn't told me about Ashe," Marco grumbled. "I wouldn't have had the information to take to Winkler and Cori wouldn't be on the outs with me. That doesn't even cover what Ashe probably thinks."

"Ashe is young, Marco. What difference does it make what he thinks?"

"Dad, that's what you don't understand. I don't understand it, either. What Ashe thinks matters to me. A lot. And any respect he might have for me is really important, somehow. I don't know how to explain it better than that."

"Nathan has always wondered at Cori—the way she calls or emails Ashe for advice," Marcus rose from his chair and tossed the television remote onto the coffee table. "He always seems to be a step ahead of his classmates. I heard from the Grand Master that he's a pure-blood Elemaiya. They've gotten confirmation somehow. He's different, Marco. I don't know whether we can trust that or not. I told Sali that he had to bring any new information on Ashe to me. And to you. I know it's terrible to place suspicion on the boy, but you saw what that Elemaiyan filth tried to do to us."

"You told Sali to break the confidence." Marco stared at his father.

"As his father and Packmaster, he's obligated to me. It isn't my intention to hurt Ashe, but the Pack has to be protected."

"Good-bye, Dad," Marco snarled and stalked out of his parents' home.

Nathan hated himself. Hated that Marcus had given him the information and hated that one of the conditions that the Head of the Council had placed upon his marriage renewal was a promise from Nathan to bring any new information on Ashe to Wlodek.

He'd made the call earlier, leaving a message for Wlodek before he woke. As if that would mitigate the guilt he felt—that indirect contact wouldn't hurt his vampire sire or his child as much. Now Wlodek was aware that somehow, against all odds, Ashe was completely Elemaiya.

In some way, the DNA of the Elemaiyan race could overcome that introduced from Aedan and Adele. He suspected it was the reason that those with a quarter or less of that blood managed to keep their mindspeech and misting abilities when they were made vampire.

Nathan and Aedan had both known of the experimentation with the older children of vampire-shapeshifter marriages. The shapeshifting ability had not survived the turn, so the experiments were halted. Nathan was glad—the female shapeshifters hadn't survived the turn attempts, either.

Wlodek had shut down that side of the experiment quickly, and that meant Nathan's girls were safe. He would never tell Wlodek that his youngest seemed to have mindspeech. Ashe would keep that secret, too. Nathan wasn't sure how he knew that, but he did. It made him feel worse that he'd betrayed Ashe and Aedan.

The only reason Wlodek didn't know that Ashe wasn't susceptible to compulsion was that Aedan, as his sire, had commanded it. A command from a sire overrode any other commands. Nathan was compelled to obey. This new information, however, Aedan didn't have and Nathan was forced to report it to the Head of the Council.

Ashe had seen so many things. Obediah Tanner hadn't gotten all of his animals for the hunt through Mexico. Polar Bears and other northern exotics, as well as shapeshifters aplenty had been funneled through Canada with the help of the Casper Pack.

Dexter Beesley had brought that lucrative business with him when he'd moved to Colorado, shortly after his former Packmaster had been killed and one of Obediah's cronies had taken over.

They'd all filtered across the southern border over the years, joining Ezekiel's end of the operation. Dexter was the last of the Pack remaining in the U.S. Matt Michaels listened impassively as Dan and Keith, Packmaster and Second, spilled everything they knew after Ashe placed compulsion.

They also revealed the names of several in the Boulder Pack who were involved with the smuggling ring. They'd suspected Dexter of the killings, but the money had started to come so they'd looked the other way.

"Ashe, go with Trajan, son," Weldon nodded to Ashe. "We have business to take care of." Ashe walked out of the building with Winkler's second.

"They'll be sent to North Dakota," Trajan squinted in the clear, bright sunlight once they were outside again. "Weldon will likely call in the Denver Pack. He knows the Second there really well. They'll send guards."

"What will they do? Are they sentenced already?" Ashe looked at Trajan curiously.

"The Grand Master or the Packmaster lays the charges according to Pack Law, kid, and then pronounces them guilty. They can say what they want in their defense then. It's a lot of whining and blaming somebody else, usually. That's why they asked me to take you out of there. I don't like listening to it either."

"They killed a lot of shifters, Trajan."

"I know. If the shifters had a Council, they could demand restitution."

"Then the shifters need a Council."

"Maybe they do." Trajan didn't tell Ashe of Bear Wright's plans. If the old grizzly was successful, Star Cove could become shapeshifter central.

"When are we leaving for D.C.?" Ashe changed the subject.

"Tomorrow morning. We have a hotel set up in Denver for the night. Winkler and Weldon will have dinner with wolves from the Denver Pack. After they round up all the guilty parties from Boulder, that is. They'll be shipped off to North Dakota tonight."

When Winkler, Weldon, Trace and Matt walked out of the building half an hour later, Weldon and Matt's bodyguards weren't with them. "Sent 'em out the back way with the bad guys," Trace said, grinning at Ashe's unspoken question. "We had a few from the Denver Pack waiting out back, too. Don't want 'em to get away from us."

‿

"Mom, the only other place I'd like to live right now is Star Cove," Randy said over the phone. His mother had waited a week before calling him. Dawn had asked him to come live with her in New Mexico. Again.

"I think I can get a transfer to the Corpus Christi Post Office or one of the surrounding cities. Pack your bags, hon; I'll have this done before the week's out." His mother was completely serious, Randy knew.

"I have to have a job, Mom," Randy muttered, although the lure of living in Star Cove with many of his old friends appealed greatly.

"I have some money put back and there's still some of your father's insurance money left. We'll use that until you find work. It shouldn't be difficult—you're good at what you do."

"Let me talk to my boss," Randy sighed.

‿

Ashe picked at his dinner. Trace and Trajan had taken him to a restaurant near the hotel while Winkler and the others had gone to a steak place recommended by the Denver Packmaster. "Ashe, if the chicken isn't any good, we'll send it back," Trajan offered.

"It's okay," Ashe said, setting his fork down. An uncertain feeling had settled in the pit of his stomach. Somehow, something had gone awry with his parents. He'd hoped to bring his father home with his mother.

Something—he couldn't say exactly what—had wrecked that opportunity. His life was shifting and there wasn't anything he could do about it. "I feel sick," Ashe lurched from his seat at the table, rushing toward the restrooms on the other side of the restaurant.

"We can't get anything out of him," Trajan spoke with Winkler over the phone. "Other than the dry heaves."

"I think there's a physician's assistant in the Denver Pack. Should I send him over?"

"The kid doesn't want anybody to touch him for some reason. He's not happy about something, boss."

"We're nearly finished here," Winkler said. "I'll come back and talk to Ashe."

A part of Ashe felt embarrassment over the queasiness; another part felt the deepest of sadness. He sat in the back seat of Trajan's rented car, head in hands, wondering if he'd make it to the hotel without heaving again. He made it, by the barest of margins.

"Father, I received this." Charles handed the letter addressed to Flavio of the Council to his vampire sire. Flavio lifted the envelope from Charles's fingers. "Father, the Honored One refused to give Aedan Evans an extension on his marriage. Everyone else who asked received one."

"You've already read this?" Flavio lifted the flap. Charles seldom called Flavio father, unless he wanted something very important from his vampire sire.

"You asked that I screen all your mail that comes through this address."

"Yes, I did, didn't I?" Flavio sat on Charles's guest chair. Charles's office furniture was seventeenth century German and quite sturdy.

Flavio was Wlodek's second oldest child, a member of the Council and high in the vampire aristocracy. Charles's office was large and filled with file cabinets, his desk, the guest chair and four computers, one of which was his laptop. Flavio watched his vampire child fidget anxiously while he drew the letter from the envelope.

Honored Flavio, the message began, *I send this to beg you to intercede on my behalf. My name is Ashe Evans and Aedan Evans is my father.*

~

"Ashe, you don't know that for sure," Winkler was trying to bring Ashe around. Ashe stared at the Dallas Packmaster.

"My gut says otherwise," Ashe muttered. "Mom will be home soon, and everything will be different."

"Kid, will you be able to fly tomorrow? Matt Michaels is riding back to D.C. on my jet."

"I'll try to have things under control by then," Ashe said. He sat on the edge of his bed—he was bunking with Trajan while Trace had settled into Winkler's suite to provide protection for the night.

"I got this," Winkler handed over a bag filled with remedies for upset stomachs he'd gotten from a nearby pharmacy.

"Mr. Winkler, I just have to come to terms with this." Ashe rose from the bed and walked toward the window. It provided a nice view of downtown Denver, with the mountains in the background. The first of August had arrived and a sliver of moon hung in the sky.

"Full moon in twelve days," Winkler said softly over Ashe's shoulder. "Ashe, did you turn last time?"

"Mr. Winkler, I don't have to turn. It was fun going out with the others, but I don't feel the pull of the moon like you and the shifters do. I understand that now, since I learned I'm all Elemaiya."

"How does that make you feel? That you're a pure-blood and not half like we thought?"

"Lost," Ashe admitted. "And it's worse now that the Council has managed to tear the only family I have apart. I'm tired, Mr. Winkler. I think I'd like to go to bed now."

~

Three rogue vampires—Aedan had taken all of them down in a single night. The ash from their bodies was drifting down the street, floating with runoff from the rain that fell. Aedan had been particularly angry and his prey unusually stupid. Streetlights reflected on the rain-soaked streets and narrow alleys that surrounded Aedan.

The Head of the Council, once called Sanguis Rex by his subordinates, had refused to renew Aedan's marriage, even with Aedan offering to come back to the Enforcers. He had nothing left to offer Adele.

The Council would not sanction his request for renewal and the companion vote would go against him. He worried for Adele—and for Ashe. That meant only one thing—he had to send Adele away. If she no longer recognized Aedan as her mate and husband, perhaps that would keep Ashe safe from an early turning.

If Wlodek thought to lure Ashe because he held Aedan's reins, then Aedan was determined to make that as difficult as possible. He fully intended to convince Alvin Wright, the new Star Cove Principal, to form a shapeshifter Council and accept Ashe into their ranks as quickly as possible through Adele. Surely, Wlodek would not offend an organized shapeshifter community.

Adele wouldn't want to leave and Aedan had only placed compulsion on his wife once. His marriage, along with his promise not to place compulsion on Adele again, would end tonight. Aedan drew out his cell and dialed a familiar number. Charles answered on the other end. "They're all dead," Aedan reported. "You can send the jet for me tomorrow evening."

"How many will be traveling?" Charles asked.

"Only one," Aedan replied gruffly and terminated the call. If anyone had been awake to see or hear at that late hour, they'd have witnessed a vampire weeping for the loss of his family on a narrow, brick lane in Amsterdam.

"Cori, how long can you keep this up?" Lavonna sat at the breakfast table next to her oldest daughter. "You and Marco—I thought you were made for one another."

"We are, Mom, but I can't deal with this right now. Ashe saved us—he saved Dori and we treat him like this?" Cori tossed a hand out in frustration. "Marco should have told me before he went to Mr. Winkler."

"Marco is a werewolf, Cori. The rules are different."

"Then we may have to stay apart." Cori got up and walked away from her mother. The sun was shining outside, the heat and humidity were already present and Cori felt betrayed and abandoned by the man—or wolf—she loved.

Closing the back door behind her, Cori sat on a deck chair and stared, unseeing, at the Anderson's back fence. Dori walked out to the deck minutes later, a plate of eggs and toast in her hand. Silently, she sat on the empty deck chair beside Cori's and began to eat.

They were expected in the exercise room in less than half an hour —Marco and Ace had taken over Sali and the girls' training since Trajan was out of town with Winkler, Trace and Ashe. Ace was quiet, efficient and thorough. He explained carefully what he wanted and then watched to make sure his instructions were followed.

Wynn was doing better than anyone expected. She even ran alongside Ace and talked with him occasionally. Cori received mostly grunts from Winkler's bodyguard, but Wynn got better answers.

"Still on the outs with Marco?" Dori ventured to ask.

"Don't start," Cori warned as she stood and stretched. "I'm going to brush my teeth before we have to exercise. Dori, you never intended to give Ashe a fair shake—it was Sali all along, so don't get all sanctimonious now."

"I said I was sorry I hit him."

"You don't get it, do you?" Cori stalked into the house, slamming the patio door behind her.

"Get what? Ashe said it was okay," Dori grumped. She chewed her toast harder than necessary.

Weather delayed the flight for an hour in Denver. Ashe and the others waited on the jet until the rain stopped coming down in buckets. Raindrops continued to pelt the tarmac as the jet backed away. Matt Michaels had made calls on his cell and fretted over the delay—he had meetings scheduled later in the day.

Ashe had wakened earlier at the hotel to find a voice message from his mother on his cell—she was getting a flight out of Amsterdam and would be back in Star Cove Friday afternoon. Not a word was said about his father. Ashe intended to call Aedan as soon as he was in D.C. It was likely his father wouldn't tell him anything, but Ashe already knew enough.

"Here, you haven't gotten enough protein lately." Trajan plunked a bottle of protein drink in front of Ashe while the jet taxied along, preparing for takeoff. "There's more where that came from," Trajan said. "Matt has arranged for us to exercise at an FBI training facility if we have time. He says they have a place there where his paranormal division works out."

"Sounds like a barrel of laughs," Ashe said.

"I always feel better after I work out. My troubles sometimes vanish completely."

"Say that to me when your parents split up." Ashe cursed before calling the Head of the Vampire Council a few names. His mother would be shocked at the words Ashe used. Trajan listened patiently and never said a thing.

The flight was bumpy over Colorado, but smoothed out and became boring. Ashe didn't want to read, although he'd brought two books along. Trajan and Trace failed to pull him into conversation—Winkler watched occasionally through hooded, worried eyes. At one point Winkler called the Grand Master, but Ashe failed to hear the conversation. He was too deep in depression to care.

The jet landed at the airport around six, local time. Winkler's cell rang. The noise of flight had abated, allowing Ashe to hear every word as the Grand Master confirmed his fears—Wlodek had refused to renew Aedan's marriage to Adele.

Weldon added that Wlodek was upset that Weldon had called about it, saying that three new vampires would be sent to Star Cove to guard at night. Ashe sighed—he'd have three more spies to avoid.

"You heard that, didn't you?" Winkler asked as Ashe pulled his backpack over his shoulder and prepared to deplane. Winkler had walked to Ashe's seat as soon as the conversation with Weldon was over.

"I heard." Ashe wasn't looking at Winkler.

"Kid, I'm sorry."

"You can't be anywhere near as sorry as I am."

Josiah Dunnigan lifted his bags from the luggage carousel at the Corpus Christi airport. He'd be meeting with his contact soon and together they would devise a plan to eliminate William Winkler. Josiah gripped the handles of his suitcases and walked through the small terminal building toward the rental car aisle. He'd get a car and drive into town, searching for a suitable hotel.

Soon—very soon—Winkler would be dead and Josiah could retire on his ranch, set for life. Josiah grinned and stepped up to the rental car agent, pulling his suitcase behind him.

CHAPTER 10

"Child, I refused to renew in order to separate them. Aedan will never willingly consent to turning the boy—I have that information from Nathan. I have no desire to fight Aedan Evans when it's time to take his son." Wlodek gave Flavio a hard look. "I'll send three to keep an eye on things and help guard the community until Ashe Evans turns eighteen. I intend to conscript immediately after."

"You're using Aedan's vampire child against his sire."

"Child, do not point the finger at me, I have already gone over this ground," Wlodek sighed and rose from his seat. He had chosen his library as a place to talk and now Wlodek pretended to gaze across a shelf of ancient titles. "Is it fair to the boy? No. Is it fair to Aedan or his wife? Certainly not. You know as well as I that the vampire race is in peril. Many of our citizens are turning to crime after the last wave of economic crises. They lost much—if not all—of what they have. We have more rogues than ever before. We need the boy, Flavio. If the information we have is halfway accurate, he will be the answer to our problems."

"Surely we need more than one boy, Father. Have you not thought to conscript others or to look among our ranks for those who might help? The boy and his family suffer, my sire."

"It is only two years. I will allow the marriage to continue after that, and Aedan can be instrumental in training the boy after he is turned."

"Father, while two years is nothing to us, it is quite a long time to others. Much can happen in two years."

"For us as well, never forget that."

"Whom do you plan to send to Texas?"

"I have contacted Hector, Edmond and Casimir. Casimir will perform the turning when the time comes. He is experienced and not so hard as some of the others might be. You see, I have some sympathy over this."

"Father, you should have left things alone. I feel this quite strongly."

"Child, we will disagree on this, I know. If Aedan gives Nathan a direct order, it will supersede anything I might command Nathan to do. This concerns me, as there may be information I have not or will not receive as a result. My three will act as spies in the community. I will have information on the boy regardless of the source."

"Father, someday your plans may backfire. I believe that is the modern term, anyway."

"Then hope it is not the term for this situation. We need the boy and we do not want him taken by the werewolves for their purposes or hired by the U.S. government for their own use against terrorists and such. We allowed the experiment, hoping for gifted vampires. This may be the most gifted of all."

"We need the kid in a suit. He'll have to look as if he belongs there—as much as we can make him look that way," Matt Michaels looked Ashe over. Ashe, slightly offended, was dressed in a pair of cargo pants and a T-shirt with sneakers. His clothes were clean, at least.

"Come on, you," Trajan pulled Ashe away from the hotel room. Matt was putting them up in one of D.C.'s best. "Trace, let's go find tall and skinny here a suit."

"Where am I going to be that I have to wear a suit?" Ashe jerked his arm away from Trajan as they walked toward the hotel elevator.

"A hearing. A couple of members of Congress will be present when we question Jack Howard."

Ashe muttered a foul word; Trace laughed and pushed him onto the elevator when it opened. Half an hour and a harrowing cab ride later, Ashe was trying on suit coats in a men's clothing store. "Can you hem these now?" Trajan was eyeing the bottom of Ashe's trousers. They'd found a decent jacket that didn't have to be altered right away but the pants were another problem.

"Know how to tie a tie?" Trace asked Ashe when the salesclerk carried the pants toward the back for an emergency hemming.

"No. Never needed one," Ashe muttered. While the pants were hemmed, Ashe received a quick lesson on tying the tie Trajan picked out. Dress shoes came next. Ashe wasn't fond of those—the hard soles were aggravating.

"Kid, your feet are nearly as big as mine," Trajan grinned.

"He's probably not finished growing," Trace pointed out. "We may make a shooting guard out of him yet."

Ashe glared at Trajan. "I thought you gave up basketball," he grumped. The tie was tight around his neck and he didn't like it. "If I want a hanging injury, I can get one easier than this," Ashe jerked on the silk annoyance. "I need to make a call," he pulled the cell from a pocket of his cargo pants. "Can you leave me alone for five minutes?"

Trajan and Trace stepped back and allowed Ashe to move toward an empty corner of the store. Ashe hit his father's cell number—it was still night in England. The call went straight to voice mail. "Dad, I don't know why you did it, but you have to take it back," Ashe choked out. "You have to, Dad. Right away. You don't know what I know. Please, Dad." Ashe wiped tears away when he ended the call.

~

"Boss, this is the worst possible time to be doing this," Trajan informed Winkler after Ashe and Trace had gone to the coffee shop in the hotel for a bottle of water. "The kid broke down when he tried to call Aedan."

Winkler cursed and tossed a pillow across the room. "What the hell are we supposed to do, Trajan? What? I'm not the boy's father. He won't come to me for anything like this."

"I don't know. I wish he trusted us. I don't think he trusts anybody, now. We pulled that rug from under his feet." Trajan flopped onto the sofa inside Winkler's suite, rubbing his forehead. The incident had given him a headache.

"We'll get this thing over with as quickly as possible tomorrow and go home," Winkler sighed. "Adele is home—I heard from Marcus. Denise went to pick her up at the airport. Said she seemed in a sort of daze and barely remembered to ask about Ashe."

"Compulsion. If Aedan thinks to protect them by doing this, I'm not sure I agree with that," Trajan looked up at Winkler, who prowled restlessly about the suite. "I don't believe for a minute he doesn't love both of them."

"This could be disastrous," Winkler said. "And Weldon called—said Wlodek is sending three vampires to help Nathan guard the community."

"Then we'll be watching them, boss."

"Yeah. We'll be watching, all right. I talked to Buck—told him he had to get the beach house finished in record time. We'll move the kid there. See how Wlodek likes that turn of events."

"How long until it's done?"

"Soon, according to Buck. Weather should hold—unless we get an unforeseen hurricane or something. The new place is fireproof and can withstand winds up to two hundred miles an hour."

"Think that will keep us safe?" Trajan searched Winkler's face. They'd lost Jimmy, Spencer and Gabe to Tanner and his Elemaiyan allies.

"As much as any building can keep us safe. There are a few hidden rooms, too. I asked Buck for those in particular."

"Hidden doorways, boss?"

"No doors or windows of any kind—only small air vents. Ashe can get inside these rooms. We can't."

"That means he can get us inside if he wants."

"Exactly. They'll all be built as safe rooms." Both werewolves heard the door open in the suite next door and stopped their discussion. Winkler tapped on the connecting door before walking inside.

Ashe handed a cup of coffee to Winkler, who lifted an eyebrow in surprise—he hadn't asked for it but was thinking about going downstairs to get some.

"Kid, I want to hug you right now," Winkler sighed.

"Maybe later," Ashe set his water bottle on the desk. Trace handed a can of soda to Trajan—he knew what his brother liked.

"Feel like eating in about an hour? I think we can get a haircut for you before we find a restaurant."

"It does look a little shaggy," Ashe admitted, settling into the chair beside the desk and lifting up a lock of hair. "It could use a trim. I wish I'd brought my laptop."

"You can borrow mine if you really need it," Winkler offered. "Take your water, we'll get a cab and go out."

Ashe got his hair cut and styled at the hotel salon, after insisting that Winkler didn't need to spend so much on a haircut. A steak and seafood restaurant was next on the list. Ashe ordered prime rib while the others had rare steaks. Ashe's cell rang while he was eating. "Mom?" He said after checking the ID on his phone. "What happened?" Winkler and the others listened as Adele explained.

"Denise said I had to call you," Adele sighed. "Your father and I decided to separate," she added. "This wasn't going to work out between us so we parted friends. Marcus says you're in Washington state?"

"D.C., Mom," Ashe sighed. "Winkler had a meeting and didn't want to leave me behind."

"Probably a good idea. Are you doing what he tells you to do?"

"Yeah. Mom, did Dad say anything about me—about you and me?"

"No. I just walked away and boarded the plane after he went to sleep."

"That's not an answer. You know that, don't you?"

"Ashe, we parted friends. He's still your father. I just don't think you'll see much of him. I get the idea he'll be really busy from now on."

Ashe wanted to curse. Scooting his chair back, he rose and walked away from the table. "Mom, I can be home in no time. If you need me," Ashe wiped dampness from his cheeks.

"I'm fine. We'll get through this. I'll just have to get the sale done on the store soon—we'll need the money. I don't have your father's bank account to draw on any longer."

"Mom? He's not even—he's not going to help?" Ashe's voice broke. His father wasn't going to help support them?

"He said you had a job, now. You can take care of yourself."

"Yeah. I guess that makes me an adult and all."

"Don't look at it that way. I don't think he meant for you to feel like this."

"How did he mean for me to feel, then? How?" Ashe punched the end button on his phone and nearly ran out of the restaurant.

"This isn't good, boss," Trajan phoned Winkler after following Ashe out the door. Ashe wandered the streets of Silver Spring, Maryland, a nearby suburb of Washington, D.C., walking aimlessly down the street. Trajan relayed the phone conversation from both ends while chasing after Ashe. "And if he turns or hops, we've lost him."

Winkler cursed. "See if you can catch up with him. Try to convince him to come back. Damn. I wish there was some way to track that kid."

"Maybe there is, boss. Let's buy him a nice watch and put a chip in it," Trace suggested quietly. He and Winkler still sat at the table inside the restaurant while Trajan tried to reach Ashe.

"I've got one better," Winkler grinned. "We'll have Matt give it to him. It'll have the time zones on it and anything else the kid might want it to do, including checking the Internet. Trace, sometimes I don't give you nearly enough credit." Winkler whipped his cell out again and called Matt Michaels.

~

"Ashe, we have to find a way to deal with this. Do you think for even one minute that Winkler will allow you or your mother to starve?" Trajan had finally caught up with Ashe. "Your food is likely cold, but we can get them to reheat it." Trajan had a hand on Ashe's shoulder as Ashe walked aimlessly, his body hunched over and hands stuffed in the pockets of his cargo pants.

"I know he has a reason for doing this, but did he mean to hurt us so much?" Ashe lifted his head to stare at Trajan.

"Kid, sometimes people do the worst things for what they think are the best of reasons. It usually turns out badly—for everybody."

"Why did he do this? Why?" Ashe leaned against Trajan for support. His mother's words had dealt a terrible blow. Perhaps his father meant to be kind by being cruel, but did he think it wouldn't hurt in the worst way possible?

Ashe didn't expect a response from his father. Aedan had cut ties with his family. Ashe hoped his father's actions were meant to protect them instead of an indication that he didn't love them.

"Come back to the restaurant, kid. We have business tomorrow and you don't need to go to bed hungry." Trajan successfully steered Ashe in the opposite direction.

~

"Can we get these two dinners reheated?" Winkler asked their waiter when Ashe and Trajan sat down again. "Ashe, I know there isn't anything I can say or do to make this better for you," Winkler watched the waiter walk away before speaking. "All I can say is to give it time. I hope things turn out better. I hope there's a happy ending somewhere. I do. In the meantime, we'll get through this, one way or another. Weldon contacted another physician in the area—he's sending somebody to our hotel with something that will help you sleep tonight."

"Fine." Ashe and Trajan's dinners were back in moments. Ashe didn't mind that his prime rib had cooked a little more but Trajan was forced to eat a medium steak instead of a rare one. Ashe wanted to apologize, but the words just wouldn't come.

～

"Brush your teeth and get into pajamas—this stuff works pretty fast."

Ashe eyed the syringe with distrust. The woman who held it looked to be in her thirties, was pretty enough and Winkler said she was werewolf, so the age estimate was likely far off.

"Drugs kill people," Ashe pointed out. He didn't want to voice his sudden suspicions aloud.

"Kid, are you saying you don't want this?" Winkler watched Ashe carefully.

"I think that's what I'm saying, Mr. Winkler. I'd like to be able to wake up if I need to."

"He doesn't want it," Winkler shrugged at the woman. He pulled a wad of money from his wallet and handed it to her. "I'll let Weldon know you did your job."

"I'd like that," the nurse snatched the bills from Winkler's hand, shoved the syringe into her purse and hefted the bag over her shoulder. Ashe knew she wasn't happy, but there wasn't anything he could do about that. "What's your name?" Ashe asked.

"Trina," she snapped.

"Sorry, Trina. Maybe next time," Ashe apologized. "I'll try to get to sleep on my own."

"You do that." Trina walked toward the door of Winkler's suite in a huff and slammed it behind her.

"I don't think she likes me," Ashe muttered.

"Kid, she just didn't want to catch a cab home. I think she wanted Winkler to drive her," Trajan grinned.

"Ah. You weren't going to uh, jump on that?" Ashe looked at Winkler.

"Nope. Got big fish to fry tomorrow. Maybe later. Come on, kid. Get your jammies on and brush your teeth. Trajan has an early morning."

"I can sleep late?" Ashe gave Winkler a wide stare.

"No, that was my tactful way of saying you have to get up with the chickens."

"I thought it was go to bed with the chickens."

"Kid, if you go to bed with chickens, it makes sense that you'd wake up with chickens. Hence the rooster crowing at sunrise or before? I thought you grew up on a farm." Winkler tousled Ashe's hair.

"We never had chickens. The Thompsons had chickens. Mom got our eggs from Mr. Thompson."

"You never chased chickens? Man, those are good memories," Trace sighed blissfully.

"Until Mom caught you and you got grounded for two weeks," Trajan observed dryly. "He was chasing them as werewolf at eighteen." Trajan offered Ashe a wide grin.

"You terrorized chickens?" Ashe stared at Trace.

"As much as I could get away with," Trace laughed. "Mom would hit me now if she knew about the times I didn't get caught. Besides, those were mean chickens."

"Come on, they have feathers and they're a foot tall," Ashe wagged a finger at Trace.

"And they'd peck if you got too close."

"Uh-huh. My friend the chicken-chaser." Ashe walked toward the bathroom to brush his teeth.

"Did you call me your friend?" Trace poked his head inside the bathroom door, watching Ashe spread toothpaste on a toothbrush.

"I said that." Ashe stuck the brush in his mouth to clean his teeth.

"Someday, I'll ask for your autograph," Trace grinned.

"Yeah. Just like Sali is gonna ride in my convertible as a wolf." Ashe scrubbed his teeth while Trace supervised.

"Want to talk about that?" Trace leaned his shoulder against the bathroom door.

"Uh-uh," Ashe mumbled around his toothbrush.

"Kid, I don't think Sali would just throw your friendship away over nothing," Trace said. "Maybe we should get to the bottom of this before we toss him away as a friend."

"Hmmph." Ashe kept brushing.

"And Marco was only keeping his oath to Winkler. He wasn't looking to upset you or destroy the friendship. He wants to protect you just as much as Winkler, Trajan and I do. Kid, we're worried. We haven't heard from those folks you're related to and we're getting a little itchy over that."

Ashe spit into the sink and rinsed his mouth. "You think I'm not worried, too? Trace, how much more can I possibly be worried about right now? Care to answer that one?"

"No. If I had my way, I'd haul you to my parents' farm and let you spend a week or two with Mom and Dad. Mom would feed you constantly and Dad would let you drive the tractor and the four-wheeler."

"That sounds like somebody's dream of grandparents." Ashe rinsed his toothbrush and slipped it inside the plastic holder.

"I think Mom and Dad would treat you like that—as a grandson," Trace smiled slightly. "They're always after Trajan to get married."

"So, nobody's on the horizon for him?" Ashe studied Trace's expression. Trace chewed his lip and hid a grin.

"I'm not supposed to ask, am I?" Ashe felt like smiling suddenly.

"Nope. Big secret. Come on, get in bed. We have to get up early tomorrow."

Trace had made Ashe feel better, but he was still restless and sleepless most of the night. What should have worried him wasn't what worried him. Trina kept forcing her way into his mind until he couldn't stand it any longer.

Trajan was snoring lightly in his bed when Ashe gathered him into his mist, and then he made his way into Winkler's room noiselessly, carrying the still-sleeping Trajan. There he gathered up Trace and Winkler.

Winkler was snoring louder than Trajan, but Trace wasn't snoring at all. Lifting his mist through the ceiling, Ashe went through the roof—Matt had arranged for the penthouse in a twelve-story hotel. He hovered overhead while three cars stopped on the street below and ten people stepped out. Ashe recognized Trina right away—she was the only female.

His sleeping cargo might have felt a bit of vertigo at the speed that Ashe dropped, but he was right behind the last man's shoulder as they made their way into the hotel. Trina flashed a key card at the desk clerk who shrugged and allowed her to pass.

Ashe wondered that she'd managed to get away with one of the cards without alerting Winkler or his bodyguards. *It might not even be one of ours*, Ashe realized. It probably wouldn't be difficult to rent another room in the hotel or bribe one away from a staff member. Ashe hovered over the heads of all ten while they rode up the elevator to the ninth floor. Guns came out of pockets and waistbands.

Mr. Michaels, Grand Master, I hope you can hear me, Ashe sent. *Trina is back with nine other people and they all have guns. I think they're trying to kill Mr. Winkler.*

CHAPTER 11

att Michaels shouted into his cell phone as he sped toward the hotel he'd booked for Winkler and his party. The Grand Master, too, was on the phone, waiting on another line. Matt had two vampires and six special agents nearly at the scene.

Matt was concerned, too, about Winkler and the others and where they were at the moment. Winkler might attempt to take the attackers himself and that could prove fatal. And, if he were honest, Matt worried about the sixteen-year-old Ashe even more than the three werewolves.

"Just get in there and stop them—there are ten attackers, likely on the top floor. I haven't notified hotel security in case they're in on it!" Matt punched another button on his phone as his driver sped through traffic lights in the darkness.

"Grand Master, the vampires have arrived—one of them knows William Winkler. I don't know whether the others with the nurse are human or werewolf, but we'll know shortly. I'll call with information as soon as I have it." Matt ended the call and held on while his driver screeched around a corner.

Ashe considered dropping his cargo in an empty room and handling the attackers himself. He had brief thoughts of gathering them inside his mist and then dropping them into the street from a great height before reconsidering. That would be ten deaths and not an easy thing to explain when someone had to clean up bodies later.

Ashe heaved a mental sigh and floated behind Trina and her companions as one of the men knelt outside Winkler's door and took Trina's key card. Someone else produced bolt cutters—the metal security latch was hooked on the inside.

Trina must have gotten a master key from someone working at the hotel—the card worked and the door opened quietly. The bolt cutters were employed immediately after and three men rushed in, guns blazing. They might have gotten out again with none the wiser, except for Matt's vampire agents.

"Kid?" Matt Michaels stepped over a pile of glass from a lamp shattered in the shooting. The vampires had gathered those who still lived among the attackers—two humans. The others, including the female werewolf, were all dead. No signs of Winkler or any of his party were inside either room.

"Here," Ashe dropped his still-sleeping cargo onto the beds inside Winkler's room, causing all three werewolves to wake with a start.

"What the hell?" Winkler was up and growling immediately, his back to a wall in no time. Trajan and Trace flanked their Packmaster, ready to defend him. Ashe solidified on the floor not far away, hanging his head and looking sheepish.

"Sorry, Mr. Winkler," Ashe apologized. "I didn't mean to scare you. I just kept seeing Trina's face in my head and then I couldn't help myself. I picked all of you up while you were sleeping and misted outside. I followed Trina and the others inside the building. I think she had a master key to get in and somebody else had bolt cutters."

"He's right." Matt nodded to one of his human agents, who held both items. "Now, we'll just take these two somewhere for a little questioning," he jerked his head toward the two humans his vampire agents held. They were hauled quickly from the room.

"I've got people checking to see whose key card this is," Matt went on. Temper flashed in his hazel eyes as he accepted the card in question from his agent. "If we find 'em, we'll haul them in, too. In the meantime, I'm moving you to another hotel, so gather your things. Nobody will know where you are after that. A car will come to pick you up around nine in the morning. I'm rescheduling the hearing for later in the day."

"Kid, come here." Winkler, dark hair disheveled and dressed only in pajama bottoms, motioned for Ashe to come to him. Ashe gulped. He was about to get in trouble with the Dallas Packmaster. Ashe's feet felt stuck to the floor and he moved them with difficulty. As soon as Ashe was within Winkler's reach, Winkler grasped Ashe's upper arm and hauled him into a tight hug while Trajan and Trace watched.

Rabis sighed. He knew—he'd been following the movements of William Winkler, the werewolf Packmaster. The Bright Elemaiyan Foreseer was successfully outmaneuvering Wildrif. Wildrif and Winkler he could see. His grandchild he could not.

Come the morning, Friesianna would ask questions that Rabis would be forced to answer truthfully. "Be safe," he whispered to the winds flowing over Montana fields. The boy had to live. *Had to.*

"Dude, Randy and his mom are moving to Star Cove!" Sali couldn't help calling Ashe, though he knew they were still at odds with each other. Ashe had always liked Randy for some reason, and had defended him when everyone thought him guilty of exposing the Pack. Sali figured Ashe would want this information, no matter the source.

"Sali, what are you saying?" Ashe rubbed his eyes and blinked for a few seconds. He felt the effects of a very short night with little sleep as he spoke with Sali on his cell. He, Winkler and the others were currently riding in the back of a limousine toward the location selected for Jack Howard's hearing. "And dude, we're still on the outs, in case you hadn't noticed," he added.

"Yeah. I get that," Sali replied. "I'm sorry, man, but I thought you'd want to know. They'll be here in three days. Randy just stored all his stuff at his uncle's house. His mom got a transfer to the Corpus Christi Post Office and Randy has an interview with the Corpus Christi newspaper."

"That's nice, dude. I'm going back to being mad now."

"Dude, we've been friends for a long time," Sali whined.

"Sali, we've been friends since I saw you the first time. But that doesn't mean anything to me right now."

"Come on, I found a burger place in Aransas Pass. I'll drive you there when you get back. You can cuss me while we eat."

"As attractive as that sounds, we have to discuss this later. I have work to do." Ashe ended the call and flopped his head against the back of the seat.

"He's trying, Ashe," Trace said softly.

"Yeah. Does he still remember what I did, or has that been wiped away again?"

"I don't know. Perhaps you should ask Nathan."

"Nathan is a vampire, Trace, and likely just as much under the Council's thumb as anyone else. I'll be careful what I show to a vampire from now on."

"Kid, when we get out of this questioning session today, you and I are going shopping. You can buy as many pairs of cargo pants and shorts as you want. Banana Republic is calling your name," Winkler grinned. "Plus, you'll get a little bonus in your paycheck."

He and Trajan sat facing Ashe and Trace in the back of the limo. Bottled water, soft drinks and a few bottles of harder stuff were lined up inside a mini-fridge in the back. Ashe held a bottle of expensive water and sipped occasionally as they were ferried by one of Matt Michaels' drivers.

When the limo pulled to a stop, the door was opened for him and Ashe stepped out of the car, looking around at the guarded parking garage. The space was constructed mostly from concrete, with steel pillars placed at regular intervals and no signs anywhere to tell him where he was. Still clutching his bottle of water, Ashe trailed the others, who followed their driver.

An elevator carried them up three flights until they arrived at an unmarked floor. The elevator doors opened to reveal a tiled foyer and a security desk, manned by a uniformed, armed guard. Ashe blinked as two more guards stepped away from both sides of the elevator to flank them as they walked toward the desk and the man waiting there for them.

Ashe hauled out his driver's license when the guard requested ID— he'd barely gotten to use his license and remembered with mixed feelings the day he'd gotten it and Sali's teasing afterward. He missed Sali, when all was said and done. That didn't mean he wasn't still angry, though.

"What's a sixteen-year-old doing here?" The guard muttered gruffly.

"Material witness," the driver snapped. "Matt will have something to say if you bother him."

"Why didn't you say that to start with?" The guard handed Ashe's license back. He took Winkler, Trace and Trajan's IDs next, looked them over and passed them back. "Go ahead." He pressed a button and a door behind the desk swung open.

Ashe, walking between Trajan and Trace, strode down a narrow hall behind Winkler and their driver. He wanted to ask where they were. That would likely get him in trouble so he remained silent. They passed several doors on both sides of the hall, Ashe noticed, but none of them were labeled with anything other than numbers.

The door at the end of the hall was their destination. It opened when they arrived and Ashe was ushered inside. Matt Michaels and eight others were waiting. Ashe recognized some of them.

Two important members of Congress sat in comfortable, high-backed seats behind a horseshoe-shaped table. Former Congressman Jack Howard, looking nervous, sat at a smaller desk in the center with someone—likely an attorney, at his side.

"Ashe, these people all know about the Special Paranormal Division of the FBI, and they are aware that vampires, werewolves and shapeshifters exist," Matt said as he led Ashe, Winkler and the others to seats around the horseshoe.

Ashe, dressed neatly in his new suit, watched Winkler closely and unbuttoned his jacket just as Winkler did as he sat down. Trace and Trajan were ahead of him in getting as comfortable as a suit might allow. Ashe was introduced to both members of Congress and he nodded respectfully to them. At any other time, he might have liked to ask questions, but this wasn't the time. He did have a question, however, that couldn't wait.

"Mr. Howard's attorney is also aware that vampires, werewolves and shifters exist?" he asked.

"Mr. Howard's attorney, unbeknownst to Mr. Howard until now, is a shapeshifter," Matt Michaels stifled a grin. Ashe wanted to grasp the shapeshifting attorney by the throat and tell him exactly what Jack Howard had attempted to do after Obediah Tanner kidnapped Wynn. Instead, he remained silent. Jack Howard, however, did not.

"I want another attorney," he sniveled.

"You can have one after today," Matt said. "Mr. James had no trouble defending you against other charges. I assume he will also defend you to the best of his ability in these proceedings as well. This is not a court of law, Mr. Howard. This is merely a fact-finding session. If you answer questions truthfully today, we might be able to present a plea bargain somewhere down the road that won't be completely unpalatable. Ashe, will you come and place compulsion upon Jack Howard?" Matt asked. "Order him to tell the truth to all inside this room. Mr. James, you do not object?"

"No, you've already assured me that this information will not go any farther and that national security is on the line. I'll allow it." Jack Howard glared at his attorney but didn't speak. Ashe figured the esteemed former Congressman was cursing his attorney silently. Ashe rose and came to stand before Jack Howard.

"You will truthfully answer all questions asked by anyone inside this room. Do you understand? Answer now."

"Yes. I understand," Jack Howard wasn't happy but he answered anyway.

"Good. Quack like a duck," Ashe said. Matt Michaels rubbed his forehead and Winkler hid a smile as Jack Howard quacked several times before Ashe stopped him. "He's ready," Ashe said and moved back to his seat.

"Does the boy know how to shield? Your best guess, Rabis," Friesianna demanded. "Can he command the visions as well?"

"I believe the answer to both questions is no," Rabis bowed before the Queen. He was sworn and compelled to answer her. "All must be taught these things—they are not something one can stumble upon accidentally. There are none to teach him, my Queen."

"Then he is vulnerable. My spies tell me Baltis still wishes to capture him. That is foolish in my opinion. We will kill him instead and eliminate this threat. I cannot understand how Baltis fails to see the boy as such."

"My Queen, the Ekdi H'Morr says," Rabis wasn't allowed to finish.

"That is not correct—my crown gives me power and authority over all my subjects. It stays where it is. We will deal with this as we deal with any other threat—we will eliminate it. If Baltis had any intelligence, he would do the same. If he is as you say, then he is responsible for the deaths of my Jewels. Find someone to go through the gates. I want as much lion snake poison as we can get. That will kill any Elemaiya."

"Yes, my Queen." Rabis bowed and walked away, dismayed. Lion snakes were the most poisonous of any viper. Death came in a blink if one were bitten. While Elemaiya were immune to many things, lion snake poison would kill them quickly. He worried for the boy and sent up a silent prayer, even as he sought for one who might capture or kill a snake that dwelt on a faraway world.

~

"May I speak?" The questioning of Jack Howard had been long and tedious, most of it dealing with his misuse of public funds and his connections to illegal foreign businesses and concerns. Little was said regarding his hunting on Obediah Tanner's game preserve. Now the former Congressman wanted to ask questions.

"What is it, Jack?" One of the Congressional representatives asked, weariness evident in his voice.

"Is that the boy those things were after?" He pointed to Ashe.

"What things?" The representative said.

"You know—those things. Those creatures. I can't remember what they called themselves."

"We're done," Matt announced. "He's hallucinating now. Jasper, get him out of here." Matt called one of his werewolf guards, who came to cuff Jack Howard. He and two others led Howard from the room.

"You're a shapeshifter?" Jack Howard's attorney grasped Ashe's arm before he could move away.

"Yeah." Ashe didn't want to elaborate past that.

"And you can lay compulsion." The attorney had sandy-brown hair, light-brown eyes and a wry smile.

"He's one of the vampire-shifter kids," Winkler came to stand behind Ashe, causing the attorney to drop his hand.

"One of those," the man shifted his briefcase. "I should have guessed. I know vampire DNA will destroy a human if they're not turned, but shifter DNA is another matter, isn't it? I heard they shut the program down."

"That's what I heard, too. I suppose you'd have to contact the Council to get the truth of it." Winkler was doing his best to pull Ashe away and out of the room.

"Not going that route," the attorney grimaced. "Anybody with any sense would stay as far away from that as possible. Kid, what's your animal?" he asked one last question.

"He's a bat," Winkler grinned and hauled Ashe out the door.

~

"As soon as they're awake, have one of our vamp agents contact me," Matt ordered after extricating himself from the congressional representatives. "I have to plant one more suggestion on Jack Howard before he goes to trial. We don't need him pointing a finger at the kid. That could bring up too many questions we don't want to answer."

"Right, boss." Jasper nodded and pulled out his cell.

~

"Ashe, you can't tell a former member of Congress to quack like a duck," Winkler sighed. "Not in a formal setting like that. Understand?" Ashe was packing his bag the following morning after breakfast so they could make the trip to the airport and fly home.

Winkler had already held a conversation with Matt Michaels while Trajan took Ashe for breakfast downstairs. Matt hadn't gotten anything out of the humans who'd survived the attack two evenings before—they'd been hired muscle and nothing more.

Weldon was doing his best to investigate Trina, but that could take time. No good explanation could be found for her attempt to kill Winkler and the others. Winkler was glad to be putting D.C. behind him; the trip had turned sour in many ways.

"The quacking was epic," Trajan whispered to Ashe, loud enough for Winkler to hear. Winkler rolled his eyes and walked through the connecting door to see to his own bags.

~

"I've only been Grand Master for fifty-two years," Weldon reminded Winkler later. Winkler had stepped behind the pilot's cabin to take a call from the Grand Master. "Records before then were spotty if they existed at all," Weldon said. "We don't have anything on where Trina came from originally; all I have is the record where she married into the D.C. Pack. Her husband, the Second, challenged and was taken down. She hasn't married again. Had a nursing degree and worked for one of our physicians there."

"But something set her off. She knew you called her employer. She had to know you'd come after her if she were implicated in any way." Winkler pinched the bridge of his nose.

"That's what concerns me. This wasn't just her—I'd bet my ranch on it. Since she's dead and the humans don't know anything, we may not find the truth of this."

"And that concerns me," Winkler said. "Look, if we come up with anything on our end, I'll get back with you." Winkler hung up and moved toward his seat—they were scheduled to land at the Corpus Christi airport in less than an hour.

Josiah cursed, then kicked the chest that held the television in his hotel room, causing the appliance to rock dangerously. His contact in D.C. was dead, Winkler was still alive and his reward money remained tantalizingly out of reach.

When he'd gotten the initial call from Trina, the circumstances had sounded too good to be true. Winkler was easily within his grasp, as was the Dallas Second and two others.

The drug injection had been refused—that would have taken care of the boy. Trina called afterward and told him that, but when he ordered her to gather a few wolves and humans willing to commit murder for the right amount of money, things had gone wrong.

Josiah didn't have information on how Trina and the others were killed—his contact couldn't get it. Now he was back to the original plan. That plan had to be put into motion before Winkler's beach house was completed—he had it on good authority that breaching the beach house would be next to impossible. According to his sources, Josiah had less than a month.

❧

"Chad, of course you'll be reinstated with the Pack," Marcus sat at the kitchen island across from his visitor.

Since Chad and Jeremy had transferred to Corpus Christi University, they'd arranged to move their belongings into an empty house near Jeremy's parents. They'd driven their rented van to Star Cove the day before. Now, Chad had to ask Marcus for a spot in the Star Cove Pack if he expected to run with them come the full moon.

"I just wanted to make sure things were cool," Chad said, staring into his cup of coffee instead of looking Marcus in the eye. Keeping one's eyes lowered was often the reaction of a submissive werewolf to his Alpha.

"I do expect you to try and get along with everyone in the community. We have three new vampires—they came in late last night. I want everyone to introduce themselves when the vamps wake —they're here to beef up security around the community—they'll be trading nights off so Nathan won't be pushed to the limit like he and Aedan were before."

"Too bad the Council recalled Aedan." Chad's words were hollow and tinged with sarcasm. Marcus noted it but made no comment, studying the twenty-year-old werewolf instead. Chad had his mother's dark hair and hazel eyes. His facial features belonged to his father, though. Marcus never forgot that Chad's father, Hollis Daniels, had challenged—and lost.

Marcus had attempted to talk Hollis out of the challenge—Chad had been eight at the time and Marcus didn't like leaving families without one of the parents. Hollis hadn't liked the fact that vampires were part of their paranormal community. Therefore, he'd challenged Marcus. It was a mistake. Marcus sighed at the memory and put it out of his mind.

"Chad, I have work to do—I'm buying a shop in Aransas Pass to set up my locksmith business again. Sit here until you finish your drink. If you need anything, ask Denise." Marcus rose and walked out of the house. Chad didn't say anything as he watched Marcus leave.

"What's your college major?" Bear Wright was moving things into the office set aside for the Principal. Jeremy Booth had come to talk for some reason.

"Psychology," Jeremy said. "But I'm still getting basics out of the way."

"And you've gone for two years?"

"Yeah."

"I see. How do you like it?" Bear hefted a box of files onto a shelf inside a tiny storage closet.

"It's okay."

"Planning to hang up a shingle when you're done with your PhD?" Bear lifted another box of files.

"I hadn't thought that far ahead," Jeremy admitted.

"What were you going to do after graduation, then?"

"Don't know. Maybe get a job on a local fishing boat or join the Navy. Mom and Dad are paying for school, so I'll get that out of the way before I look for a job."

"Why didn't you go for history instead of psychology? I saw you had decent marks in Dodd's classes."

"Mr. Dodd was pretty cool. He made history interesting. But the classes in college? Boring."

"I always thought that some teachers should have found something else to occupy their time, and some that went into other fields should have been teachers. Some people just have the knack for it. Others couldn't care less."

"I heard you were thinking about trying to organize the shapeshifter community." Jeremy said what he'd come to say.

"Ah. Finally the truth." Bear shifted the boxes of files on the shelf to fit another in. He'd dressed in a checkered shirt with sleeves rolled back, his bushy, light-brown hair was more disheveled than normal and his jeans were frayed around the hems. Star Cove's new Principal had come prepared for physical activity. Jeremy found it unattractive. Principal Billings had never dressed that way.

"Mom told me," Jeremy shrugged, as if the subject didn't interest him.

"Are you opposed to being organized?" Bear leveled a thoughtful glance at Jeremy.

"No. The werewolves are organized. The vampires are *really* organized."

"I suspect that not much will change, if we do organize," Bear said carefully. "But a Shifter Council might have some leverage when it comes to criminal activity, both committed by and against shapeshifters. I have no idea how much you know about that game preserve they shut down in the Texas Panhandle, but plenty of evidence was found indicating shifters were hunted and killed there. Most of them were rare shifters—ones we can't replace."

"Don't know about that," Jeremy scuffed a toe of his athletic shoe on the polished tile floor of Bear's office.

"Maybe you should know about it. Ask Marcus—see if he'll tell you," Bear lifted the last file box and maneuvered it into place. Each box was neatly labeled with the contents inside.

"I'll ask," Jeremy lied. "Is there anything I can do to help?" Jeremy raised his eyes and asked.

"Nope. Just finished. Have to make calls now. See you later." Jeremy took the hint and left.

Andy was waiting at the airport with a van and a pile of messages for Winkler. Winkler looked through the stack while Andy drove Ashe and the others toward Star Cove. "Mom, I'm back; we're between Corpus and Star Cove right now," Ashe told his mother.

"Hi, hon. Buck and I were going over the plans for the school cafeteria, and we'll update the kitchen at Victoria's when that's finished," she said brightly. Ashe wanted to sigh. Whatever his father had done, he'd been thorough about it.

"I'll see you when we get in," Ashe said and hung up.

"Kid, don't let it get you down," Trace pulled Ashe into a bear hug. "We'll work this out. You'll see."

Ashe sat back when Trace let him go and stared at his new watch—Matt Michaels had given him the timepiece before he'd boarded Winkler's jet. The watch was a nice one—it gave temperatures, elevations, time zones and even had an Internet connection. The manufacturer was committed to the idea of keeping up with cell phones and other devices while still looking elegant on a wrist.

Ashe had looked the watch up on its Internet connection, whistling at the price. Matt said it was in appreciation for what he'd done for the country so far and patted Ashe on the shoulder. "Here's my card, kid. That's my private number," Matt added. "If you have information for me or ever need anything from me, I'll answer if possible."

"All right," Ashe promised. "Thanks for the watch." Ashe had boarded the jet shortly after that, pulling the watch out of the box and placing it on his wrist. Made of platinum, it had a square face and a few diamonds around the bezel.

"That's a nice gift," Trace nodded at the watch as Andy drove them home.

"Yeah. I guess." Ashe would give that up and more if he could have his family together again.

"Good news," Buck was waiting for Winkler when the van pulled into the drive of Winkler's home in Star Cove. "You can move into the beach house in a week. We won't be done, but what's left can be finished while you're there. The kitchens and the bathrooms are done and carpet laid in the bedrooms. We're putting up stucco this week and painting next week."

"I'll come look after dinner tonight," Winkler promised. "How's the Star Cove restaurant doing?"

"Just fine—it'll be ready right before school starts. Adele is working out menus with the cooks and putting cost sheets together for you. You'll have those in a day or two. We're storing canned goods and supplies in the school for now—we might hire some of the kids to move those over when the time comes."

Buck was happy with what he'd accomplished so far, Ashe could tell. He was certainly motivated. Ashe didn't want to examine that thought closely at the moment. He wanted to lie down somewhere and go to sleep.

"Dude?" Sali was suddenly beside him, dressed in shorts, flip-flops and a tank top, with his hands stuffed in pockets. He lifted his head shyly to give Ashe half a grin. "Want to get a burger?"

"Where's Dori?" Ashe couldn't help but ask.

"I told her we had business, so she and Wynn are lying in the sun on Wynn's deck right now."

"And Marco?"

"Cori and Marco are still fighting, so Marco went to Winkler's beach house to help do some stuff over there. You should see the place —it's like an anthill, they're so busy."

"Fine. Let's get a burger and then you can drive me by the beach house." Ashe gestured for Sali to lead the way.

"Do I need to go?" Trace looked at Winkler. Winkler thought for a moment before shaking his head. Ashe followed Sali around the U-shaped street toward the other side. His feet and legs felt cramped after the flight and he needed to work out a few kinks. Trajan would likely put him through hell over the next few days since he hadn't exercised while they were gone.

"Slow down, dude." Ashe was running without realizing it while Sali called after him. Adele had come out of the house and was standing in the driveway of their home. Ashe ran up and hugged his mother.

"Ashe, don't be upset," Adele held him away from her. "Your father —I'm sure he still loves you." Her expression was nearly blank.

Ashe watched his mother's face carefully. He was going to call his father again. Aedan hadn't replied to the last message, but that didn't mean he hadn't gotten it. His mother seemed a bit dazed to see Ashe and the mention of his father had no emotion crossing her face.

His father was much better at compulsion than Ashe realized. He cursed it and the Head of the Council silently. "I'm going to Aransas Pass to get a burger with Sali. Want anything?"

"No, I just finished lunch a little while ago. Go have fun." Adele shooed him away.

~

"What did you do in D.C.?" Sali asked as he drove his Honda toward Aransas Pass.

"Winkler took me to Banana Republic and I bought a ton of clothes," Ashe said. "We had to buy another suitcase to carry all of it."

"Dude, that's not all you went for."

"It's all I'll tell you."

"Fair enough." Sali's words held a growl.

"Come on, Sal; tell me why we're fighting. Tell me. Or do you not remember. Like always?"

"Dad let me remember."

"How nice for you." Ashe leaned his elbow on the armrest and stared out the passenger side window.

"Ashe, we've been friends for a long time."

"Yeah, but I never ratted you out."

"Yeah. I'll give you that." Sali made a turn after going through a yellow light that turned red. Less than twenty seconds later, a local policeman pulled Sali over.

"The light was yellow when I started through," Sali complained as he handed his license to the officer.

"But you were going forty-five in a thirty-five mile per hour zone," the officer pointed out. "And then you went through a nearly red light. I'm not ticketing you for that—I'm ticketing you for speeding. Here's the ticket," he passed the slip of paper to Sali. "The court date is on the back if you want to dispute the ticket. Have a nice day." The officer walked back to his car and drove past Sali and Ashe seconds later.

"Dude, you could have put your mojo on him," Sali grumbled as he put the car in gear and pulled away from the curb.

"Putting my mojo on somebody got us where we are today. Maybe I should have let you tear into those drunks and then get hauled off to jail. Look at it this way—you only got a ticket this time and I'll pay half."

"It's ninety-five dollars, dude." Sali handed the ticket to Ashe.

"Then I'll pay the whole thing. Since it appears to be my fault." Ashe couldn't keep the sarcasm out of his voice.

"Do you want a ride home or not?" Sali snapped.

"Dude, I don't need a car to get around."

"Yeah. I remember that, too." Sali pulled into the parking lot surrounding a low, square building. Dandee Burgers was spelled out in red neon over the doorway.

"Dandee Burgers? Could they come up with a worse name?" Ashe climbed out of the car and shut the door.

"The burgers are good." Sali's voice was sullen.

"Dude, maybe we should have waited. As reconciliations go, this one isn't going so well," Ashe pointed out as they walked to the entrance. The door was dark glass with a paper *Open* sign hanging on the inside.

"Ashe, just go in and sit down. I have something to say and it isn't gonna be easy," Sali muttered, knowing Ashe would hear. Sali went to the counter and ordered for Ashe and himself before coming to the table with two soft drinks in his hands.

"So, what is it, Sal? What do you have to say? We were already on the outs. Maybe you should have left it that way."

"Dude, that's not the whole story," Sali muttered. "Dad—he didn't like it that I almost got hauled off by Zeke Tanner and a bunch of your people."

"My people?" Ashe goggled at Sali, confused.

"You know—what you are." Sali flushed uncomfortably.

Ashe stared. Started to speak and went back to staring. "Are you telling me that your dad suspects me because of what those people did?" He finally spoke, unwilling to believe what Sali was telling him.

"Sort of." Sali wouldn't look at Ashe.

"So. I pull you and the others off that stupid island and bring you home, and Marcus DeLuca thinks I'm like them. Sali, I'm leaving." Ashe pulled what cash he had from his pocket and dumped it on the table.

"There's more," Sali whispered before Ashe could take three steps away from the table.

"Oh, this is too good to pass up. What else do you have, Sali? What else can you do to me? I suppose your father ordered you to tell him everything you know about me. Is that it? Marcus thinks I'm a murderous criminal now. Is that what you're saying?" Ashe whirled to face Sali.

"Sort of," Sali hung his head. "He's my dad, Ashe. What was I supposed to do?"

"I don't know, defend me, maybe? Say I'm not like that? But then you don't know, do you? Your brains are scrambled, so I'll let that go. If Marcus doesn't want me in Star Cove, I think I can fix that." Ashe stalked out of the restaurant.

"Mr. Winkler, I messed things up. That's why Ashe didn't come back here." Sali fidgeted in Winkler's guest chair.

"What did you do, Salidar? Where do you think Ashe went?" Trajan stood near the door to Winkler's study, ready to go if Sali gave him a location.

"I told him the truth—that Dad doesn't trust him because he's Elemaiyan. Dad told me to bring everything I saw Ashe do to him and to Marco."

Winkler was cursing and dialing Marcus at the same time. "Get your ass over here. Now," Winkler snapped when Marcus answered the phone. "Salidar, you need to go. This is between the Grand Master, your father and me. I don't want your name in this. Trajan, get Sali out of here. Try Ashe's cell. See if he'll answer." Trajan grabbed Sali by the collar and hauled him from the room.

"What?" Marcus was inside Winkler's study within ten minutes. The Grand Master was on speakerphone, waiting for Marcus to appear.

"Marcus," the Grand Master spoke, "If I have to take you down myself to keep you from torturing that boy, I will."

CHAPTER 12

"*I*t doesn't matter how he found out. He likely has foresight, in addition to a few other things. And we have this." Winkler slapped a copy of the email sent by the one claiming to be Ashe's grandfather. Marcus read it quickly, and then again, more slowly the second time.

"What does he mean, *guard him closely if you value your lives and your planet?*" Marcus handed the sheet back to Winkler.

"I might have dismissed this as a prank or a lie of some sort, except that someone else has taken an interest in Ashe," Winkler snapped. Marcus knew he wasn't in Winkler's or the Grand Master's good graces at the moment.

"Who?" Marcus couldn't help asking.

Weldon Harper cursed over the speakerphone before saying one word; "Griffin."

"It's not something we can discuss—he and his race cannot directly interfere," Winkler sighed. "They're not dangerous to you, me or any of us unless we attempt to attack them. If you want to die and do it quickly, then by all means," Winkler flung out a hand. "Griffin has come to Ashe twice now. He's interested in this for some reason. Interested in Ashe for some reason. Marcus, do you believe that Ashe means you harm in any way? Do you? This is preposterous," Winkler rose and shoved his chair beneath the desk with another curse. "I don't think this one is lying when he says the survival of the planet depends on keeping Ashe safe. As much as we can, anyway. Marcus, if you've lost him for us," Winkler growled.

"What am I supposed to think?" Marcus defended himself. "I am Packmaster, here. It is my responsibility to keep the inhabitants of this community safe."

"And everything you've seen Ashe do up to this point leads you to think he'll turn on you?" Weldon Harper snarled. "He saved Winkler and the others in D.C. two nights ago. That doesn't sound like someone who means harm to me."

"Those things took my boy," Marcus snarled back.

"And Ashe got Sali back. The Elemaiya came because they wanted Ashe. Zeke Tanner wanted your son and the other kids. Dom Pruitt led him right to your boy and the others. The Elemaiya came for Ashe, not Sali or the others. They only agreed to help Tanner to get to him. Dom Pruitt and Zeke Tanner led them here because they were after Dom's boy, Sali and the others. Now you're punishing the one who killed the Elemaiya that helped take Sali and the others. Ashe killed them, Marcus, to protect that community you're so worried about." Weldon was throwing things—Winkler could hear it in the background of Weldon's phone conversation.

"He won't be a nuisance to Marcus much longer—I'll take him with me to the beach house and then to Dallas," Winkler pointed out. "I'm not worried that he'll turn on me. The boy lifted me, Trajan and Trace into his mist the other night. Just picked us right up while we slept. He could have killed us in so many ways. Ashe saved our lives instead."

"What I'm concerned about is where he is right now." Weldon said. "Marcus, you'd better hope we find him and quick. The vampires took Aedan away, and that was one line of defense Ashe had. They've sent those other three to act as spies, no doubt. I'd watch my back with them instead of Ashe."

"Next time, maybe you'll let me in on your schemes and secrets before I start thinking what any normal werewolf might think," Marcus snapped.

"You forget who you're talking to, *Packmaster*."

Marcus jerked back in his seat. "My apologies, Grand Master," Marcus muttered.

"This talk is getting us nowhere. I need to look for Ashe," Winkler said. "Grand Master, I'll keep you informed."

"See that you do," Weldon ordered. "You, too, Marcus. Get some of those wolves of yours off their asses to help."

"I'm on my way, Grand Master." Marcus stood and walked through the door of Winkler's study without a backward glance.

"Marcus is pissed," Winkler muttered to Trace as he walked toward the door. "Any word from Trajan?"

"None, boss. I'll call him now."

"Nothing," Trajan said when he answered Trace's call. "I drove by the beach house and didn't see anything. With Ashe, that doesn't mean a thing, though. I asked the workers—they haven't seen the boy."

"Keep looking," Winkler said. "We'll do the same."

Winkler's cell rang shortly after Trace ended the call with his brother. Andy was calling. "Boss," Andy said, "I got a hit on Ashe's debit card—he used it in the café at the bookstore in Corpus."

"Drive," Winkler snapped out the order. Ace, who was driving a Winkler Security van with Winkler and Trace inside, hit the gas and sped toward Corpus Christi.

Ashe settled into a comfortable chair to sip his frozen caramel mocha and read a science-fiction book. An employee recommended it and Ashe was engrossed from the first page. "Ashe, we were worried." Winkler knelt next to Ashe's chair.

"Marcus doesn't want me in Star Cove," Ashe stuck a thumb in the book to mark his place.

"We heard. The Grand Master had a talk with him and set things straight," Winkler explained. "Your mother is probably wondering where you are."

"My mother has been brainwashed. She barely remembers she has a son."

"Ashe, come home with us now. We'll put you up in the beach house soon and you won't have to deal with Marcus."

"Why did he believe that? Why did he set Sali to spy on me?" Ashe gazed levelly into Winkler's nearly black eyes.

"Ashe, you know Marcus was in the military. He dealt with terrorists. He didn't trust anyone from certain tribes or races. I think that has tainted his views on this. I'm not making excuses for him; I'm just explaining things as I see them. He should never have involved Sali in this. I'm sorry that your friendships have soured with Sali and Marco. I think Marco still likes you—very much. You'll just have to play it by ear with him. And with Sali, too, if that's what you want."

"Mr. Winkler, I don't really know what I want anymore. I want my dad back, but that's not gonna happen."

"Son, I can't do anything about that," Winkler sighed. "I wish I could. Come on, I'll buy your book and we'll go to a restaurant down the street for dinner."

"Yeah. I didn't get my burger earlier."

"I heard. Let's go."

~

"Did you mean to do this, Dad?" Ashe left another message for his father. "Mom barely recognizes me. I might as well be a distant relative. Thanks for fighting for us." Ashe hung up angrily.

When Winkler had gone home with Ashe to help explain why he'd been missing, Adele dismissed it lightly, as if nothing had happened and her son hadn't been away from everyone for hours.

Winkler asked Adele if he could put Ashe up at his house again. Adele agreed readily, as if that were perfectly normal and acceptable. "I'll have breakfast ready for you and the others tomorrow morning," she promised as Ashe walked out of the house with Winkler, Trace and Trajan.

Ignoring the upheaval in his life, Ashe spent the rest of the evening doing laundry and reading his new book. He barely glanced at the GED study guides in his makeshift office and bedroom. All his new clothes were clean and hung inside the small closet when he went to bed.

~

Nathan was patrolling the community with Edmond when his cell vibrated. Aedan's number appeared on the screen. "Aedan?" Nathan's question was in his father's name.

"Child, I may have made a mistake," Aedan said quietly. "Are you alone?"

"No, father."

"This conversation needs to be held in private."

"Sorry, Edmond," Nathan walked away from the other vampire. "Father, I am near the ocean and am away from the others, now. What mistake?"

"I placed compulsion on Adele before she left, as you likely know. Ashe left a message earlier, saying she barely recognized him. I was too zealous in my instructions, I think."

"What did you tell her?"

"To forget me and what we had together."

"And that includes Ashe."

"Yes. I see that now."

"Father, I cannot undo your compulsion. Layering more compulsion over yours may cause damage."

"I know that, Nathan. I know not what to do. My boy is suffering as a result of my stupidity and haste to do the deed."

"There was a problem earlier," Nathan ventured to say. "Marcus has Sali spying on Ashe because he distrusts the boy. His worries are baseless, but he now suspects anyone with ties to the Elemaiya. He thinks of Ashe as one of them and set his own son to spy on Ashe and bring any new information to him. I hear there was quite a meeting between Marcus, Winkler and the Grand Master, who was teleconferencing. And all this happened while Ashe was missing for hours."

Aedan cursed. "Did they find him?"

"Eventually, yes. When Winkler went with him to explain why he'd gone missing, Adele treated the whole thing lightly. Casimir was listening from outside and heard what was said. He says it wasn't the way any normal mother would act when her son was lost or missing. She then blithely allowed Ashe to go home with Winkler to stay."

"Casimir is there?"

"Yes, father. Casimir is here."

"Wlodek is determined to take my son."

"It looks that way."

"Nathan?"

"Yes, father?"

"You will give no information to any other vampire concerning my son. I command it."

"Yes, father."

Ashe didn't speak to Sali or Marco when they came to the exercise room to work out Saturday morning. Cori, Dori and Wynn came, too. The girls worked out with Ace, who was quite patient with them. Ashe caught the white werewolf smiling now and then as he instructed Wynn. Trajan watched over Ashe; Trace worked with Marco and Sali.

Ashe ran ahead of the others on the beach later so he wouldn't be forced to acknowledge the DeLuca brothers. Cori ignored Marco as well. Ashe found a perverse sort of satisfaction from that. Marco cornered Ashe later in his office and Ashe didn't think he could just throw Marco out without getting into a huge fight. Marco settled on Ashe's guest chair with a sigh.

"Ashe, hear me out first and then decide whether you hate me or not," Marco said. "First off, I'm sorry. I know it's a betrayal of sorts, and that's what bothers me so much. I owe you. Just like Sali and Winkler and the others owe you. At least I remember that I owe you. Most of the others don't, so you have to overlook that. I'd give anything to go back to the place where this hadn't happened yet. Things might have been different, if I'd known Dad was involved. We're not speaking right now, Dad and I. That doesn't make me feel good because I care about my parents—like I know you care about yours. All I can do is apologize and tell you not to let anything slip. Ever again. Cori says she won't come back to me until I make things right with you. But that's not the only reason I'm here. I want things to be right between us, Ashe. I think of you as a friend. A good friend."

"People have a funny way of showing friendship around here," Ashe muttered, tapping on his computer. He was taking a practice exam online for the GED.

"They call it the Fraternity of the Wolf," Marco admitted. "The blood of the race binding one werewolf to another. It's the ritual all young werewolves go through when we run with the Pack the first time and swear the oaths to our Packmaster."

"I guess Obediah and Zeke Tanner forgot those parts," Ashe observed dryly.

"Ashe, you know that every race has its outlaws. The Tanners were werewolf outlaws. Well, Zeke is still out there, so he can cause more trouble after he recovers from the loss of most of his wolves."

"With the way things are in Mexico, that won't take long," Ashe observed. Actually, Marco's mention of the Tanners made Ashe think for a moment. "Marco, did the Grand Master ever find the leak he suspected in the Amarillo Pack?"

"I don't know, but I'll ask Winkler."

"Okay. Let me know what you find out."

"Will do. Can we at least declare a truce?"

"Should have brought in a white flag, dude." Ashe answered three questions on the computer while Marco stared.

"If I bring in a white flag, will you at least keep talking to me?"

"Here." Ashe lifted a tissue from the box inside a desk drawer. "Wave that. I can't do anything about Cori. You have to make your own peace with her."

"Is that what this is? A kind of peace?"

"Some kind. I just won't trust you again. Or Sali." Ashe's voice was bitter on Sali's name.

"That's too bad. I have a feeling you could ruin Sali with Dad if you wanted. But I'm not about to pry," Marco held up both hands when Ashe glared. "I'll leave you alone to finish whatever that is. Ashe, I really am sorry."

"Then we'll agree to a truce. And we'll talk. It just won't be any exchange of confidences." Ashe waved Marco out of the room.

"Rather hard, isn't it, not having anyone to confide in," the tall, hazel-eyed man was back and sitting in the chair Marco had just vacated.

"You have no idea," Ashe grumbled. "Why are you here? Come to rub it in?"

"No, I came to give you this." Ashe stared as papers appeared from nowhere and now dangled from the man's hand. Reaching out hesitantly, Ashe lifted them from the man's fingers. "I translated more for a friend, and he made the mistake of handing it to someone else, who withheld most of it. This isn't all, but it's what you need right now." The man disappeared as quickly as Ashe could blink.

When Ashe got himself back in hand, he stared at the first sentence on the top page. *When the Destroyer appears and the Bright and Dark of the races are at war, the Ir'Indicti will come*, it announced.

Ashe misted the new pages inside his father's safe. He discovered that his mother had removed much of what had been inside. Most of it

dealt with her marriage to Aedan. He sighed again over what his father had done.

Had Aedan truly meant to leave his wife and son with no contact or support? It made no sense to Ashe. His mother never knew he'd been inside the house—he misted away again without letting her know.

~

"How are the sample tests coming along?" Winkler dropped into a deck chair beside Ashe. Winkler had brought furniture from somewhere and piled it on the covered patio behind the house in Star Cove.

"Good. I squeaked by on the first two. I'll study those books a little more and do another tomorrow."

"After you finish your book?" Winkler's mouth twisted into a half-grin—Ashe's finger held a place two-thirds through the book he'd gotten the night before.

"Sort of."

"Let's go see the beach house. We'll grab lunch on the way," Winkler patted Ashe's shoulder. Ashe rose and followed Winkler into the house.

~

"So things didn't go very well with Ashe." Sali looked up at his father's words.

"Dad, I had to tell Mr. Winkler why Ashe disappeared."

"Both my sons, loyal to another Packmaster," Marcus growled.

"That's not it. I told you what you wanted to know. Sold out my best friend to do it and you're still not happy. What would you have done if I'd come to tell you that Ashe figured everything out and took off? Would you have said good riddance and left it at that?" Sali stabbed the spaghetti on his plate. His mother remained silent as she set a plate in front of Marcus.

"Son, I saw those pages the vamps sent. Winkler showed them to me last night. He wouldn't tell me how many of those things Ashe can do. You probably know better than I ever will."

"If you're fishing Dad, you know everything I know."

~

"The father is in the London area for the second day," Wildrif informed Baltis.

"Good. One more day and I will send my guards," Baltis replied. "Be sure that the boy's parents are not with others. I do not wish to lose more of our people."

"Of course, my King." Wildrif bowed and was escorted from Baltis' chambers.

"I am stifled so far underground and do not have the ability to relocate as you do," Wildrif informed his companion, a rather short, white-blond Elemaiya. "Might it be possible to find an entrance somewhere to breathe purer air?" Wildrif's mismatched eyes begged pitifully.

"Very well. Come, we will find one of those round openings nearby."

"That is all I ask," Wildrif nodded deferentially. Sunlight filtered through the keyhole of a metal cover somewhere along the way and Wildrif was allowed to climb up the ladder to sniff better air. He concealed his actions from the guard as he pulled a cell phone from a hidden pocket and sent a quick text before climbing down again and thanking the guard for his indulgence.

~

"My spy has information," Friesianna stared at her new Assassins. "Baltis plans to send someone to London—that is where the boy's father is and they suspect the boy is with him. Follow them. I want the boy dead. They want to keep him alive to serve their purposes, clearly expecting to keep his true nature from him. That will not be. Kill the boy and Baltis' guards. They have spilled enough of our blood. Let the Dark King worry about replacing his assassins with what he has left of his people." Friesianna's voice was cold and determined.

If she could locate Baltis' encampment, she planned to send as much of an army against it as she could gather. Her spy informed her that Baltis left the majority of his people elsewhere, under Prince Beldris' supervision. She wanted the Prince's death just as much as she wanted Baltis'.

~

"She won't know, I promise." Rabis led a small group of Bright Elemaiya to a copse of trees. Two had come originally, worried that they and their children would become fodder for the Queen's army. She'd turned to conscripting artisans and weavers.

"Jump from here," Rabis pointed to the ground, "to this spot and then to the gate." He tapped a dot on a human map. "Take this map with you. You should still have enough strength to get through the gate and to the place I described to you. Go there. The old Queen is waiting." He handed the paper map to his companions.

"Your daughter, if I remember correctly," the weaver said softly.

"Do not say that where anyone can hear. Friesianna thinks her dead. Go now or you will be taken on the morrow to serve in the army."

"We leave you with our thanks." The man bowed low to Rabis and he and his party disappeared.

Rabis sighed helplessly. "Only six that see sense," he muttered. "Friesianna will kill us all."

~

"This is one of three safe rooms," Winkler tapped the wall with a finger.

"How do you get in?" Ashe asked. He could see no evidence of a door, even a hidden one.

"I don't. *You* do. Go through the wall, Ashe. There's a room inside, with everything you might need. I count on you taking the rest of us with you if you go—and getting us out again when it's safe. But just in case, there's emergency equipment inside that'll cut through the walls." Winkler's grin belied the seriousness of his voice.

Ashe, Winkler and Trace were in the basement of the new beach house. Buck had studied the situation seriously, drawing up plans to keep the Dallas Packmaster safe from just about anything.

"Have you seen inside it?" Ashe asked.

"Not yet—I only have Buck's word that he furnished it comfortably and that it had a working bathroom and shower inside before he sealed it off. There are small air vents, but those are the only openings."

"Want to check on that?" Ashe asked, a mischievous glint in his eyes.

"Thought you'd never ask," Winkler laughed. Ashe gathered Winkler and Trace into his mist and went right through the wall.

"This is better than I thought," Trace sat down at the small table inside. The room was long and narrow, running the length of the beach house, with a full bath on one end, a small kitchen on the other. In between was a sitting area with a flat screen on the wall, a computer on a desk nearby, a telephone, printer and any other electronic gadget one might need to conduct business. The space was already carpeted, painted and had a hidden closet and laundry area behind the sofa in the center of the room.

"Buck did a great job," Winkler agreed, examining the walls, cabinets and office space. Ashe settled on the sofa and used the remote to turn on the television.

"I think I could live here," Ashe said, flipping through cable channels.

"You have a bedroom upstairs. It's a suite, actually. Trajan and Trace have one on either side—those take up the southern half of the second story. Mine takes up the northern half," Winkler said.

"Cause he's the boss," Trace agreed good-naturedly.

"Take us upstairs, Ashe, and you'll see what you're getting." Ashe turned off the television, tossed the remote on the sofa and turned to mist a second time.

"Wow." Ashe looked around at the suite Winkler was building for him. Carpet had just been laid and the walls were ready to be painted, but windows were bare of blinds or curtains and light fixtures were missing. Nevertheless, the suite was large.

The bedroom was separated from an adjoining media room, and a small study lined with bookshelves was just off the bedroom. A sink and space for a small refrigerator was located at the back of the media room, as were a few shelves and cabinets.

"You can live here," Winkler pointed out. "The basement is for emergencies only."

"Keep it to yourself, but we may be able to move in next week," Trace whispered. "We don't want our enemies learning our movements ahead of time." Trace's words were humorous, but Ashe recognized the gravity underneath.

"We will," Winkler acknowledged. "And we'll do it right after sunrise. Those vamps won't see a thing." Winkler found that more humorous than anything.

"Have you met them?" Ashe queried.

"Last night. Seem all right on the surface." Winkler turned away. He didn't tell Ashe what else he was planning. Not then, anyway. He had some calls to make and explanations to give beforehand. "Now, let's go pull Trajan away from our construction supervisor." Winkler jerked his head toward the door.

"Where are we going?" Ashe asked as Trace drove toward Corpus Christi.

"Men's clothing," Trajan heaved a patient sigh. Winkler, sitting in the passenger seat, grinned at Trajan over the back of his seat.

"I'm not getting more monkey clothes," Ashe insisted.

"You're not, Trajan is," Winkler was still grinning at Trajan.

"But you had a nice suit on the other day," Ashe stated the obvious.

"I need a new one, apparently." Trajan sounded somewhat bewildered. "Boss, this can wait, you know."

"No, I want to do it now. Before school starts at the end of the month. We'll get together the day we move into the new beach house. That's a good beginning, don't you think?"

"What? What's going on?" Ashe felt just as bewildered as Trajan.

"Trajan's getting engaged, that's what," Trace chortled.

"Bro, if I have to come up there," Trajan gripped the back of Trace's seat with a very large hand. Large enough to palm basketballs, Ashe noticed.

"You'd think they were six and eight, instead of fifty-six and fifty-eight," Winkler laughed.

"That's funny now. You have to tell my mother." Trajan poked a finger at Winkler.

"Yes, I suppose I do." Winkler was still grinning when he turned around in his seat.

"Dude, you're that old? I thought you were twenty-five or something," Ashe whispered to Trajan. Trajan and Trace burst out laughing.

"I like this one best," Trace looked his brother over with a critical eye. The suit—a dark-gray pinstripe, looked good on Trajan, although it needed alterations. The tall werewolf was broad across the shoulders, narrow at the waist and his legs—any basketball player would want those.

Lean and powerful, Ashe thought as he watched Trajan turn this way and that for the store clerk to make small chalk markings on the coat and pants. Winkler was looking through expensive shirts and tossing several to Trace, who caught them expertly and placed them in a pile. Ties came next—Winkler pulled out six and handed those to Trace, who placed them in the growing pile. Shoes, socks and a few other items came after that.

"Your feet are almost too long for me to fit," the clerk grimaced, using a shoehorn to get dress shoes onto Trajan's feet. Ashe grinned helplessly—Trajan had mocked him when he'd tried on shoes only days ago. Now Ashe was getting payback.

"Dude, your pinkie toe is as big as someone else's foot," Ashe teased.

"Are you mocking me?" Trajan lifted an eyebrow at Ashe.

"Yep."

"Just checking," Trajan grunted as the second shoe went on.

"We'll special order the next ones," Winkler promised as two pairs of shoes were boxed up and added to the waiting pile.

"When's the wedding?" Ashe asked.

"Not for another two years—it'll be a long engagement," Trace murmured as he and Ashe watched Winkler pay nearly six thousand dollars for what they'd purchased. "This will give Trajan enough time to get to know his intended. And vice-versa."

"An arranged marriage."

"Yeah. Seconds are good marriage material. As are Packmasters, but most of those are married already. There are three hundred twelve Packs, so that means over three hundred Packmasters and more than three hundred Seconds. That's leaving room for the female Packmasters, who don't have any trouble finding a male. Females aren't common among the werewolves. Not anymore."

"What happened?" Ashe asked, his curiosity forcing the question.

"The race war," Trace said softly as he ushered Ashe through the door, following Winkler and Trajan who were loaded down with bags and boxes. The suit would be ready in two days, or so the clerk promised. "The vamps targeted the weakest among us, and those were often the females. Fewer females mean fewer births. The vamps regulate how many of them get turned, so when the wolves took down a vamp, it decimated their numbers as well."

"Trace, decimate by definition means one in ten. I think those numbers would have to be elevated to account for actual losses," Ashe pointed out as he climbed inside the van.

"Okay, on both sides, the deaths accounted for around two-thirds of both races."

"Holy cow," Ashe hissed.

"That's the bigger picture," Winkler had listened to both sides of the conversation. "We don't know how many shifters died—the vamps, some of them anyway, didn't like them either."

"Have they stopped killing shifters?"

"That was the agreement when they married some of them to the vamps. Shifters aren't organized, but a few are powerful enough and have enough connections throughout the race that they can bargain at times with Wlodek. Wlodek wanted shifters to marry vamps and see if they could have kids, substituting DNA into the egg. In exchange for the vampires leaving shifters alone. You're a result of that, Ashe."

"But Mom and Dad met in a bar in London. That wasn't arranged."

"You don't know that, Ashe. What if somebody knew your mother was going to be where she was? And conveniently sent in a vampire?"

"Trace, I have a headache." Ashe didn't want to continue the discussion. Too many ugly possibilities crowded his brain.

"Trace, enough." Winkler nodded to Trace, who settled into the driver's seat and started the van. "Ashe, we only speculate. We don't know truth. It won't ever change who your parents are. Remember that. If things were normal, you wouldn't be having this conversation or worrying about it. Trace, drive." Trace put the van in gear and drove.

CHAPTER 13

"You're kidding?" Dawn sat at Denise's table on the deck, while she and Randy sipped iced tea in the Texas summer heat. "He just up and left her behind?" Denise had explained Aedan's recall by the Council.

"Unfortunately, yes. Now we have three new vampires guarding at night. Marcus met them, I haven't."

"How dangerous do you think they are? Will they come after wolves again?"

"The Council sent them, so I assume they're safe enough."

"How did Adele and Ashe react to the whole thing?"

"Adele barely remembers she had a vampire husband, or a child with him. Compulsion, more than likely. I thought he loved her more than anything, so this has me completely confused." Denise poured more iced tea and pushed a plate of finger sandwiches toward Randy, who was eating and content to listen.

Randy wasn't about to tell anyone that Ashe appeared and disappeared from his tiny Chicago apartment not long ago. Randy had made the move, too, and gone out on a date with veterinarian Sara Dillon shortly before his move to Texas. Sara knew about the move and promised to keep in touch. He hadn't told his mother yet, but Sara and he—well, Randy wanted to marry Sara, after only one date.

～

"My King, my spies report that our encampment may be attacked soon." Beldris informed his brother. He'd made the trek from Canada to speak with Baltis regarding the impending attack.

"Friesianna thinks to do this when I am not present to help protect our own," Baltis paced restlessly. The painting that hung on his brick wall was getting old. Perhaps he would ask his guards to change it.

"I believe that as well," Beldris agreed.

"Then we will exchange places. You know of the plan for London. Execute that for me, brother, and we will give the Bright Queen a surprise she will not soon forget."

"That is the brother I admire," Beldris smiled.

～

"Gather as many as we can send, and station them here," Friesianna tapped appropriate locations on a map laid out atop a makeshift table.

"My Queen, I counsel against this," Rabis said softly as Friesianna spoke with Parlethis, who was now captain of her guards.

"You will not interfere with this. We have not had such an opportunity in many years. This is our chance to take our Dark cousins by surprise and eliminate many of them, including the Prince. We will cripple them in one blow and they will be forced to admit defeat. Perhaps I will allow Baltis to live, after he offers his crown to me."

"My Queen, you may not wield the Dark Crown," Rabis interjected. "It is forbidden."

"You think that Baltis will hesitate to take mine and use it?" Friesianna snapped. "Go. I do not have any questions for you concerning this."

"As you will it, my Queen."

"Yes, I will it. Take yourself from my sight." Rabis was more than happy to do as the Queen dictated.

~

"Ashe, we're going to a movie." Ashe looked up from his study guide to find Cori and Marco standing before him. It was Sunday afternoon and he'd taken (and passed) three sample tests since breakfast.

"So the reconciliation is complete and you want my blessing?" Ashe asked, setting his book aside. Cori's hand was firmly held in Marco's. Her expression was hopeful as she smiled at Ashe.

"No, we're asking you to come with us."

"Dude, that's just—I'd be an extra," Ashe admitted lamely.

"Sali and Dori are coming," Cori said, trying to coax Ashe.

"Cori, that's not—it doesn't feel cool," Ashe said. "You're dating. I'm not." *And thanks for making it so obvious*, he added silently. He wanted to sit in a dark theater with his arm around a girl. Perhaps steal a kiss now and then. Ashe had no girl, hence none of the other things as well.

"Wynn's coming," Cori said brightly.

"But does Wynn want to come with me?" That was the trouble. Ashe had seen the way Wynn looked at Ace. The way she'd gone out of her way to touch Ace. Somehow, he knew it was right, though Ace was likely much older than Wynn. He wondered if the werewolf had enough courage to approach the O'Neills with his request to date their daughter. Ashe might have leaped at the chance not long ago, but he had other things on his mind. Chasing after Wynn when she was destined to belong to another, well, that was an exercise in futility.

"Ask Ace if he wants to go," Ashe suggested. "I have studying to do." He deliberately raised the study guide and pretended to read.

"Ace is outside," Marco said, steering Cori out of Ashe's room. Ashe went to mist and followed behind them. "Ace, want to go to the movies with us? Wynn's going," Cori said.

The werewolf was kneeling beside Winkler's van, checking tire pressure on a rear wheel. Lifting his head and grinning, Ace nodded.

Ashe misted to his room again, sighing once he came back to himself. No doubt about it, Ace was smitten with Wynn syndrome. Ashe was surprised three hours later to get a call from Marco, saying they'd gone to a pizza restaurant in Port Aransas after the movie. Ashe was invited to come eat with the others.

"All right, I'll come," Ashe dumped the study guide on his cot and stood to stretch. Pizza Neetsa was in a dome-shaped building on the outskirts of town, about three miles from Winkler's beach house. Ashe knew where it was—he'd seen it every time he'd passed through Port A.

He hopped to a spot right over the building, turning to mist before he became visible. Dropping through the roof, he landed in an empty stall inside the restroom and walked out to find the others sitting at a long table.

Sure enough, Wynn was leaning against Ace, who wore a bemused look on his face, as if someone had given him a winning lottery ticket. For a *lot*. Ashe scooted into the chair next to Cori, who didn't mind leaning into Marco to give Ashe room. Marco put his arm around Cori possessively.

"He'll want sausage and mushroom," Sali said when Ashe was about to place his order. Dori slapped Sali's hand for being rude.

"It is what I want," Ashe handed his menu to the waitress. "With extra of both." He hadn't had lunch and it was nearly time for dinner. Winkler, Trajan and Ace had been absent most of the day, *on business*, Winkler said before they'd taken off in one of the two vans Winkler kept in Star Cove, leaving Ace and Andy there to stand guard.

"See, I am good for something," Sali hung his head.

"I never said you weren't," Ashe pointed out. "I just said I didn't trust you. That's all." Ashe wished he could take the words back as quickly as he'd said them. "Dude, I didn't mean it quite like it sounded," Ashe apologized as best he could.

"Let's leave that for now. We'll agree to disagree," Ace said. "Salidar, sit up straight. You're mortifying your date." Dori was certainly staring at Sali.

Dude, I'm sorry. I think Dori wants you to put an arm around her or something. Ashe's silent sending had Sali straightening up and slipping an arm around Dori. He went one better and kissed Dori's temple. Dori leaned against Sali with a sigh of contentment. Sali gave a brief nod to Ashe and things were better after that.

"I can get myself home," Ashe said when they went to load into the van later.

"No, ride home with us," Cori held out a hand. Ashe squeezed in beside Cori, and that's how he ended up hopping Cori and Marco to London when he knew his father was in trouble.

~

"Winkler, I don't know what happened—Ashe yelled 'Dad' and he, Marco and Cori disappeared from the van. We're on the side of the road—I pulled over as soon as they were gone." Ace phoned Winkler after stopping the van.

"He's in London," Winkler's voice held little doubt. "I'll get the Head of the Council on the phone right away." Winkler hung up, leaving a frustrated Ace kicking a tire he'd aired up earlier.

~

Marco and Cori had turned. Cori's panther yowled at the six Elemaiya who were threatening her and Marco, her tail flipping angrily at them. Ashe, as invisible mist, hovered over Marco and Cori's heads, sending mindspeech. *Don't let them attack you—just look menacing,* Ashe instructed.

His father's body was nearby—the Elemaiya had managed to drag it out of a nearby house, securely wrapped in a black cloth. Ashe figured they wanted to question Aedan as soon as he woke; that meant they were looking for him and they hadn't found him near his father.

Sunset was close, too, and Ashe knew his father would wake fighting—Aedan always drew in a heavy breath when he woke. That would tell him he was outside and not inside—a vampire's nose was as sensitive as any wolf's.

At the moment, Aedan's wrapped body lay on the grass outside a large cottage, somewhere in the English countryside. Ashe might have thought it was pretty where they were if not for the direness of the situation.

The Elemaiya intended to use Aedan—perhaps blackmail him, in order to find Ashe. Ashe was determined to remain mist as long as possible, allowing Cori and Marco to hold off the kidnappers.

"Just let us have this—it's dead anyway," one of the Elemaiya cajoled, pointing to Aedan's wrapped body. Cori yowled louder. The Elemaiya stepped back. They weren't prepared to take on a panther and a werewolf.

Things might have gone well; sunset was very close and Marco and Cori were holding the Elemaiya off, but another half dozen appeared from nowhere. When the Elemaiya already present saw the newcomers, turmoil erupted.

Winkler checked his watch and hit the number again. Sunset would arrive any moment in Great Britain. Many older vampires woke a short while before sunset if they were inside a dark, safe place. They moved sluggishly at first and would, as long as any sunlight might reach them. Once the sun dipped below the horizon, they were prepared for anything. "Come on, pick up," Winkler muttered frantically.

"Charles speaking," Wlodek's assistant answered the call.

"Charles, this is William Winkler. I have reason to believe Aedan Evans is in trouble and that his son has gone to help," Winkler's voice was breathless. The Dallas Packmaster was rattled and he was never rattled.

"I'm dialing one of our Assassins on another phone," Charles was calm in a crisis. "Gavin, how long will it take to get to Aedan Evans' home?" Charles had placed the call on speaker.

"I can be there in twenty." The line went dead.

"That's one on the way," Charles announced and placed a second call.

Twelve Elemaiya, six on six, now stared one another down after a brief altercation that had turned into a standoff. Ashe, feeling itchy, became corporeal and jerked the cloth off his father the moment the sun dropped below the horizon.

Marco's wolf and Cori's panther held their ground between the Bright and Dark Elemaiya when Ashe and Aedan joined them. Aedan had claws and fangs out in a blink. "Go home," Ashe snapped, glaring at the twelve. "You have no business here." He lifted the short sleeve of his shirt, displaying the gold medallions. Elemaiya on both sides stepped back in surprise.

"You have no authority over us," one of the Bright Ones said.

"Come closer and find out for yourself," Ashe snapped. "Your people need you. You have no business here."

"How would you know that our people need us?" The same Elemaiya demanded.

"Jeez, you really are stupid, aren't you?" Ashe muttered. "It doesn't take a genius to figure out where the Dark King is. Or where the Bright Queen is."

Ashe spoke mentally to both sides after that, telling them exactly what he knew and giving precise locations—telling the Bright Ones where the Queen was, the Dark Ones where the King might be located. "What are you, idiots or something? Go home. Hide better than that if you expect to live."

"Are you going to stop us? We were instructed to bring you to the Dark King," a Dark Elemaiya guard bluffed while he backed further away. Neither he nor his companions could fathom how Ashe knew where their camp was.

"No. The boy dies here," one of the Bright Elemaiya snapped. Aedan had listened patiently to the dialogue, but at that statement, he growled. The Bright Elemaiya who spoke took another step back. Vampires could kill Elemaiya easily; they all knew it. In addition, the boy held all eight of the talismans, Bright and Dark. Perhaps there was truth in the H'Morr after all.

"How do you think I got these?" Ashe pointed to the talismans on his arm. "I killed the ones who held them. Go home. Whoever sent you after my father made a mistake. This isn't my father. My father is Elemaiya." One of the Elemaiya hissed in a breath.

"How can you know this?" The first one spoke again.

"Someone who can't lie told me," Ashe said. "Go home. I'm not in the mood to kill anybody today."

"You lie." The second Bright Elemaiya accused.

"He does not." The brown-haired man appeared and all the Elemaiya took another step back, looking frightened. "He is pure-blood. Tell the Queen that. And your King." The tall man nodded to each speaker. "If they are using that as an excuse, then they should rethink their motives. Do as the boy says. Go home. Live to fight another day. Two more vampires are coming. They will not allow you to live. Ashe is offering a generous gift. I suggest you accept."

The Elemaiya looked frightened to Ashe. Cori's panther leaned against Ashe's legs and growled low. Marco's wolf stood nearby, snarling at the Elemaiya. Aedan had claws and fangs at the ready. "More vampires are coming," one of the Elemaiya squeaked. All twelve disappeared shortly before two vampires ran up in a blur.

"You missed it, Gavin," the brown-haired man observed as a tall, wide-shouldered vampire appeared at his side. "Twelve Elemaiya, gone in a blink." He snapped his fingers.

"Griffin, I'd appreciate it if you'd leave the continent," Gavin snapped.

"But I haven't had dinner yet."

"Gavin, you have no control over this one. Leave it." The other vampire said.

"Russell, you have always had more patience than I. I have only heard that I shouldn't attack this one." Gavin wasn't giving up easily, his dark eyes focused on Griffin.

"By the Honored One's command. Don't risk your life. Aedan, are you well?" The vampire called Russell asked. Russell stood at six-six, only a bit taller than Aedan and Ashe. He had dark-brown hair, brown eyes and was built like a boxer.

"I am fine." Aedan retracted claws and fangs. "It appears I need a new place to stay."

"There are safe houses in the area. You may have one of them if you want. Contact Charles." Gavin was finished since the enemy had fled.

"Dad?" Ashe said. He sounded lost. Aedan hadn't spoken to him.

"Ashe, go home. I'm not sure how you arrived, but you should leave now." Aedan wasn't looking at Ashe. Instead, he kept his gray eyes focused on Griffin, deeming him the greater threat.

"Someday, you will regret those words. And your actions," Griffin informed Aedan in an icy voice before he disappeared.

"Cori?" Marco was human again and pulling clothing on hastily.

"Here," Ashe pulled up the cloth the Elemaiya had used to cover his father. Draping it over Cori, he waited for her to change. She appeared under his arm and he helped her wrap herself in the heavy black drape. Marco gathered her scattered clothing, some of it ripped in Cori's haste to help.

"I guess we'll go, Dad. Since you don't want us." Ashe lifted Cori and Marco in his mist and hopped to Star Cove. Aedan cursed as they disappeared.

"Thank goodness," Winkler muttered when Ashe appeared in Winkler's kitchen with Cori and Marco. "Kid, what happened?"

"Six Elemaiya pulled Dad out of his house and had him lying on the ground, wrapped in this," Ashe pointed to the cloth in which Cori was wrapped. "And then another six showed up from the opposing camp. Since they didn't find me with Dad, they intended to get information from him on where I was. One side wants to kill me, the other side wants to take me and make me work for them. We had a few words before that Griffin guy showed up. They all took a step back when they saw him."

"If they'd attacked him, they'd have died," Winkler said. "They wouldn't have enough to take him down if they'd had thirty times their numbers. How's your father? Did those two vampires get there in time?"

"Yeah. Two showed up, right after Griffin convinced the Elemaiya to leave. Somebody named Gavin and Russell. Dad's fine. He told us to leave." Ashe wanted to go to his room and sulk instead of answering questions.

"Gavin is Chief of Wlodek's Assassins and Tony Hancock's surrogate sire. Russell is Chief of Enforcers," Winkler said. "Charles sent the best he could."

"Now I know why Hancock's so grumpy, if that's his surrogate sire," Ashe said. Winkler pulled him into a hug.

Ashe found himself on a conference call with the Grand Master shortly after that. Cori and Marco had to come, too, and give their account. Bear Wright had come to sit with Cori, since she was a shapeshifter. "Just to make sure Weldon doesn't get away with anything," Bear grinned and patted Cori's shoulder. Nathan might have come, but it was still daylight.

Ashe relayed the incident to Weldon, while Winkler and Trajan listened and Andy recorded everything. Cori and Marco added their bit; Weldon and Winkler asked questions after that.

"Ashe, how did you know you could do that hopping thing to England?" Weldon asked.

"I don't know. I just knew Dad was in trouble. I didn't even think about the distance."

"If I'm asking about this, you can be sure your Dad is getting grilled by Wlodek. If not now, then very soon. He'll want to know."

"Not surprising," Ashe said, ducking his head and staring at his shoes. A few blades of grass clung to one of his sneakers—grass from England. Grass from his father's front yard. The house had looked to be a country house, with London in the distance. Somehow, the

Elemaiya had found his father. Ashe hoped Aedan would be well hidden from then on.

"Ashe, there's something else we have to tell you," Weldon said when the questioning was done. "We've worked this out with your mother. Your father has officially refused to support you—I learned this from Wlodek. And, with the way things stand with your mother, well, Winkler has asked to be appointed your guardian. Your mother signed the papers in Corpus Christi today. If you agree to sign, too, Winkler will make sure your expenses are covered and you have everything you need. Your mother seems a bit confused, so we think this is for the best. If you object, we'll work this out."

Ashe sat, his wrists and hands dangling over his knees. Confused was a mild description of his mother's condition. "No. It's probably for the best right now," Ashe agreed. Taking the offered pen, he signed the paper the Dallas Packmaster placed before him. Then, rising swiftly, he stalked from Winkler's study.

"One of those we cannot name appeared. He verified it," Parlethis said, hoping the Queen would sense his sincerity and not blast him for the news he brought. "And we saw all eight talismans. Here, on the boy's arm." Parlethis tapped a spot on his left arm.

"We cannot have this. I will not accept it. I still want the boy killed. You realize what kind of threat this might be." The Queen was agitated and paced before her throne. A canopy had been spread above it—a late summer storm threatened. "Who held the poisoned dart?"

"I did." Parlethis admitted.

"Keep it. The opportunity may come again. Meanwhile, we have an attack upon the Dark camp to execute. Prince Beldris does not hold the Dark Crown. He will be little more than a common soldier against us." Friesianna swished her skirts aside so she could sit, adjusting the crown that afforded her the power to rule.

"Randy." Ashe leaned against the wall beside his cot and stared at Randy Smith. "I heard you and your mom were moving to Star Cove."

"It was a compromise. I told her this was the only other place I'd consider, never thinking she'd do it. And here we are." Randy flung up his hands in surrender. "The gods pull our strings and we dance."

"I'd prefer to do the waltz, then, and not the samba," Ashe grumped.

"It's all in the hips," Randy laughed. "I've got an interview tomorrow morning. Any advice, man?"

"None whatsoever," Ashe said. "Just don't sound so much like a city slicker."

"Should I pick hayseeds out of my teeth?"

"I wouldn't go that far. Tell them you're from New Mexico. I get the idea that Chicago might be a dirty word."

"Got it. How've you been, man?" Randy sat on Ashe's guest chair.

"Not bad. Working for Winkler is okay."

"Dude, I hear wolves would kill to get a job with him. Winkler's the man. Er, wolf."

"Have you talked to him? He might have pull with the local paper."

"Hadn't thought about that. Maybe I will. In the meantime, I think I'd like to go out sometime. Feel like a burger or something later in the week?"

"Maybe. Let me know." Ashe nodded to Randy.

"I need to get back. I think Mom wants to unpack kitchen stuff." Randy stood.

"I'll walk out with you. Maybe I'll catch sight of the new vamps," Ashe grinned.

"Didn't see anything on the way in," Randy said, walking ahead of Ashe.

"Maybe we will this time." Ashe walked out of the house with Randy, then down the narrow street toward the house Randy and his mother had taken. Two vampires appeared at their side as if magic had breathed them onto the pavement.

"I can pull that trick too," Ashe said to no one in particular, causing one of the vampires to blink in surprise. Ashe wanted to laugh over getting a response from a stone-faced vampire, but he didn't. Neither vampire was Nathan—both of these were new to the neighborhood.

"I am Hector," the one who'd shown surprise said.

"I am Casimir, at your service," the other nodded to Ashe. Ashe knew, somehow, that Casimir might be older than any vampire he'd seen before. With the exception of Wlodek, of course. He wasn't tall—perhaps five-eight or so, with dark blond hair carefully brushed back from his forehead. He seemed to Ashe like an old-world gentleman, one who'd sat in a drawing room at one time or another and served brandy to his guests. Before he drank from them, of course.

Aedan drank bagged blood, but that convenience hadn't always been available. Vampires seldom killed their donors—their laws forbade it. Preservation of the race was paramount, after all. If a vampire killed a human and threatened exposure of the race, they were declared rogue and hunted.

Ashe doubted if Casimir would ever be hunted. Hector, on the other hand—Ashe shook himself to get rid of the thoughts. Hector was taller and thin as a blade. His face was narrow, his nose hawkish. Darker-skinned than Casimir, Ashe imagined that Hector might have come from Turkish origins.

"Good to meet you," Ashe said. "I'm Ashe. But you know that already. This is Randy. He's going to work for the Corpus Christi newspaper." Ashe introduced his human acquaintance.

"Haven't gotten the job yet—have to interview first." Randy was nervous about being so close to strange vampires; Ashe sensed it.

"I'm walking Randy to his house," Ashe said. "Want to come?"

"You are a precocious child," Hector said. "I shall decline."

"I must do my work, protecting the community," Casimir was more polite. Both vampires whisked away.

"Hear that? I'm a precocious child," Ashe chuckled.

"You weren't afraid just then?" Randy asked softly.

"After what I saw earlier? No."

CHAPTER 14

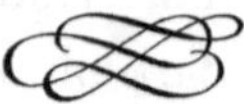

"**W**hatcha doin', *empty*," Chad couldn't resist. Ashe was walking toward his mother's house—that's how he saw it now—as belonging to his mother. He no longer lived there. Adele barely recognized Ashe and had willingly signed the papers, making Winkler his guardian.

How had his father done this? Ashe shivered at what vampire compulsion could accomplish. He'd move his things out as soon as Winkler opened the beach house. There was enough space in the beach house study for all his books; Winkler had seen to that. He'd known what Ashe might like and worked to get it. Ashe wanted to weep for his losses—both parents no longer claimed him for any reason. To make matters worse, Chad was back and calling him names. Again.

"Muck for brains," Ashe handed out the old insult, for which he'd garnered a black eye in the seventh grade. Chad wasn't fast enough. Ashe ducked out of the way easily when Chad threw a punch and when Trajan grasped Chad by the collar, Chad yelped in surprise.

"If I were you," Trajan settled Chad on the pavement, "I'd stay away from what you can't defend yourself against."

"I can defend myself against that." Chad wasn't giving in, although Trajan could bite him in half as a wolf.

"What does your nose tell you?" Trajan said amiably. "You know what humans and shifters smell like."

"He's only half shifter," Chad insisted. "The rest is all empty."

"Try again. Get close. Ashe, if he touches you, you have my permission to teach him a lesson." Trajan offered Ashe a wicked grin.

Chad came closer. And sniffed. "That's different," Chad muttered, pulling away.

"Now, go home and think about that," Trajan slapped Chad on the back, sending him down the street.

"Bigoted jerk," Ashe muttered when Chad was out of hearing range.

"Certainly that. We'll keep an eye on him and Mr. Booth. Come on, Winkler will be having breakfast before we get there."

"Thanks, Mom," Ashe said as Adele placed a plate of food in front of him.

"I hope you like ham, dear," she said. Ashe blinked. Was it getting worse? His mother knew he loved ham and she always called him honey. She never said *dear.*

"Ashe, it's all right," Winkler held out a hand. He must have seen Ashe's face fall. "Mrs. Evans, how are we doing at Victoria's?" Winkler asked.

Adele sounded perfectly normal as she rattled off expenses and problems that had cropped up. Ashe sighed and ate what he could, although everything had turned to sawdust in his mouth. Later, he sat at his tiny desk, sorting through files Andy had given him. Ashe called his father.

"Dad, this is the last call you'll get from me," he said. "Unless you call me first. Dad, Mom told me she hoped I liked ham today at breakfast. I have to tell you, you're damn good at compulsion. How can you wipe love away like that? How? She told me once that she'd always be my mother and you'd always be my dad. Only that wasn't true, was it? If somebody asked her, she'd probably tell them she didn't have any children. Thanks, Dad. Thanks a lot." Ashe sniffled as he hung up.

"Son, it's all right." Winkler knelt next to Ashe's chair. Ashe, for once in his life, didn't hold back. He held onto Winkler and wept.

∾

"Two and a half weeks before Winkler's new beach house is finished," Josiah told Zeke over the phone. "We'll have him before then." Josiah stood outside a popular sushi restaurant in Corpus Christi while he talked.

"See that you do. I want his head, remember? Wolf head is best, but I'll take whatever you can get."

"I'll see what we can do on the full moon. We might kill two wolves with one silver bullet, don't you think?" Josiah chuckled at his own humor.

"Just do it and spare me the lame jokes. That's about as funny as a boil on my butt." Zeke terminated the call.

∾

"Why should I move? If the boy thinks to come against your guards, then we will provide a surprise for him, don't you think? Besides, Wildrif says he likely can't shield or command the visions. That makes him vulnerable," Beldris reassured Baltis. "Our spies predict the Queen's movements. She will try her hand in the north. We shall stay put," Beldris added.

He and Baltis sat inside Baltis' chamber beneath Chicago's streets. The Dark King would return to the camp in Canada the moment he finished the conversation with his brother.

Baltis agreed with Beldris' assessment. "I believe we will resolve the issue surrounding the boy, but first we will eliminate the Queen. If the boy refuses to serve us, then he will die. No loss to us; once the Queen is no more, we will rule." Baltis seemed happy with his conclusions. "Wildrif, too, will be forced away again. We have no need for mortals, no matter how gifted."

"Yes. My guards and I have talked and we believe it was the vampires and werewolves who eliminated your Destroyers, brother. It cannot be otherwise. They would not have fallen to any untaught youngling, even if he is quite talented."

"Yes. I have come to the same conclusion myself. That is why I want the boy—we can train him and he will obey us. Will it not be fitting, brother, to use a Bright one against his own race?" Baltis accepted the cordial his brother offered, the reddish liquid glinting in the dim, artificial light. "We failed in Great Britain, because the vampires came. We will not fail a second time."

~

"Ashe, I got the job." Randy flopped into Ashe's guest chair for the second time in as many days.

"Knew you would," Ashe shut a folder and placed it in the *all clear* basket, which sat next to another basket Ashe referred to as *the trouble pile*. Only a handful of folders lay in the trouble pile; Ashe had marked figures on a few of those file pages for Andy to review.

"I'm curious. How did you get to my place in Chicago?" Randy asked.

"Hocus-pocus," Ashe fluttered his fingers dramatically. He wasn't about to tell anybody anything. Not anymore. Randy didn't remember being saved by Ashe—twice. Neither did Randy's mother. He wasn't going to remind them.

"I have a girlfriend," Randy said, changing the subject. "She's a vet in Chicago."

"A veterinarian? That's cool. Bring her down and have her take a look at Sali."

"I heard you were on the outs with him," Randy said. "I'd have said that was impossible, three years ago. You were inseparable."

"Yeah. Things change."

"Actually, I was thinking about inviting Sara down. Maybe she'd like the beach."

"Just about everybody does," Ashe flipped through another file.

"She was the one who did the autopsies for me—on all those dead rats." Ashe jerked his head up.

"Randy, she's not going back down there, is she? To the tunnels?" Ashe recalled then that he hadn't told Winkler about his suspicions.

"She never went—city workers hauled the rats out for her to examine."

"Randy, this is important; get on the phone and tell her and anybody else not to go near any of that. The rats are expendable. People aren't." Ashe hauled out his cell and sent a text to Winkler. He hardly used his cell anymore; his mindspeech was much more direct and reliable. Winkler arrived in Ashe's office quickly, in response to the text.

"Randy, tell Mr. Winkler about exploding rat hearts," Ashe instructed.

❧

"Matt, we think some of them are holed up in the Chicago narrow gauge rail tunnels," Winkler was on a conference call with Matt Michaels and the Grand Master.

"I'll get with the City—see if anybody has detected anything," Matt said.

"I can get some wolves on it," Weldon offered.

"Don't get close enough to get anybody killed," Winkler warned.

"Don't worry. I think we can use sensors," Matt suggested. "And if we find them, maybe we can flush them out."

"There's a thriving vampire community in Chicago. I'll get Wlodek on the phone. He may be interested in this," Weldon offered. "If I send my wolves in with his vamps, we might be able to take care of this with none the wiser."

"That's less conspicuous than sending in Special Forces," Matt agreed. "I'll send a task force in right away. We'll know by tomorrow."

"If Wlodek agrees, we can get our forces together by Wednesday night," Weldon suggested.

"Good enough. Let's get what we can. Maybe we can force them off the planet after all," Matt agreed. He'd had several meetings with the President, with specific discussions over this particular alien invasion. The trouble was, none of his agents had been able to locate them. This was good information and Ashe Evans and Randy Smith had collaborated, giving him the best intelligence he'd received to date. Matt itched to get to Chicago himself.

"Winkler, what's in the tunnels under Chicago is just a portion of them," Ashe pointed out quietly over dinner. Trajan and Trace were listening carefully to Ashe's words.

"You know where the others are," Winkler stared at his ward.

"There are young with the camps. I'm not about to send Matt Michaels and a bunch of vampires and werewolves after kids."

"Ashe, the adults can do more damage," Winkler frowned.

"They're after me. If they find me, the rest of you need to stand out of the way and let me handle it." Ashe was having meatloaf at a local diner in Star Cove. He'd never gotten his burger at Dandee Burgers, so he wasn't sure which might be his favorite restaurant so far.

"Kid, I know you're talented, but," Trajan began.

"Here." Ashe pulled his cell phone out and hit a few keys. "Randy forwarded this to me. He didn't know what it was. You didn't see this because you were on St. Joseph Island. I never knew Randy recorded it." Ashe handed the iPhone to Trajan. Winkler and Trace leaned in to watch as the canal in the center of their Star Cove community burst into flames, burning high into the night sky. Ashe hunched down in his seat when the screams sounded. Winkler cursed in wonder. Trace whistled.

"I'll get Randy to erase those images. Send this to me, Ashe, if you wouldn't mind," Winkler said, handing the phone back. Ashe sent the images to Winkler's email and pocketed his phone. "Now, Ashe, would you mind telling us how you managed to burn everything else and get out of there alive?"

"I'm not talking about that," Ashe replied and refused to say anything else.

❧

"He wouldn't say how he got out of that," Winkler sighed. He'd made a conference call to Matt and Weldon after arriving in Star Cove. Ashe had gone out for ice cream with Trajan and Trace. Winkler forwarded the images from Star Cove during the last full moon.

Winkler felt itchy—the full moon was four days away. He'd talked to Buck—they could move into the beach house on Friday before the full moon on Sunday. Winkler was brought back from his thoughts by Matt's words. "If we could recruit that kid, think of the possibilities. He could get in anywhere and do anything. Hostages rescued, terrorists eliminated," Matt sounded euphoric.

"You're talking from a purely human point of view," Weldon said. "We need him too, remember? We have rogues that can be more dangerous than any human. Same with the vamps. Wlodek's Enforcers and Assassins are working overtime, while my Trackers haven't seen time off in I don't know how long. I'm working to recruit more, but that's harder than it sounds. Face it, Director, we all need him. The shifters, too, unless I miss my guess. The trouble is, he's only sixteen. Won't be of legal age for another two years—can't drink for three years past that. Those deaths in Star Cove bother him, even though they were trying to kill his friends and capture him. I don't know what effect dealing with terrorists and rogues will have on the boy."

"I think we'll have to wait two years, but he's already been a big help," Winkler said. "We'll utilize him for special assignments but as my ward, I don't want him anywhere near the Middle East. He stays in the U.S. and works here."

"That's fine, but when he turns eighteen," Matt began.

"We get it. We'll all come knocking and he'll make up his own mind. What we have to do is keep him out of Wlodek's clutches when the time comes." Weldon wasn't mincing words. He knew Matt depended upon his vampire agents. He was trusting Matt to do the right thing and work to keep Ashe the way he was.

~

"Sara, I know this is a little forward, but you could come for a visit," Randy coaxed. "There's a beach just a few yards away, a boat slip that runs down the center of the community and we could spend a little time together. I told the newspaper that I could start work on the fifteenth. Come down for a few days."

Sara Dillon was quite shocked. "I don't know," she said over the phone, hesitating at the suggestion.

"Come on, they haul shrimp straight from the gulf. It'll be the best you've ever had. Baby, you said you had some frequent flyer miles. Use them. Come and see me this weekend."

"I'll think about it. Give me until tomorrow and I'll call back with an answer," she promised.

"All right, but the answer should be yes." Randy was smiling.

"I'll give you an answer tomorrow," Sara was smiling, too.

"I'll be waiting. On the beach, cell phone in hand, walking through the surf in nice, clean air." Randy was teasing.

"Then I'll think harder," Sara laughed. Randy hung up reluctantly.

~

"Honored One," Edmond reported, "Nathan received a call from Aedan. I was not privy to the conversation past Aedan's orders that the call be private."

"He likely ordered Nathan not to reveal further information on the boy," Wlodek agreed. Edmond had waited until his own call might be made in private to the Head of the Council. "No matter, that is why I sent Hector, Casimir and you. You will report the information.

Nathan need not worry any longer that he is betraying his sire's trust. Have you anything new on the boy?"

"What you know already—that the boy managed to disappear from a van not far from here and appear at his father's home outside London with two others."

"Yes, Gavin has informed me from this end."

"I have nothing else," Edmond said. "We will contact you when we have news."

"I expect no less." Wlodek ended the call. "Charles?" Wlodek looked up at his assistant, who stood near his desk, waiting expectantly. Charles wasn't as tall as Wlodek, with slightly curly brown hair and hazel eyes. Thinner, too, and not as broad across the shoulders as Wlodek. Many people (and vampires) had underestimated Charles through the years.

"Honored One?" Charles replied.

"Take the rest of the evening off. I have personal business to conduct." Wlodek rose from the seat at his desk.

"Of course, Honored One." Charles nodded respectfully. "I feel like a trip to London. Haven't been in months." Charles turned and strode from Wlodek's private study. Wlodek watched him go before pulling his private cell phone from a pocket. "Radomir, bring the car around," he said.

Charles closed the door on his own vehicle. He didn't drive much, but he certainly enjoyed it when the opportunity came. His Wiesmann GT Lizard King hugged the road and drove like a dream. Misty silver in color, it could blend with the fog in London if Charles chose to drive it there.

Charles shifted and flew through the front gates outside Wlodek's manor. Halfway down a private country lane, Charles pulled over and shut off the lights. Hauling out his cell, he began tapping out an email before attaching a file and sending it on its way. Breathing a sigh of concerned relief, Charles put the car in gear again, left the lights off and drove toward London.

~

"Mr. Winkler, Ashe asked not long ago about the possible leak in the Amarillo pack. Did we ever get anything on that?" Marco settled into the seat beside Winkler's desk.

Winkler had just gotten off the phone with the Grand Master; Wlodek had authorized several vampires from the Chicago area to coordinate with wolves from the Chicago Pack, in addition to some of Matt Michaels' best human operatives.

A strike would be made against the Elemaiya who were occupying the narrow gauge rail tunnels in the Chicago area on Thursday evening. The full moon wasn't long past that and the wolves would love a fight. Winkler thought about going, but decided to stay put and let others handle things for a change. Marco's question caught him off guard.

"No—nothing ever came from that. The Grand Master suspected something, but the Packmaster swears by his members and we couldn't find a thing. You say Ashe was asking?"

"Yeah. Don't know why."

"Ashe plays his cards close to his vest," Winkler sighed. "There may be something we missed. I'll ask the Grand Master for any records or information he might have and we'll take another look."

"I'd like to help, if that's possible," Marco offered.

"I'll consider it. A new set of eyes is never a bad thing. I'll let you know." Marco recognized a dismissal when he heard one. Lifting himself easily out of the chair, he walked softly from Winkler's office.

Marco could move as quietly as a cat when he wanted; it was one of the qualities Winkler valued in the young werewolf. Andy walked in after Marco left Winkler's office.

"Here's the information on the Little Rock thing, boss. Fergus fired the accountant. According to Fergus, the man was sniffing after Eudora. Said it was a relief to get rid of the guy."

"Any way to get the money back? Eudora should have reported it instead of taking the money. That's Fergus' Second's wife, you know. We could bring the matter up with the Grand Master. Weldon could remove Fergus' Second, Jarrett Long, if Jarrett knew anything about his wife accepting some mighty big paychecks. Eudora works as a secretary in Fergus' regional office and got paid three times what she was supposed to get." Winkler had offices located in many the major cities across the U.S., plus several in foreign countries. "Ask Fergus about that."

"I'll ask," Andy agreed. "Probably won't know anything until tomorrow, at the earliest."

"If you can't get it that way, see about bringing charges against that fool accountant. That's nearly fifty thousand, Andy. See what evidence Fergus has against the man."

"Yeah. I'll work on that. Find what kind of proof Fergus can produce and then hand it over to the D.A. in Little Rock."

"Do that. Email the Grand Master, too, and see if he's got any information from the investigation on the Amarillo Pack."

"Will do, boss." Andy walked out of Winkler's office.

"Now, what else can I do before the day's over?" Winkler grinned.

"You think they'll take the bait?" Trajan sat at the all-night diner in Port Aransas, nursing a cup of coffee and staring across the table at Winkler.

"I'd bet money on it," Winkler grinned. "Around fifty thousand ought to do it."

"Expect any trouble?"

"Nah. Piece of cake," Winkler said. "I've got several in the area already. When Fergus tries to run, probably with Eudora, they'll have both of 'em."

"What about Jarrett?"

"He probably doesn't suspect a thing, more's the pity," Winkler's grin faded. "He's decent. Have to see what he wants to do after Fergus and Eudora are hauled in. The accountant is locked up already; Fergus just doesn't know about it."

"Since Andy doesn't know the details, his emails will put Fergus on the run," Trajan sighed. "Boss, you're always a step ahead."

"I wish I was as far ahead as Ashe is, most of the time," Winkler dumped sugar into his coffee and stirred.

"Kid knows more than is good for him," Trajan agreed. "And he's only sixteen. What do you think he'll be like when he's twenty?"

"Scary as hell," Winkler muttered and sipped his coffee.

"Ashe, Sara's coming for the weekend," Randy was nearly vibrating with happiness. Ashe sat at the kitchen island, having a soda and reading one of his GED study guides. Andy had invited the newest reporter for the Corpus Christi newspaper into the house when he rang the doorbell.

"That's great, dude," Ashe said. "Want a soda?"

"Yeah. Whatever you got," Randy nodded. "My boss gave me an assignment already so I could do a little research before starting officially at the paper. My next story will be covering all the garbage that people dump on the beach. Right now, the only way to pay for cleanup is through the hotel tax."

"So, somebody is thinking about getting tax money from another source to pay, or organizing the locals or something?" Ashe poured a can of soda into a glass of ice for Randy.

"Among other things. It'll be a fight, more than likely. Costs are going up for those tractors that rake the beaches. I did research already on other states—Florida has taxes allocated for beach maintenance, but Texas doesn't collect state income tax. Can't do it that way."

"So, that's where the fight will be the fiercest," Ashe grinned.

"Yeah. It'll be fun," Randy settled back on a barstool and sipped his soda. Ashe's cell phone beeped to let him know he had email. Hardly anyone emailed him anymore. Curious, Ashe pulled out the cell to check his message.

"What is it?" Randy asked when Ashe's eyes widened.

"Uh, nothing. Just something I wasn't expecting to get," Ashe pocketed the cell. "How's your mom? She gonna be all right with Sara coming?"

"I haven't told her. I figure Sara and I can stay at a hotel on the beach, since Sunday is full moon. Honestly, I forgot to check the calendar," Randy muttered guiltily.

"Yeah. Been there, done that," Ashe said, hauling chips out of a cabinet and passing the bag to Randy. Randy opened it and pulled out a handful of crisps.

"Too bad Billings is dead now—it used to be funny telling that story about graduation," Randy said. "Now that he's gone, it's speaking ill of the dead."

"I don't mind badmouthing Hitler, and he's dead," Ashe observed.

"Well, that's different," Randy crunched into a potato chip. "Mom won't talk about him at all—she somehow found out that Billings wanted to take the execution."

"What execution?" Ashe watched Randy pull more chips from the bag.

"Mine. Sounds weird, doesn't it, that they were ready to kill me?"

"Randy," Ashe sighed. "What do you remember about all that?"

"It gets blurry after the Trackers hauled me in. I was hiding out in a mountain cabin that one of Mom's friends from the post office built as a ski lodge," Randy replied. "But they found me anyway. Figured they would."

"Did your mom ever say who contacted her from Cloud Chief?"

"No. Mom doesn't talk about that. And if you mention my dad, she has a meltdown."

"Yeah. I can understand that," Ashe said. Terry Smith, Randy's father, had been killed by Paul Harris, the werewolf English teacher at Cloud Chief Combined. "I know that you and James still talked," Ashe said softly. Randy jerked his head up.

"Ashe, that can get me in trouble, still," Randy said breathlessly.

"And that's why nobody else will ever know. I figure you didn't get to mourn James properly, either," Ashe went on. "I just wanted you to know how he died, dude."

"How? That memory is a little fuzzy, too."

"Those rats in the tunnels? James died the same way." Randy was standing and staring at Ashe in a blink.

"That can't be," Randy had difficulty breathing. "That just can't be."

"If they can make rat hearts explode," Ashe shrugged.

"They who? Who did that? I thought Paul Harris did it," Randy said.

"He had a few allies," Ashe said. "Randy, this isn't something to discuss with anybody else. Most people just don't remember the exact circumstances. With a little help, you understand."

"Yeah. Vampire help," Randy sounded angry.

"Dude, don't badmouth my dad. Everybody else had a hand in it, too. Maybe it is safer if nobody knows."

"You just handed a mystery to an investigative journalist. You think I won't figure out the truth?" Randy emptied his glass of soda and thumped the tumbler on the island. "Thanks for the info, Ashe. I'll get to the bottom of this."

"I hope you do," Ashe murmured quietly as Randy shut the front door behind him.

CHAPTER 15

"**I** don't like this, man." Jeremy handled the case of darts carefully. Chad glared at his friend—they'd borrowed Jeremy's mother's car to drive to the beach. "I can't believe they expect us to do this on the full moon."

"Look, just load darts into both guns, get two shots off and then turn," Chad hissed. "And make sure you do it near a tree in case somebody comes after you."

"That's easy for you to say; you'll be out in the crowd, looking innocent while the guilty wildcat is up the tree."

"They probably won't even notice. If we let that deer out, they'll be chasing it instead. You know how it is—if a wolf gets the scent of prey, that's all they focus on. So what if two go down? Less competition for the others." Chad nodded for Jeremy to get on with the task of loading both tranquilizer guns with poisoned darts.

"Too bad we can't get the stupid bat-boy while we're at it."

"Too small, man." Chad snickered at the thought. Ashe's bumblebee bat was too insignificant to hit with a dart. "We can get him later, though. When he's asleep in his coffin."

"Nah, that's just his dad," Jeremy hooted. "Ashe hangs upside down in a cave with little, tiny claws." Jeremy held up a hand in a claw-like

194

gesture. "Maybe if his parents had worked a little harder, he'd be a sparrow." Chad guffawed at Jeremy's description.

"Besides," Jeremy continued, "Fergus says Zeke Tanner will offer jobs to us after we do this," he loaded the second dart. "Good paying jobs. All we have to do is make runs back and forth across the border. We'll have anything we want after we work just a few months for him. Fergus figures Zeke might pay for the information we have on the shifters trying to organize, too." The dart case was closed carefully—it held an extra four darts. "There, all loaded up. We can break into the six-pack, now." Jeremy settled both guns into a case inside his mother's trunk and lifted the cooler lid.

With fingers shaking slightly, Ashe opened the email he'd received earlier. *I am risking my life to send you this,* the message began. *I have to trust that you keep it hidden or my life will be forfeit. This was yours—was meant for you all along. I have no desire to see more injustice aimed in your direction. Therefore, I hope you accept this in the spirit that it was meant and someday, I hope to meet you in person and call you friend—Charles.* What followed was every bit of the H'Morr that had been translated by the strange man he'd met—*Griffin.* Wiping away a bit of moisture from his eyes, Ashe began to read.

"Late night?" Ashe was yawning at breakfast the following morning. Winkler accepted a cup of coffee from Adele with murmured thanks.

"Yeah. Did some studying." Ashe's watch proclaimed it to be Wednesday, August sixth.

"That doesn't get you out of working," Trace tousled Ashe's hair.

"Never thought it would," Ashe yawned again. "But I learned a few things." Ashe stuffed a bite of sausage into his mouth and watched his mother move about the kitchen while he chewed.

She barely acknowledged him any longer. Sighing over his vow never to call his father again, Ashe went back to his breakfast. When Winkler and the others rose to leave, Ashe stayed behind for a few moments.

"Mom?" he said, watching Adele pile dishes into the dishwasher.

"Did you say something, dear?" Adele looked up at him, much like she might have looked at Sali or one of the others.

"You told me once you'd always be my mother. I think you meant it at the time." Ashe turned on his heel and nearly ran from the house.

"Dude?" Sali ran up beside Ashe. They barely spoke during their workout sessions before breakfast. Ashe had started watching Ace work with Wynn and the others—Ace was becoming more and more protective of Wynn.

"What, Sali?" Ashe huffed. The weather was muggy, the air thick with moisture from the gulf and the insects were already singing their daily song. Ashe felt like chucking everything and misting to the dunes to allow the gulf breeze to cool him off. He noticed that Nathan had replaced the boat he'd lost nearly a month before, and it looked expensive. Ashe, in a former life, might have asked for a ride. That likely wasn't an option any longer. He hadn't seen Nathan in days.

"Is that all there's gonna be from now on? You snapping at me?" Sali asked.

"Sali, is this my fault?" Ashe stuffed hands in the pockets of his cargo shorts.

"No. Well—no."

"Look Sal, I'd like to go into the past and trust you again. That's not gonna happen. I can't discuss anything with my best friend, or former best friend, because he'll run to his dad and blab."

"Is that what we are? Former best friends?"

"What would you call it, Salidar?" Ashe never called Sali by his first name. Never. Sali jerked back when Ashe said it. "Did I ever tell your dad you used to spy on the pack in that old oak tree outside Cloud Chief? Or tattle about the dozens of other things that would have gotten you grounded at the very least? That answer is no, dude. You're the one who broke faith."

"Ashe, it's not all his fault." Marco had come up silently on both of them.

"No. But the betrayal feels the same." Ashe misted away.

"You spied on the Pack?" Marco stared at Sali with new respect.

"Yeah." Sali hung his head and scuffed the toe of his flip-flop on the pavement.

"Way to go," Marco grinned, slapping Sali on the back. Sali lifted his head and grinned at his brother.

Winkler gave Ashe half an hour before calling his cell. Surprisingly, Ashe answered right away. "Son, don't you think it's time you came to work?" Winkler asked.

"Yeah. I'll be right there." Winkler barely had time to end the call before Ashe was standing in front of his desk.

"Kid, maybe you should knock or something. That's just scary," Winkler drew attention to Ashe's sudden appearance.

"I will." Ashe turned to go.

"No. Ashe, sit down. Let's talk."

"About what?"

"About Trajan's engagement. I want to know what you think. Trajan is sweating bullets over this, even though he thinks I don't suspect. I know you know things. I want you to tell me what you think and be brutally honest. I picked Trajan for Wynter. They'll be engaged come Saturday unless you give me a reason to call it off. Honestly, I think Trajan would be relieved. I have no idea how Wynter would feel—she likes Trajan well enough and I know he'd take care of her and never mistreat her, but that's not everything."

"Yeah. I already figured that out," Ashe picked at a thread that escaped the hem of his shorts.

"Well, are you going to tell me or what?"

"Mr. Winkler, I really don't want to scare you that much. More than just appearing in front of you, that is."

"Kid, I'm already scared. A little more won't make that much difference."

"Mr. Winkler, look at me. Look me in the eye," Ashe said. Winkler lifted his eyes and watched as Ashe's eyes changed. Became completely blue. Not the normal blue of his eyes, but midnight blue. The blue that surrounds a full moon at night. Stars appeared in their depths. No other white showed.

Winkler cursed softly in wonder. "Wynter will not love Trajan, and he deserves that," Ashe said, his voice deepening. "Trajan will provide for her but she will bear her children and leave."

"But who would she love? Tell me that," Winkler begged.

"Trajan said his name once," Ashe went on. "Thomas Williams, Jr.—from the Sacramento Pack." Ashe blinked and the spell was broken. Winkler watched as his eyes became normal again.

"The Sacramento Packmaster?" Winkler stared at Ashe in amazement.

"Yeah. That's the one." Ashe started to rise.

"No. Sit right there. Hold on." Winkler motioned Ashe down again and hit a button on his cell. Ashe heard when the call was answered.

"Winkler?" The voice sounded surprised.

"Thomas, you're not engaged or anything, are you?"

"No. Not many prospects in the area right now," Thomas replied.

"Good. My daughter needs a husband in two years. Would you like to meet her?" Several seconds of quiet met Winkler's straightforward question.

"Well," Thomas Williams found his voice, "When?"

"How about this Saturday? I'll send the jet out to pick you up. You can run with the Pack here. Let your brother take your Pack out on Sunday."

"All right," Thomas agreed. "Call me when you get everything arranged." Thomas hung up.

"You're sure about this?" Winkler looked at Ashe.

"Yeah."

"Trajan will be relieved."

"I sure hope so. I don't want him to feel slighted or upset."

"Let's find out." Winkler grinned. "Kid, I don't know what that was, but it really is scary as hell. Trajan!"

~

"Boss, this is such a relief." Trajan sighed. Ashe hadn't waited around after Trajan whooped with joy when Winkler gave him the news. He'd scooted straight out of Winkler's office and disappeared inside his bedroom. "Mom always wanted it to be a love match," Trajan added.

"Then you'll have that chance. Ashe said Thomas Williams, so she's getting Thomas Williams."

"Boss, try not to shove him down her throat. Why don't you just casually introduce them and see how that works out?"

"All right, we'll go the politically correct route," Winkler agreed. "You can wear that new suit at the engagement party."

"Suits me," Trajan laughed.

~

"They are here—the humans call this Lac Savard. It is in Quebec, in the country of Canada," Parlethis was proud of his newly developed map-reading skills.

"Then let us make arrangements to be there tomorrow evening. That will take them by surprise, I think." Friesianna pretended to study the paper map. Rabis had offered to bring her an electronic version. She'd refused.

"I will bring Prince Beldris to you personally," Parlethis bowed deferentially. Rabis held his breath and counted. He had no desire to display his distaste over Parlethis' obsequiousness. That would court disaster with the Queen. She wasn't listening to Rabis anyway. He wished she'd just let him go. He knew where he'd like to be—somewhere watching his grandchild grow into adulthood and come into his talents.

"I care not if he is dead or alive when you bring him," Friesianna remarked icily. "Just bring him. Perhaps we shall offer the Prince to his brother, in exchange for the Dark crown."

"A fitting reward, my Queen." Rabis wanted to relocate just to get away from the fawning Parlethis.

"Rabis," the Queen snapped, bringing Rabis out of his thoughts. "Show my Captain the most advantageous location to mount our attack," she shook the map at her Foreseer.

"Respectfully, my Queen, one place is no better than another," Rabis replied softly.

~

"My contact is ready to go," Josiah spoke to a waiting Ezekiel Tanner. "I'll be nearby, ready to help if necessary. We have things well in hand. William Winkler will be dead and you'll have your trophy soon."

"Don't muck this up, Dunnigan. I'm warning you. You've already lost a good contact to that moth-infested patch of fur. Fail me in this and I'll send someone after you."

"There will be no need for that, I assure you," Josiah was glad he was speaking with Zeke on the phone instead of in person. A werewolf as old and experienced as Ezekiel Tanner could smell fear a mile away, and Josiah was certainly afraid. Josiah worked to keep that emotion from his voice. It made him more determined than ever to take William Winkler down quickly.

"When you get done with that, I could use some help here," Zeke suggested. "Supply problems, you understand."

"But," Josiah sputtered. He wanted his ranch in Wyoming, no strings attached.

"Had you worried, didn't I?" Zeke cackled. "Do this for me and we're done unless you need another favor sometime."

"I appreciate the offer," Josiah lied.

~

"School starts in two weeks," Sali grumbled to Dori.

"I'm looking forward to it," she said. Sali leaned against Dori's legs on the Anderson's deck. Dori sat in a deck chair, Sali lounging at her feet and sipping iced tea that Cori made. Cori lay on her stomach on a chaise nearby, dressed in a bikini. "I can't wait to get into college," Dori added.

"Two more years," Cori muttered into the chaise cushion.

"We'll be juniors, Sal," Dori wiggled a toe against Sali's side.

"Randy's girlfriend from Chicago is coming in on Friday," Sali leaned back to squint at Dori. The sun was shining right in his face.

"He's taking her to a hotel near the beach," Cori said. "But he still hasn't told his mother that she's coming. That ought to be a surprise."

"She's not leaving before the run?" Sali couldn't believe Randy so remiss as to forget about a full moon.

"Flight back is Monday morning early," Cori said, turning over. "She's a vet. Makes good money, according to Randy."

"Maybe she can take a look at Sali," Dori snickered.

"Hey, now," Sali slapped Dori's leg playfully. Dori dumped her iced tea down Sali's back, forcing him off the deck in a blink. Sali tickled her mercilessly after that, making Dori squeal with laughter.

"What's going on?" Wynn came through the patio door to witness Sali and Dori wrestling playfully.

"Kids," Cori muttered.

"Mom and Dad gave permission for me to date Ace," Wynn sat on the deck beside Cori's chaise.

"How old is he?" Cori asked quietly. Sali and Dori were still play fighting.

"He's forty-six; young for a werewolf," Wynn sighed. "I know there's an age gap, but he's just," she didn't finish.

"He's the right one? I think I got that vibe from Ashe, too. He thinks the same."

"I think we'll miss Ashe in school this year," Wynn said. "I can't believe he's just going to leave all of us behind like that."

"Ashe is different," Cori said and left it at that. "What did your parents say to Ace?"

"That he had to mind his manners," Wynn blushed. "He said he understood."

"The werewolf-shifter community is different, too," Cori agreed. "Werewolf females can be married off to somebody three or four times their age. I heard Mr. Winkler's wife was twenty-two when he married her at age eighty-six."

"Really? He's over a hundred now? He doesn't look it," Wynn breathed.

"Yeah. Mr. Winkler comes from strong stock," Cori said. "Anyway, that's what Marco says."

"Ace says he wants to give me a ring the minute I turn eighteen," Wynn said dreamily.

"Wynnie, are you sure you want all that so fast?" Cori sat up and looked at Wynn.

"I think so. Anyway, Mom said she was glad I had somebody who would protect me."

"Understandable," Cori sighed, leaning back again.

"What about you and Marco?"

"We're not ready to jump into anything," Cori replied. "But it's nice to know he's there."

"Hey, Sal," Hayes and Jeff walked onto the deck. "Dori's mom said you were here. How about a trip to the beach? We haven't been in days." The two young werewolves looked hopefully at Sali.

"That sounds great," Wynn said. "Sali, will you drive us? I'll ask Mom if I can go."

"I'm ready, if everybody chips in for gas money," Sali said.

"Let's go to the beach, man." Chad slapped Jeremy on the back. Diane Booth, Jeremy's mother, was running the vacuum. Chad hated the sound. He and Jeremy had been watching television at Jeremy's parents' home, but the vacuum interrupted.

"Mom," Jeremy half-shouted over the cleaning din, "Chad and I are going out." Diane waved a hand at them and kept vacuuming the living room.

"I hate it when she cleans," Chad muttered as they walked out of the house. The keys jingled in Jeremy's hand as they opened the doors to Diane's small Chevy.

∼

Ashe lifted his head twice to watch Sali's car speed out of the community, followed shortly after by Jeremy and Chad, driving Mrs. Booth's little white car. Sighing, Ashe went back to checking records Andy had given him.

"Kid, Winkler wants lunch in Port A and then we'll check on the beach house after that," Trace poked his head inside Ashe's doorway. "So drop those folders and shake a leg."

"Your leg or mine?" Ashe grinned at the werewolf.

"Yours—mine's already shakin'," Trace said. Ashe stood and stretched, allowing Trace enough time to walk over and pull one of Ashe's ears, hauling him out of his office.

"They're moving the kitchen equipment into the restaurant," Trajan pointed out as Ashe opened the van's back door. Winkler was already loaded into the front seat and Trace had climbed in on the driver's side. Ashe watched for a few seconds as a delivery crew unloaded a huge stove. Two large freezers were parked on the driveway, waiting their turn.

"Buck will have that finished before school starts," Winkler said as Ashe slid onto the seat behind him and shut the door.

"Where's Ace and Marco?" Ashe asked.

"Ace, Marco and Andy are at the beach house, getting Andy's and my office put together." Winkler leaned around the back of his seat to look at Ashe. "Don't tell anybody, but we're moving in on Friday, first thing after breakfast."

"Good," Ashe said. Perhaps that would take the sting out of seeing his friends drive past on their way to a day spent amid sand and surf.

"We're going to Victoria's, and your mother will be there," Winkler added. "Is that gonna bother you, son?"

"No, Mr. Winkler," Ashe sighed heavily and stared out the window. "Has she already taken it over for you?"

"Yeah. A couple of days ago. Kid, I'd fix this if I could." Winkler settled in his seat and stared out the windshield.

"I know. Nobody can fix this, Mr. Winkler, except my dad. And he's not returning my phone calls."

"Ashe, we'll get through this." Trajan reached over and patted Ashe's shoulder.

"Yeah." Ashe was sinking into the mire of his misery as he watched the coastal community of Star Cove fly past his window.

"You're kidding." The service station attendant stared at the pile of bills and coins Sali dumped on the counter.

"Nope. Twenty-three dollars and seventy-six cents," Sali grinned at the man, who appeared to be in his early twenties. "Everybody chipped in so we could go to the beach."

"Which beach?" The attendant asked as he counted out bills and coins.

"Padre Island. At least we have a permit and don't have to pay to get into the park," Sali said.

"Yeah. I like going there, too, and the price of the permit is definitely worth it."

"My dad said it was cheaper than paying every time," Sali agreed.

"You're set," the attendant raked the money into his register and turned on the pump. "Have fun at the beach. That's where I'd be if I had time off."

"Yeah. School starts in a couple of weeks so we're going out while we can."

"Understood," the attendant said.

Hayes was already pumping gas when Sali got back to the car, and

Jeff was washing beach scum off the windshield and windows while Wynn, Dori and Cori watched.

"Cori, did you pack any soda?" Sali opened the trunk to scavenge from the cooler.

"It's in there," Cori said. "I want an orange." Sali tossed the bottle of orange to Cori and lifted out a cola for himself. "Dori, what do you want?" he asked. Everybody had soft drinks in hand before they pulled away from the service station.

~

"Look—that's Sali's car," Chad pointed to a car waiting in line to get onto Padre Island. Sali's small red vehicle was three cars ahead of them.

"Let's follow them," Jeremy suggested. "Maybe the empty is with them."

"Yeah. Nobody here to protect the stupid little bat this time."

~

"Ashe, I've set up your new bank account in both our names; it'll make the deposits simpler," Winkler handed over a new debit card while they waited for their server to bring lunch.

Ashe had seen his mother going into the manager's office near the kitchen but she hadn't stopped to talk with them. "All the funds have been transferred from your old account already. You can set up something online to keep track of everything. Half of your wages are going straight to a savings account and I have to approve any withdrawals."

"That's fine," Ashe said absently as he watched his mother walk out of her office and into the kitchen.

"Kid, do you even know how much you make?" Trajan tapped Ashe's shoulder.

"What?" Ashe turned to Trajan.

"He hasn't been listening," Trajan sighed.

"But," Ashe began.

"Kid, it'll work out," Trajan leaned back and sipped his iced tea.

~

"Jeremy, go away."

"What? We paid to be here, too. Where's the empty?" Jeremy lounged against the side of his mother's car while Chad growled at Sali. Hayes was pulling on Sali's arm.

"Dude, this isn't the time—it's too close to the full moon," Hayes whispered as Sali growled at Chad. Chad bristled right back and growled louder.

"Chad, Ashe isn't here. He's working, but that's something you wouldn't know about," Dori snapped. "Get out of here. We don't need a fight; there are humans!" The last word was hissed at Chad. Humans were all around them; Sali had parked in a popular spot on the beach and Jeremy pulled in right beside him.

"Look, we don't need to get into a fight," Hayes said. Jeff was now on Sali's other side, trying to pull Sali away. Cori was hugging Dori to keep her from helping Sali. Wynn was backing away, frightened by the potential conflict. Chad lunged at Sali, snapping his teeth at him. Sali broke away from Hayes and Jeff and the fight began. Chad had no idea how angry—or tough—Sali really was. Chad was shrieking in no time while the others watched helplessly.

"He's killing Chad!" Jeremy shouted as Chad shrieked again. Sali, being the werewolf that he was, bit Chad as he pounded and pummeled.

"Get back, you'll get hit!" Cori shouted as Jeremy attempted to get close. When he didn't back away, Cori grabbed his arm to pull him back. Jeremy flung Cori's arm away, nearly knocking her to the ground.

"Hey!" Dori shouted. In a blink Dori had changed, lunging at Jeremy in ocelot form. Cori shouted at her sister, Wynn screamed, Hayes and Jeff attempted to separate Chad and Sali only to be rebuffed and Jeremy, angry and desperate to help Chad, ran to the trunk of his mother's car and pulled out both tranquilizer guns.

~

Ashe watched as Buck, Winkler's werewolf contractor, walked in and began talking with Adele. Then Ashe blinked and stiffened. First, because Buck leaned down and kissed his mother, and second because he knew there was trouble.

"You have to come," Ashe whispered and pulled all three werewolves away from the table, disappearing amid shouts and screams from the other patrons. Buck, jerking around, guessed what had happened.

"Adele, we have to get Marcus," Buck said and hauled out his cell.

~

"Dori!" Cori shouted when she saw the two guns in Jeremy's hands. Dori was hissing and spitting at Jeremy as he raised the first gun and pointed it at Sali. He had to wait—Sali and Chad were locked together, Chad still fighting for any advantage over Sali.

Sali, four years younger than Chad, was tougher and more determined. He growled as he shoved Chad to the ground, preparing to follow and deliver more blows. When the two young werewolves separated, Jeremy lifted the gun. Dori's ocelot leapt at him, clawing his arm and locking her teeth in his wrist. Cursing, Jeremy knocked her away with the butt of the gun and aimed at the spitting ocelot.

"No!" Cori screamed and sprang toward Dori, attempting to snatch her sister away. Jeremy fired the gun, hitting Cori in the side with the poisoned dart as she dropped to cover Dori's body. The moment Cori fell, Jeremy jerked around and fired at Sali.

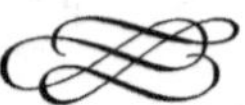

ynn couldn't stop screaming. Cori was convulsing on the ground and Hayes, who'd stepped between Jeremy and Sali, was doing the same. Jeremy stood, staring at the ones he'd shot with poisoned darts while Sali shoved Chad away and dropped to his knees beside Hayes.

Jeff tilted his head back and howled in grief. Humans nearby were beginning to walk in their direction. "No," Jeremy whispered, dropping the guns and running down the beach. Chad was soon behind him.

Ashe, Winkler, Trace and Trajan appeared at that moment. Frightened by the scene before him, Ashe glanced from Hayes to Cori, moaned softly and dropped to his knees beside Cori's convulsing body.

"Trajan, Trace, go!" Winkler jerked his head toward the fleeing Chad and Jeremy. Both werewolves took off at a run.

"Ashe, please," Wynn held onto Dori, who was still in ocelot form. Ashe placed his hands on Cori, looked up at Wynn with stars in his eyes and blinked.

"What the hell happened?" Marcus demanded. Buck rounded up several patrons who'd seen Ashe disappear with Winkler and the others.

"That boy and the others just—vanished," Adele whispered.

"Adele, that boy is your son," Marcus snapped. "What the hell was he doing?"

"No idea," Buck said. "But we need somebody to tell these folks they didn't see anything."

"Get names and numbers; sunset isn't for another four hours," Marcus growled. "Tell them to go home and not discuss it until they're contacted by the authorities. All right?" Marcus pulled his cell out and dialed Winkler's number. Adele and Buck both listened when Winkler answered.

"Cori?" Cori stared around her. All was muted light. It felt comfortable, wherever she was. She was weightless. Happy. Had no desire to leave. She recognized the voice, though. *Ashe.*

"Cori, I neutralized the poison," Ashe said gently. "But you have to decide to come back. Come back with me now, all right?"

"But," Cori said. Something else was pulling on her.

"Cori, Marco is waiting. He'll be hurt and upset if you don't come back," Ashe coaxed. "Come on, Cori. We've been friends for a long time. Come back with me now so I won't have to tell Marco I lost you."

"But I'm not lost," Cori said.

"Cori, come on, pretty girl. Come home with me."

"Oh, all right," Cori turned away from the beckoning light. Somehow, without even being there with her, Ashe pulled her away.

"Hayes is dead," Jeff wept as Cori opened her eyes to stare up at Ashe. How had she gotten flat on her back on the hot sand? Confused, she blinked at Ashe, who seemed to have deep blue eyes with stars in them.

Dori, wrapped in a beach towel, was hovering nearby, wiping tears away while Wynn held onto her. Jeff was crying for some reason and Sali stalked past, growling.

"Did he say Hayes is dead?" Cori attempted to sit up. Ashe, whose eyes went from darkest blue to normal in a blink, helped her.

"Cori, Jeremy shot both of you. I didn't have time to help Hayes." Ashe sounded upset about that. The afternoon sun blazed down on all of them and seagulls rode the breeze nearby. The drama playing out on the sand held no concern for them. Cori watched as William Winkler passed through her field of vision. He had a cell phone tucked against an ear, talking with someone.

"Ashe, we need help over here," Winkler jerked his head. Ashe stood on unsteady legs and gazed at the gathered crowd of humans.

"Yeah," Ashe muttered. "Wynn, get something for Cori to drink." Ashe walked toward the waiting crowd.

"Mr. President, take a look at these records," Matt Michaels handed an electronic tablet to the President. Matt Michaels had been in the oval office many times. Never with news such as this before, however.

"What is this?" The President tapped the tablet as he examined an image that appeared to be a map of GPS coordinates.

"We have a subject wearing a watch with a chip embedded, so we can track him," Matt said. "The first map shows the start point. The second map shows the destination. Elapsed time from start to finish is less than one second, sir."

"But the start point is in Texas and the destination is somewhere near, let's see—London? That can't be right. Am I operating this correctly?" The President turned the tablet around to show the Director of the Joint NSA/Homeland Security Department.

"You're operating it correctly, sir. This has been confirmed by firsthand witnesses. The kid relocated from Texas to England in less than a second."

"Kid?"

"Yes, sir. It's time you knew, sir, since I intend to recruit him the minute he turns eighteen."

~

"You'll sit there and behave or I'll come back there as my wolf and we'll have a chat," Trajan threatened Chad and Jeremy. The two boys sat in the back of Diane Booth's car while Trace drove. Winkler was driving Sali's car home with Hayes's body in the back seat—Ashe had already transported the others to Winkler's temporary home in Star Cove.

"Hayes is dead?" Jeremy sounded bewildered.

"You pulled the trigger; why act so surprised now?" Trajan growled. "If Ashe hadn't come, Cori would be dead, too."

"I was aiming for Sali," Jeremy still sounded confused.

"Even worse. You expect Packmaster DeLuca to have any mercy for you when you tell him that?" Jeremy huddled farther into his seat. Chad was sullen and refused to speak.

"Doesn't matter, bro," Trace said. "As soon as those vampires are up, we'll find out what these two were planning."

~

Ashe rubbed his forehead. He had the worst headache imaginable. Marco sat on the sofa nearby, his arms wrapped protectively around Cori, who huddled against him. Wynn was still shaking while Ace attempted to calm her. Dori and Sali stood together in the corner, wrapped in one another's arms.

Jeff sat on the floor near Marco's feet, staring at his shoes. All of them waited for Mr. Winkler to arrive and for parents to come. Ashe knew Hayes had been Jeff's best friend since first grade. Now, Winkler was bringing Hayes's body back to his parents. Mr. and Mrs. Howard would be devastated; Hayes was their only child.

"What kind of poison was that?" Jeff looked up at Ashe. "Werewolves don't usually die from poisoning."

"Jeff, this was batrachotoxin, from those poison arrow frogs in South America," Ashe sighed. "That stuff can kill just about anything. I have no idea how those two got it. I don't think they even knew how dangerous it was. Stupid, stupid, stupid," Ashe pounded his forehead with a fist.

"Ashe, son, come with me for a minute," Winkler walked into the living room. Ashe felt weary as he followed Winkler into the kitchen. Marcus was standing there with Micah, his Second. Ashe wanted to snap at Marcus. Marcus was responsible for ruining his friendship with Sali.

"Kid, we've got Weldon's forensics team coming in to examine Hayes. We need to know what killed him," Marcus sighed, raking a hand through black hair in frustration.

"You can bring 'em in, but I already know what killed him. It's Batrachotoxin, from the poison arrow frog," Ashe said. Marcus cursed. Ashe figured Marcus knew what it was—he'd been Special Ops for the military.

"The kind that can kill a man in just a few seconds?" Winkler asked.

"Yeah. Only it took a little longer to kill Hayes. Almost killed Cori," Ashe muttered. "If she'd been human, I wouldn't have been able to save her, either. I didn't have time to save both, Winkler. I wish I did."

"I know, son. I just don't understand how you saved Cori to begin with."

"I don't want you to know." Ashe stared at Marcus when he said it. Marcus tossed a hand out helplessly and stalked off, muttering.

"Ashe, one of our Pack died today, and another member of our Pack is likely responsible. I don't think Jeremy would have any hand in this if Chad wasn't urging him on," Marcus turned back and leveled his gaze on Ashe.

"They're both guilty," Ashe said. "I'm sure those vampires can lay compulsion and get the truth. I suggest you have Jeremy's parents and Hayes's parents there when you question them."

"We'll do that," Micah said gently. "Ashe, you did a good thing—an impossible thing—today. I know we've persecuted you lately, and I want to apologize for that. Winkler says that Jeremy was aiming for Sali when Hayes stepped between them. If you hadn't arrived with Winkler and the others, the rest of them might have been killed as well. We found four more darts inside that case."

"Something to ask them about," Ashe nodded, settling on a barstool and staring at the kitchen wall. Whoever had lived in the house before had left a calendar hanging there. Winkler hadn't bothered to change it and it was still on July.

Ashe recalled that a month ago, his life hadn't been so complicated and he still had parents. Now everything was different and he found himself navigating unfamiliar terrain.

"Hayes was always the peacemaker," Ashe said softly. "He would joke around or do something to distract everybody and ease the tension. I know you don't think of your submissives as particularly brave, but Hayes may have been the bravest of all of us."

"I'm not going to argue with you on that," Marcus said. "He certainly proved it today—gave his life to do it, too. No Packmaster can ask for more than that."

"Somebody grilling one of mine?" Bear Wright walked into Winkler's kitchen.

"It's okay, Mr. Wright," Ashe sighed. "We were just talking about Hayes."

"Good. I don't like arguing with werewolves," Bear sat next to Ashe. "Has anyone informed Mrs. Evans?"

"She knows." Marcus said the words flatly. Bear Wright hunched his shoulders and didn't mention it again.

"Aedan, Casimir and I just finished placing compulsion on those restaurant guests," Nathan reported. He'd called his vampire sire as quickly as he could afterward. "Ashe, as I understand it, managed to save my oldest today. Nobody seems to understand how he did it—the same kind of poison dart killed Hayes Howard."

"Nathan, what are you saying?" Aedan was confused.

"We'll get the particulars, once we place compulsion on Jeremy Booth and Chad Daniels. They had tranquilizer guns, loaded with poison darts. Marcus says the poison was deadly—from those poison arrow frogs in South America. That will kill werewolves and just about anything else short of a vampire. Cori took a hit, as did Hayes after Salidar got into a fight with Chad Daniels. Chad started the fight but Sali was taking him down. Jeremy pulled the guns from the boot of his mother's car and shot Cori, who was protecting my youngest, and then Hayes, because Hayes stepped between Jeremy and Sali."

"And Ashe showed up immediately," Aedan sighed.

"Yes. Somehow, I'm not sure exactly, he managed to neutralize the poison in Cori's system. That's what she told me when I woke tonight —that Ashe told her that."

"Child, I'm alive because Ashe intervened. Those creatures had me hauled out into full sunlight when he showed up with Marco and Cori. We'd both be dead if not for my son."

"Aedan, he walks around in a daze. Adele called him *that boy* today. She doesn't recognize him any longer. Father, how could you do that?"

"I didn't intend for that to happen," Aedan said sadly. "He thinks we've both abandoned him."

"Father, you have abandoned him. There's no mistake, there. I might have thought otherwise, but to pull away all support? What would you have done if Winkler hadn't stepped in to support the boy?"

"I don't know. It was a rash decision, I should have left something with you," Aedan admitted.

"If he wasn't being cared for, he would be now. I owe him for both my daughters' lives, Aedan. And for mine. I owe him blood debt. As do you."

"I know. But this—I don't know how to deal with it, Nathan. Wlodek wants to turn him when he's eighteen—I'd bet my life on it. I don't want that for my boy."

"Aedan, if we don't make this right somehow, I have a feeling we'll all lose him. That he'll just walk away and we'll never get him back."

"I don't know what to do about that, child. In the meantime, I'll work on getting an assignment somewhere close. Perhaps if I can get to Adele, I can remove that portion of the compulsion. She needs to recognize our son at least. I know he's heartbroken over this, but the way things stand, I can't do anything about it at the moment."

"You could try to explain things," Nathan suggested quietly.

"I'm not sure I can. I don't think I'm strong enough," Aedan sighed.

~

"Kid, somebody else I know used to climb up on roofs and sit," Winkler settled beside Ashe. Ashe had misted through the ceiling to sit atop the roof of Winkler's temporary home. Ashe was high enough now to see the waxing moon over the gulf waters in the east. Winkler had been forced to climb onto the roof in a more conventional manner.

"How are Cori and the others?" Ashe asked.

"Shaky," Winkler said. "We questioned Jeremy and Chad under compulsion. They intended to kill both of us, kid."

"I know. Trajan, too," Ashe added. "But they got into a fight with Sali and the others, and since the guns were handy."

"Yeah. Boys sent to do a man's job, by somebody I'm hunting," Winkler agreed. "Jeremy's parents are devastated. It was a kindness to take Chad in, but he's done nothing except lead Jeremy astray. Now, since Jeremy was the one to pull the trigger, he won't live over it. Bear won't even defend him and the Grand Master has already passed sentence on Chad. We'll do the executions Sunday before the run."

"What happens to people, Mr. Winkler? What turns them in that direction?"

"I don't know, Ashe. As a Packmaster and Weldon's peacekeeper, I've seen more than my share. Some of them I've seen grow up from babies and they turn out like that. I figure Nathan and your father have seen the same. Some people, raised in the best of circumstances turn out bad, and some growing up in the worst of circumstances turn out good. I can't explain any of it."

"Is that your official title? Peacekeeper?" Ashe asked.

"More like an unofficial title," Winkler placed an arm around Ashe's shoulders. "Weldon's son is his official Second, to keep everybody's eyes off me. It allows me to move freely, and since I own a security company, I can have eyes and ears everywhere. It works out for the best, all the way around."

"I'll keep that to myself," Ashe said.

"I know you will. Just so you'll know, right now you're earning a little more than eight thousand a month. Half that goes into the savings account." Winkler patted Ashe's shoulder, then stood and stretched before walking to the edge of the roof to let himself down. "Don't stay up there too long," Winkler's voice floated up from the ground.

"You'll have to send your Trackers, Grand Master; Fergus and Eudora took off like frightened rabbits and managed to elude the wolves I had set up in the area." Winkler grimaced as he passed the news to Weldon Thursday morning.

Everybody in Star Cove had a rough night and now Winkler was dealing with an early morning. Andy set a cup of coffee in front of his Packmaster. It was six a.m. and Winkler was waiting for Trajan and the others to rise so they could go out for breakfast.

He'd notified Adele the night before that they were having morning meals elsewhere from then on. He thought it best, since Ashe had witnessed his mother kissing Buck the day before. The problem would be solved after Friday anyway—he had a cook coming down from Dallas to prepare meals at the new beach house.

Jeremy and Chad were imprisoned inside a vacant home with three of Marcus' wolves standing guard. The boys had been bound with silver—both wore cuffs and chains on wrists and ankles. Silver didn't kill but it weakened dramatically. Werewolves and shifters never wore silver jewelry.

"I'll send the Trackers after Fergus and Eudora this morning," Weldon promised before hanging up.

"Andy, check the online records—I know you changed the passwords, but I want to know if those two got away with any more money," Winkler said.

"Sure, boss." Andy walked out of Winkler's office, heading toward his own. Winkler pulled up his email account to read the message he'd gotten from Matt Michaels.

Matt was in Chicago already, preparing his team to go into the tunnels come nightfall. The sensors had been successful, locating the nest of Elemaiya in the oldest part of Chicago's underground tunnel system. Those areas were constructed of bricks and mortar and hadn't been used in a very long time. Matt had targeted those right away—he couldn't imagine that anyone, alien or not, would want to stay there for any length of time.

Winkler sighed as he closed the email. Wlodek and Weldon were cooperating to destroy the nest. Winkler didn't want to push Ashe on where the others were camped. That might be a dangerous prospect anyway; he had no idea what kind of power or ability both sides might possess.

He'd risked his life once before, tracking down the Bright Ones. They'd considered killing him before they'd heard him out. Winkler shook away the memory. It hadn't been pleasant.

~

"I have a message for my King," Wildrif insisted. "It must be taken to him directly."

"You will give it to me. I will determine whether he should be interrupted," Prince Beldris snapped. Wildrif, bearing long experience at this sort of thing, fell onto the floor of Beldris' tunnel, jerking and weeping uncontrollably. Beldris watched as this went on for an interminable amount of time. "Very well, transport him to my brother," Beldris tossed up his hands and surrendered to the inevitable.

Liridael bowed to Beldris. Liridael and his brother Laridael, were the only two remaining Dark Elemaiya with the ability to transport many others at once. Most Elemaiya could transport one or two others when they relocated—parents could easily transport their children, after all.

There weren't many Dark Elemaiya remaining who could relocate with half the camp, however. Baltis' Destroyers had the talent when using their medallions, but now the Destroyers were dead. The talent in any other was quite rare and exceptional among the Dark Ones. The Bright Ones still had several who could accomplish it. Consequently, Laridael remained with the King; Liridael was constantly beside Beldris.

"Come, filth, you will bathe before going to the King," Liridael muttered, hauling Wildrif away.

"Boss, everything is ready except for a few last-minute details." Buck spoke to Winkler but watched as Ashe explored the spacious kitchen. The island was nearly as big as Ashe's bedroom back in Cloud Chief, with an extra sink and two dishwashers.

The last-minute details included paint, some tile work in the entry and other minor construction issues. Winkler gave a slight hand gesture to Buck, telling him to back off for now. Buck wanted to talk to Ashe about his developing relationship with Adele. Winkler's small gesture told Buck that Ashe wasn't ready.

"Hey, Ashe," Marco walked in with Ace. Both had been staying at the beach house, helping the crew get everything ready.

"Kid, I want to thank you for yesterday," Ace said.

"It wasn't anything. I wish I could have saved Hayes."

"I know." Ace patted Ashe on the back and moved away.

"Come out and look at the new deck, Ashe," Marco broke the ensuing silence. Ashe was glad to leave the kitchen. He didn't know what to say to Buck.

"This is really cool." Ashe admired the massive, multilevel deck. The last one had been much smaller and only one level, with one set of steps leading to the walkway that in turn led to the beach. This one had steps going down and converging from three separate locations.

"We've ordered the furniture already," Winkler walked up behind Ashe. "All of it will be delivered tomorrow while we're here and we'll decide where to put it. It'll take our minds off other things."

"Yeah."

"Ashe, let's go for a walk on the beach," Marco suggested. "Boss, we'll be okay," Marco waved Winkler off; he was ready to send Trajan with Marco and Ashe.

Winkler nodded curtly and went inside the house, Trajan following behind him. Marco waited until they were on the sand, the midmorning light glaring off the water and making it difficult to see.

Ashe held out his hand and two baseball caps appeared from his old bedroom in Star Cove. Handing one to a shocked Marco, Ashe slipped on the other. The hat helped him see as they walked down the beach. Marco, still unsure of what he'd just seen, put his cap on as well.

"Ashe, if you hadn't helped yesterday," Marco said.

"I did it for Cori, dude."

"No part of that was for me? Or for Sali?"

"Maybe a little. Mostly it was for Cori. Cori's always been my friend. Even when the others thought I was empty. Granted she blabbed about Billings' letter to my parents to keep everybody from knowing about James being in contact with Randy, but that's understandable."

"Yeah. She told me about that."

"So you can keep secrets."

"Ashe, I know how to do that. And I understand a little better just how important it really is."

"You mean you don't run to Winkler about everything?"

"That's in the past, dude. When I made my oaths to Winkler, it states specifically *from this day forward*."

"That's how it's done." Ashe nodded, squinting over the water and purposely not looking at Marco.

"Ashe, I didn't come to open old wounds. I came to thank you for Cori's life. And Sali's and the others. Jeremy could have reloaded. There were four more darts. Humans could have gotten killed, too."

"I know. I had to place compulsion *and* wipe a few cell phones."

"I hear the Grand Master may come down for the full moon." Ashe jerked his head around at Marco's statement.

"Marco, come on. We have to talk to Winkler."

"I'm asking you to trust me," Ashe said. Winkler, Trajan and Marcus sat inside Winkler's study inside the beach house. Marcus had been summoned and the Grand Master was on a conference call.

"Kid, this is a big thing to put in your hands," Marcus growled.

"Marcus, you can't say this to anyone else. Not Sali, not Marco, not even your wife. Do you understand?" Ashe had stars in his eyes. Marcus swallowed with difficulty. It wasn't easy looking at Ashe when he was like that.

"He'll keep quiet or I'll have him locked up," the Grand Master said on speakerphone. "I'll come down. I want to see this."

"I'll handle everything from this end," Winkler said. "See you Sunday, Grand Master." Weldon ended the call. Winkler punched the end button on his handset. "Marcus, we have a little planning to do," Winkler stood and jerked his head toward the door. Marcus dutifully rose and followed Winkler.

"I sure hope you know what you're doing," Trajan stood too, coming over to wrap Ashe in a hug. "Ashe, if Winkler hadn't signed up to be your guardian," Trajan released Ashe and walked out behind his Packmaster.

"Yeah. I know," Ashe muttered.

"My King," Wildrif bowed low before Baltis. The Dark Elemaiya camp was quite cold and Wildrif was used to a much warmer climate. "I would have come sooner, but my escort insisted on my bathing. Twice."

"What is it, Wildrif?" Baltis wasn't in any sort of humor to deal with the half-crazy foreseer.

"My King, I feel your brother and those you keep in Chicago are in danger," Wildrif moaned. "The outcome is not clear, but I fear the human military is leading an attack against them."

"*Human* military? Hmmph," Baltis waved away the threat.

"But my King, the incident is still murky and unclear. Terrible things might happen." Wildrif groveled, his blue and brown eyes pleading insincerely with Baltis.

"Did you discuss this with my brother? I feel he might be more than capable of taking on a few humans," Baltis had nothing but contempt for most things human, though they did have good food and a comfortable habitat, most of the time. Baltis had spent time on worlds where things weren't nearly as hospitable.

"But my King," Wildrif wept. "Please—let me stay here with you until it is over. I beg you."

"You're that frightened? Very well, I will send mindspeech to Beldris. He may make the final decision." Baltis waved Wildrif away. "Take him to a space on the far side, near the lake. I have no wish for his stench to reach my tent," Baltis growled. He'd been in the middle of making preparations for the pending attack by the Bright Ones. That attack could come at any time. Wildrif had been consulted, but as the outcome was once again murky, he was more useless than not on the matter.

Brother? Beldris was surprised to receive mindspeech from Baltis. *I thought you would be making preparations for the coming attack.*

I am, Baltis replied. *But Wildrif seems convinced that humans are preparing an attack upon you.*

Humans? What humans?

He says the human military is leading an attack against you. He cannot see the outcome—it is murky to him.

Many things are murky to him—he's three-quarters human. Beldris' amusement came through in his mental voice.

As you say, Baltis was also amused. *What say you, brother? Do you wish to join me here, or does a threat from humans frighten you?*

I do not fear humans, Beldris declared. *We will stay and if they find us, they will regret their attack, I assure you. I have the two blasters and Treydis —he will destroy their hearts if they think to take us down.*

Wildrif is frightened and wishes to stay with me, Baltis said.

Let him stay, then. Send Liridael back to me. We will sort this out after the Bright Ones fall.

That will be the most welcome of events, brother. We will celebrate it. Baltis turned to Liridael. "Go back to my brother—he is staying in Chicago to handle any threat from the humans. Assist him in his efforts." Liridael bowed to the Dark King and relocated.

For the moment, Ashe was content to sit on the floor of his new suite, an elbow leaning on the window as he stared out at the ocean. He could see it easily from this bedroom; the new design had seen to that.

His other hand gripped his cell—Cori had left three messages. Each message begged him to call or come see her. Ashe ducked his head, leaning it against his arm on the windowsill. Hesitantly, he lifted the cell and dialed Cori's number.

"Ashe, where are you?" Cori asked immediately.

"At the new beach house. Winkler wanted to see how it's coming along."

"You're not going to ignore me, are you?"

"No, Cori. You'll always be my friend."

"Ashe, I feel so guilty," Cori wept. "That you came to me first, and let Hayes go."

"Cori, do you think I don't feel guilt over that too? That I can't go to Hayes's mom and dad and explain myself? Even I can't be in two places at once. Not for that. I don't have the ability to bring back the dead, either. Hayes left us while I was working on you."

"Ashe, I was trying to protect Dori. She turned and jumped on Jeremy, to keep him from shooting Sali. Jeremy hit her in the head with one of those stupid guns and aimed at her. I tried to stop him. He shot me instead and then aimed at Sali again."

"Cori, hush," Ashe soothed as Cori sobbed. "Hold on, I'll be there in a minute." Ashe was there in only a second or two. Cori sat on the back porch of her parents' home, weeping. "Come here," Ashe settled on the chaise beside her. Cori wrapped her arms around his neck while Ashe tried to get her to stop crying.

"What's going on?" Dori stopped dead as she walked onto the deck carrying a glass of juice. "Sis, what happened?" Dori sat beside Ashe as he rubbed Cori's back gently and murmured soft words against her hair.

She's upset about Hayes—that she lived and he didn't, Ashe sent, knowing Dori would hear him perfectly. And be able to reply if she so chose.

I'm sorry you had to choose. I feel responsible, Dori replied.

The one responsible is Jeremy. His parents are wondering right now how this happened. Don't blame yourself for someone else's temper and shortsightedness. Or whom they choose as their friends. Chad sent Jeremy in this direction. Now both will pay the price.

Then take your own advice, Ashe. Don't blame yourself because you couldn't save two people at once, Dori returned. *Nobody blames you. You did the best that you could.*

Dori, right now I don't know what my best is.

"Ashe?" Cori pulled away, wiping moisture from her cheeks.

"Cori, do you want me to take you to Marco?" Ashe brushed strands of blonde hair away from Cori's face.

"Would you?"

"Yeah. Dori, tell your mom that I'm taking Cori to Marco." Dori nodded and Ashe and Cori disappeared.

"Cori?" Marco was sanding drywall compound but stopped immediately when Ashe appeared with Cori.

"Marco," Cori was in tears again as she flung herself into Marco's arms.

"I'd take a break on the beach, dude," Ashe suggested before misting away.

"Kid?" Winkler stood in Ashe's doorway as he settled in front of his window again.

"Mr. Winkler?" Ashe stood.

"Come on, let's go into Corpus. We'll have lunch while we're there. Like sushi?"

"Never tried it, Mr. Winkler." Ashe followed Winkler out of the house.

"You might like a spider roll," Winkler grinned, draping an arm around Ashe's shoulders. "And no, there aren't any spiders in it."

Ashe tried a spider roll but liked the salmon and cream cheese better. Trajan taught him how to eat with chopsticks while Trace teased. Winkler watched, smiling slightly while having an enormous platter of sushi. Ashe was dipping a tuna roll in soy sauce when he stiffened slightly.

∼

Josiah stopped short as the hostess was about to seat him. William Winkler and three others sat at a table not far away. The werewolves hadn't caught his scent yet; the restaurant was too crowded and smelled of food. "You know, I just remembered an appointment," Josiah lied to the young woman. "I'll come back later." Josiah turned and left the restaurant quickly.

∼

"Hell, no I don't put all my eggs in one basket," Ezekiel growled at Josiah over the phone. Josiah should have known better than to call Zeke when the full moon was so close. "But I have to tell you, if I catch up with Fergus before the Grand Master does, he'll wish he'd handed himself over tied up with a ribbon. Sending kids to do what I asked?" Zeke was quite inventive in his cursing.

"You had Fergus?" Josiah worked to keep his voice steady.

"I got a lot of wolves in the palm of my hand. All askin' for favors, just like you did. He stole from our target and wanted me to take Winkler out so's he could get away with it. Plus, he snatched away his Second's wife while he was at it. And since his favor so closely aligned with what I wanted anyway," Zeke said.

"You mean he wanted to shove Winkler's son into his father's position before he was ready, and in the ensuing chaos, Fergus could get away with theft from Winkler Securities? Talk about a death wish," Josiah muttered.

"Yeah, I thought it was stupid, too, but I wasn't about to tell Fergus that." Josiah imagined that Zeke was grinning. "It got me another one for my hit. Except he was too chicken to do it himself. Gotta hand it to him, though, if those kids were older and had more sense, he might have pulled it off. As it is, he's on the run now. I've got some of mine on his tail."

Josiah didn't say anything. You didn't cross Ezekiel Tanner and expect to live over it. The only good thing, as Josiah saw it, was that the two boys hadn't been informed that Tanner was behind the hit. Winkler would believe that Fergus pulled their strings.

Josiah hunched his shoulders. Ezekiel Tanner had pulled his strings for a long time through his brother Obediah. Now he was doing the pulling himself. If Josiah could accomplish this last assignment, however, he'd be free of Zeke Tanner and have his ranch as well. The prospect brightened his day considerably.

Josiah didn't like it, though, that Zeke had brought in someone else without telling him. No matter, those boys were as good as dead and Fergus was on the run. Zeke's decisions weren't always sound but he frightened everyone too much to have that pointed out to him.

"We're still on," Josiah said. "We'll get it done."

"Good. I'm counting on it." Zeke hung up.

CHAPTER 17

"Ashe?" Sali sat on the chair beside Ashe's desk. Ashe was working late to make up for time spent at the beach house and in Corpus Christi—Winkler had driven to the airport after lunch to talk with his werewolf pilots before sending them after Thomas Williams in Sacramento.

"What, Sal?" Ashe pecked away at his desktop keyboard, finishing emails to Andy on some of the files he was working.

"Hayes—they're gonna have the service tomorrow morning."

"That's what Trace said."

"Dude, are you going?" Ashe looked up at Sali.

"I don't know." Ashe lowered his head again.

"His mom and dad—they want all of us there. All his classmates."

"Are you sure about that? I could have saved Hayes instead of Cori. I made a choice, Sali. I chose one friend over another."

"Ashe, Hayes saved me." Ashe jerked his head up again as Sali crumpled.

Trace rushed into the room as Ashe tried to hold up a sobbing Sali. *Help me*, Ashe begged mentally.

"Ashe, being gay doesn't mean I'm any better at this than anyone else," Trace muttered dryly, but he helped get Sali onto the chair again and patted his shoulder awkwardly.

"Sali, Hayes gave you a gift," Ashe finally broke down and hugged his friend. "You have to accept it, dude."

"Ashe, I'm sorry. I'm so sorry," Sali wept. "I was stupid."

"Sal, is this about Hayes or about us?" Ashe pulled away and offered Sali his box of tissues.

"Both, I guess." Sali wiped his eyes. "Sorry, dude. Didn't mean for that to happen."

"It's okay."

"Look, you two need to sort this out." Trace nodded to Ashe and walked out.

"Yeah. There's a lot to sort," Sali muttered.

"Dude, there's someplace I need to be," Ashe said, checking his watch. "Want to come?" Sali looked up at Ashe, confused.

"Where?" Sali asked.

"Canada," Ashe said. Gripping Sali's arm, Ashe relocated.

~

"They're here," Matt pointed out the location on his map. "We have to take them by surprise." He and a small army of humans, vampires and werewolves stood outside an entrance into the rail tunnels beneath Chicago.

"Then let us go in first," Gerard offered. He led the contingent of five vampires Wlodek sent. "We have the map memorized and can go in swiftly. We'll take out their front line of defense before they expect the attack, which will allow the wolves and the rest of you to finish what's left."

"Sounds good," Matt said. "Are we ready?" Everyone nodded. "Good. Let's go."

~

"Dude, where are we?" Sali hissed. They were standing on the shore of a lake in twilight, and it was cold. Sali stared about him—tall firs surrounded the area, making it the perfect hiding place. Or hunting ground, he corrected mentally. The wolves would love to run there. *He'd* love to run there.

"They're shielding the camp; you won't see it until we're in the middle of it," Ashe whispered. "I've got us shielded so they won't see," Ashe grabbed Sali's arm and pulled him along.

"But can they hear?" Sali was worried, suddenly.

"Shhh, I don't know if I have the kinks worked out on the auditory shields," Ashe hushed Sali. "Be quiet. I'll turn us to mist if there's a problem." Ashe hauled Sali farther along the lake's edge. *Lac Savard*, Ashe spoke mentally to Sali. Sali shuddered as they walked through something intangibly colder, and then he saw them. Elemaiya. Everywhere. Preparing for battle.

He and Ashe walked right through them, with none of them even noticing. Sali wanted to talk so badly, he could taste the words on his tongue. The questions crowded behind his teeth, settling at the back of his throat, bitter as bile. What were they doing here? Had his father been right all along? Was Ashe going over to the enemy? One nearly grown werewolf had no chance against the thousands in this camp, most dressed in metal or painted leather armor, much of it decorated with gems and gold. Elaborate helmets graced heads. *Even the Romans would have been impressed*, Sali thought, his head turning this way and that as Ashe dragged him through the camp.

At times, they stepped around piles of equipment or warriors donning gear. He saw an ornate, hammered gold breastplate that would bring enough money to pay for college with a little left over for a car or three. *Steady, Sali, we're on a mission*, Ashe sent. Sali turned back to Ashe and left the thing lying in the grass.

Stay with me, Sal, Ashe reassured Sali as they came to the western edge of the camp. A long line of Elemaiya stood there, all dressed in battle gear, their eyes turned toward the west as if they were watching for something. Waiting for something. Sali saw what it was soon enough.

∾

"Where's the kid?" Winkler strode through the house, raking fingers through his hair.

"He was here a few minutes ago—Sali came and well, there was an emotional meltdown," Trace said.

"Where did they go?" Winkler stared at Trace.

"He didn't leave the house. Not in the conventional sense, anyway," Trace said, rising from his seat. He'd helped himself to a soda from the fridge and sat down at the kitchen island to drink it. Now he was up and ready to look for Ashe.

"Matt's hitting those tunnels in Chicago tonight. If I find out Ashe went," Winkler huffed out a frustrated breath.

"Boss, settle down. It's too close to the full moon," Trace said. "Let me get Trajan." Trace pulled his cell from a pocket and dialed.

∾

"And he said not to tell me, too?" Denise was shocked at Marcus' words. Marcus couldn't fathom why Ashe and Winkler had been so secretive about the whole thing. Denise, as the Packmaster's wife, had just as much right to know as Trajan did. Denise shook her head in bewilderment. "Surely not, Marcus," she said. "How can this happen?"

"You know as much as I do, sweetheart. Just keep it to yourself, all right? There'll be hell to pay if Winkler hears that I told you."

"He won't know. I promise." Denise went to make Marcus a cup of coffee.

∾

"I'll pick you up at the airport tomorrow evening," Randy said.

"I have something to tell you when I get there," Sara told him.

"I hope it's that you love me," Randy said, emboldened by the fact that he was talking on his cell and not face-to-face.

"We'll get to that," Sara suddenly sounded shy.

"I sure hope so," Randy was encouraged by Sara's answer. He stood on the sand of the public beach in Port Aransas, leaning against the fender of the car he'd purchased two hours earlier.

The vehicle was smaller than he might like but it suited him and his needs. Sara wouldn't mind. The moon was close to full and rising above the waters as he spoke with Sara. Randy appreciated the path the moonlight made, as if you could walk on it to the eastern horizon. "I wish you were here right now," he said. "The moon is beautiful."

"Yeah. I wish I were there too. Love you, Randall. Bye."

~

Sali, you're shielded, they can't see you, Ashe assured his friend. Sali gulped as his eyes roamed the lines of opposing Elemaiya. He and Ashe stood in a grassy space between two armies as twilight deepened around them.

The moon was up and stars twinkled overhead, oblivious of the war about to take place. Sali watched the line of warriors they'd passed through moments earlier. Were they aware that another army had appeared? They didn't seem to be.

They're shielded, too, Ashe answered Sali's unspoken question. *But if their attackers come closer, the two shields surrounding each army will intersect and both sides will be visible. I'm about to lower both shields a little early.*

~

"My Prince!" Liridael shouted as the vampires attacked. Lengthy claws sliced out before the Prince or his trusted guard could relocate. Beldris died, his eyes staring at the rounded brick ceiling overhead. His last thought was of the skies of Morningsun, homeworld to the Dark Elemaiya. Why had he and the others thought to leave it? It no longer mattered; the light was fading. Shouts and screams around Beldris dimmed with the light, and then winked out altogether.

~

"Ashe," Sali whispered, terrified. The shields had come down as Ashe raised his arms and then lowered them.

Sal, now's the time for you to keep quiet, Ashe warned mentally. *They can see me now. They can't see you, but they might hear.* Sali nodded mutely as both sides, Bright and Dark, muttered among themselves. Here was a boy, standing between them and their enemy, and somehow the shields had been lowered without contact.

"You!" Parlethis stepped forward from the Bright army.

"Me," Ashe agreed quietly. "You represent the Bright Queen?"

"Yes. I intend to kill you, but that will wait. I want Prince Beldris to step forward or his people will die."

"Beldris is not here," Baltis came from behind his first line of soldiers to stand before them. "My brother is elsewhere."

"Your brother has been attacked in Chicago," Ashe turned to Baltis with stars in his eyes. Ashe stood in the center, Parlethis and Baltis perhaps twenty feet away on opposing sides. Baltis did not fail to see Ashe's eyes. Frightened, he wanted to step behind his troops again. He was King, however. He was expected to be braver than his bravest warrior.

"My brother?"

"Is dead," Ashe sighed. "As you likely know, none of us can truly be in two places at once. A difficult lesson I learned only recently. The Bright Ones decided to attack your camp. Others attacked your brother in Chicago. I came because you have children here. I will not see them killed. Leave now and I will not pursue."

"I have no plans to leave," Parlethis snarled. "I will do my Queen's bidding. She asked me to destroy the Dark race and take the King's crown. I will not fail her."

"But you have young in your camp as well," Ashe turned to Parlethis. "Surely your Queen has no desire to see the children die."

"She knows this and sent me anyway. The Dark Ones have murdered too many of our race. We will not back down. I will kill you, Dark King," Parlethis snarled at Baltis, raising a jeweled sword.

Light played along its edge, causing it to glow brightly in the dim moonlight.

"I stand in your way, Bright fool," Baltis hissed. "Warriors, attack!"

Ashe pulled Sali into his mist as the front lines clashed together. Energy blasts flew and exploded. Elemaiya on both sides screamed and shouted as bodies hurled through the air. Weapons clanged and huge chunks of earth and rock were thrown and blocked. Water from the lake was doused onto both sides. Those who slipped struggled to rise again.

Many still standing took advantage of the situation and fell on their enemy, until the ground began to shake beneath the feet of both armies. The quake was so violent it threw everyone to the ground. The shaking increased—so much so that none could rise again.

Ashe materialized with Sali at his side at a safe distance. "Go now!" His voice boomed through the trees and across the lake. Elemaiya warriors began disappearing by the hundreds. The ground still shook. Sali, though, stared at his feet. The earth beneath him was as still and calm as anything could be.

"How?" he stared at Ashe.

"Don't break my concentration, Sal," Ashe murmured. Sali saw tall firs break and fall. The lake formed waves and engulfed many. Parents disappeared with their children, followed closely by others. Ashe's jaw tightened as he concentrated and the ground continued to tremble violently.

Sali wanted to speak again but held back; frightened of the answers he might receive to the questions struggling against his clenched teeth. Finally, after roughly ten minutes of continuous ground shaking, the tremors subsided. Every Elemaiya was gone, including the dead. Ashe went limp, dropping to the ground in a heap. "Ashe?" Sali knelt beside his friend. "Ashe?" Sali was alone.

The End